hands of the ripper

'Guy Adams is either barking mad or a genius, I haven't decided.' Mark Chadbourn

The author of the novels *The World House* and its sequel *Restoration*, Guy Adams gave up acting five years ago to become a full-time writer. This was silly, but thankfully he's kept busy, writing bestselling humour titles based on TV show *Life on Mars* or *Torchwood* novels *The House That Jack Built* and *The Men Who Sold The World*.

He has also written a pair of original Sherlock Holmes novels, *The Breath of God* and *The Army of Doctor Moreau* as well as a biography of actor Leonard Rossiter and an updated version of Neil Gaiman's *Don't Panic: Douglas Adams & The Hitch-Hiker's Guide to the Galaxy* and *Kronos*, a novelisation of the classic Hammer film, *Captain Kronos Vampire Hunter*.

His website is: www.guyadamsauthor.com

GUY ADAMS

hands of the ripper

HAMMER

AN EXCLUSIVE MEDIA COMPANY

Published by Arrow Books in association with Hammer 2012

2 4 6 8 10 9 7 5 3 1

First published in Great Britain in 2011 by
Arrow Books in association with Hammer
Random House, 20 Vauxhall Bridge Road,
London SW1V 2SA

www.randomhouse.co.uk
www.hammerfilms.com

Addresses for companies within The Random House Group Limited can be
found at: www.randomhouse.co.uk/offices.htm

The Random House Group Limited Reg. No. 954009

A CIP catalogue record for this book
is available from the British Library

ISBN 9780099553854

The Random House Group Limited supports The Forest Stewardship
Council (FSC®), the leading international forest certification organisation.
Our books carrying the FSC label are printed on FSC® certified paper.
FSC is the only forest certification scheme endorsed by the leading
environmental organisations, including Greenpeace. Our paper
procurement policy can be found at:
www.randomhouse.co.uk/environment

Typeset by SX Composing DTP, Rayleigh, Essex
Printed and bound by CPI Group (UK) Ltd, Croydon, CR0 4YY

Foreword

You get the impression the story is set around 1901, shortly after the death of Queen Victoria. More to the point, about 13 years after the hideous Whitechapel murders popularly ascribed to Jack the Ripper.

The protagonists are Dr John Pritchard, a well-heeled London psychiatrist, and a mentally disturbed 17-year-old orphan called Anna. With Pritchard taking Anna under his wing and making every effort to mould her into a well-adjusted young woman, it's hard to resist the idea that *Hands of the Ripper* is Hammer Film Productions' blood-spattered take on the Bernard Shaw play *Pygmalion*.

It was an ingenious notion, replacing Shaw's capricious phoneticist with a stiff-backed psychiatrist and his Cockney flower girl with a tragically conflicted teenage murderess. And it resulted – thanks, in large part, to moving performances from Eric Porter and Angharad Rees, plus a rhapsodic score by Christopher Gunning – in a film that is as much a warped weepie as a gruesome body-count thriller. But where did that ingenious notion originate?

Sadly, the genesis of *Hands of the Ripper* survives only sketchily in Hammer's records. The first reference to the project is in September 1970, when company minutes merely record the title and the name of the proposed screenwriter – Spencer Shew. The next reference is in December, when Peter Sasdy is hired as director. Then, before you know it, it's January 1971 and the film is actually in production at Pinewood.

But, on release in October, the film disclosed an interesting detail in its opening credits. For the screenplay was attributed to television writer L W (Lewis) Davidson, 'from an original story by Edward Spencer Shew'. Then, to muddy the waters yet further, Sphere Books brought out a 'novelisation' by Shew himself, gaudily decorated with a front-cover photo of Porter discovering Marjie Lawrence lying very dead in a blood-filled bathtub.

I use inverted commas around the word 'novelisation' because it's by no means clear that that's what the book actually was. For Shew's version differs from the film in many fundamental ways, suggesting that it may have been an as-yet-unpublished novel when submitted to Hammer, or perhaps even an epic-length 'treatment'. Pritchard, for a start, isn't a psychiatrist; he's a physiologist. (And he's Sir Giles, not plain Dr John.) What's more, the story is set in 1888 and deals in quite a lot of circumstantial detail with the Ripper murders themselves. In other words, Anna is not Jack the Ripper's daughter, struggling with her inherited homicidal compulsions. She actually *is* Jack the Ripper.

Clearly, then, profound changes were made in translating Shew's 'treatment' to the screen, and it has to be said that most of them were for the better. Shew's prose is often quirkily diverting, and his story certainly contains the germ of the *Pygmalion* parody referred to above. But the novel's credibility is severely compromised by the fact that Anna is possessed by not one, but two, departed souls.

One of them is Franz Liszt, no less, making Anna something of a piano prodigy. The other is a notional serial killer who terrorised Liverpool back in the 1820s, a murder spree reproduced in London by Anna. The book, therefore, is divided into two sections – 'Hands Beneficent' and 'Hands Malevolent'. Maybe Hammer were worried about the Shew version's similarity to Maurice Renard's classic 1920 novel *The Hands of Orlac*, which had already been filmed three times.

Shew was for many years a crime correspondent for the *Daily Express*, and was also the author of two highly regarded true crime collections published in the early 1960s. Among other things, these books revealed his uninhibited approach to subtitles. The first, *A Companion to Murder*, was subtitled so: 'A Dictionary of Death by Poison, Death by Shooting, Death by Suffocation and Drowning, Death by the Strangler's Hand 1900-1950.'

That should be quite enough to be going on with, you might think, but Shew was only getting started. For the next volume, *A Second Companion to Murder*, he really went for broke with a truly staggering litany: 'A Dictionary of Death by the Knife, the Dagger, the Razor, the Axe, the Chopper, the Chisel; Death by the Iron File, the Marline Spike, the Hammer, the Poker, the Bottle; Death by the Jemmy, the Spanner, the Tyre Lever, the Iron Bar, the Starting Handle; Death by the Sandbag, the Sash Weight, the Mallet, the Half-Brick, the Stick, the Stone; Death by the Fire Tongs, the Butt End of a Revolver, the

Metal Chair, etc. 1900-1950.' Commendably, Shew's publishers managed to squeeze this astounding recital, not just onto the title page, but even onto the front cover.

Shew, then, was intrigued by the more imaginative, not to say baroque, forms of murder, which makes his version of *Hands of the Ripper* all the more surprising. For, ghastly though the real Ripper's murders were, they featured none of the startling variations in weaponry so scrupulously catalogued in Shew's subtitles. Oddly enough, the killings in the film version of *Hands of the Ripper* are much more in Shew's outré line, picking up the murderous poker specified in Shew's list but adding such nasty innovations as a pair of lorgnettes, a handful of hat-pins, and a truly novel conjunction of a broken hand-mirror and a full-length cheval glass.

And now, four decades later, *Hands of the Ripper* has been given a new and exciting makeover by the estimable Guy Adams. Radical, too. Apart from anything else, the story is updated to the present day – which, of course, brings with it a whole new Ripper. It just goes to show that Spencer Shew got hold, however shakily, of a truly durable idea all those years ago. To see how that idea works out in the 21st century, just read on...

Jonathan Rigby

Jonathan Rigby is the author of *English Gothic: A Century of Horror Cinema*, *American Gothic: Sixty Years of Horror Cinema* and *Studies in Terror: Landmarks of Horror Cinema*.

hands of the ripper

Prologue

An Overture of Night Music

Firelight glitters like exploding stars against the metal bars of her cot. Anna extends a finger, trying to catch the light and own it. It escapes her but she laughs anyway.

The shouting of her parents seems to come from far away when she focuses on the light. As if it's not in the same room at all. As if it comes from somewhere so perfectly elsewhere that it could never possibly harm her.

Sometimes the cot feels like a cage. She has outgrown it now but Daddy likes her to be kept inside it when he is home. It makes her think of the pictures of the lions and tigers that she sees in the picture books Mummy lets her read. One day, she thinks, she may even roar like them. She may even roar as loud as Daddy.

He is roaring now, burning as brightly as the fire in the grate.

No, she thinks, not quite. And returns her gaze to the sparkle on the cot bars.

She doesn't see the first spray of blood that spits against the cheap wallpaper. She only becomes aware that Mummy's broken when she drops to her knees in front of the cot, a bloody, cupped palm held to her face. This is not unusual. Daddy often has to help both of them shut their mouths. Daddy is clever like that; he knows how to make silence happen. He also knows how to make the world fill with noise. It's the latter he seems to be doing now because it's not just Mummy's screaming that threatens to tear her attention away from the glittering beauty of the firelight. There is the building sound of sirens, 'Night Music' her daddy often calls it as he looks out of the window and watches the police cars and fire engines as they drive past.

'The natives are getting restless,' he'd often say, 'the jungle is alive with them!'

Anna is sometimes confused by this. She has seen pictures of jungle and it doesn't look like the grey concrete world outside their front door. The jungle is a wild place, full of colour and brilliant, beautiful animals.

Mummy is holding up her hands, showing Daddy that she understands, showing him that she will be quiet now. Her words come jumbled up with bubbles, because her nose is bleeding so badly. Like the Little Mermaid singing under the sea. Daddy's not sure he believes Mummy's promises, Anna can tell, he's pacing up and down, circling Mummy like . . .

(A tiger in the jungle?)

The Night Music is getting louder and it seems to be driving Daddy mad. Normally he likes the noise it makes, sings along with it in front of the window, howling at the glass. Tonight it makes him twitch and shout. He is scratching at himself, tearing at his shirt as if he is covered in small insects. He reminds Anna of the cat they had for a short while, the way it used to scratch, kicking at itself with its hind leg. Daddy didn't like it doing that, that's why he made it go away.

Daddy walks over to the fireplace and reaches for the poker. Anna is pleased, she thinks that he is going to make the fire burn even brighter now, make the light dance more brilliantly than ever before. He is not. For Daddy, the fire has never burned brighter.

He carries the poker over to Mummy and beats at her with it. Perhaps she is full of coals, thinks Anna, perhaps she needs to be made better, encouraged into heat. It doesn't seem to be working. It's making her cry out again and Anna knows that is never a good idea and wishes she could tell her mummy to shut up as she'll only make Daddy angry with all that noise. But Anna doesn't say a word, Anna just wants to be invisible behind the bars of her cot. She watches the fire, choosing its warm orange over Mummy's deep red. She listens to the crackling of the flames rather than the pop and brittle snap of Mummy as Daddy hits her again and again with the poker.

The Night Music is almost deafening now. Anna thinks that Daddy may have brought it to their home by his singing, for she can hear the sound of feet on the stairs, then fists on the door. The noise scares her at first but then, out of the corner of her eye, she notices that Daddy has stopped beating Mummy and that scares her more. Daddy doesn't look quite empty yet. He has that, quivering, excited look of a man who still has lessons to give. Anna knows that look and usually it means that it's her turn.

Someone is shouting outside the door but Anna can't hear the words, she's too busy staring at her daddy. Watching as he lifts the poker (which is dripping on the carpet and if it stains, oh dear, that will only make him angrier still).

'Daddy?' she asks, because she's never seen him look this angry and she is scared. Scared that she won't be able to please him, scared that she won't be able to say the right things to make him stop. He doesn't look like he's even in the same room, painted red, eyes empty, he is walking towards her but is so removed that she doesn't think she will be able to stop him doing anything.

The banging on the front door gets heavier. Anna thinks that if they hit the wood any harder they'll break it and then what will Daddy say? She stares at the firelight on the bars of her cot, tries to fill her head with that and nothing else. But then she sees her father reflected in the metal, stretched thin, like a smear of red paint. He is raising the poker again and Anna bites her lower lip so hard she chokes a little in the blood that runs down her throat.

The door bursts open.

One

In the Rain with the Dead

John Pritchard looked into his son's eyes and tried to ignore what he saw in them. There is nothing more embarrassing than being pitied by one's child.

'I know, I know,' he insisted, 'the whole thing's a con. Still, you've got to admit it could be interesting.'

'A bunch of OAPs trying to chat to the gaps in their address book? Fascinating.'

Michael Pritchard stirred his tea, encouraging it to cool down. Always in such a hurry, thought his father.

'These things aren't like that,' John said, 'they're all white teeth and peroxide highlights these days. Talking to the dead is a glamorous business.'

'I doubt Derek Acorah makes many public appearances round here,' observed Michael, looking down his nose at the dreary terraced houses through the rain-streaked window. 'This place isn't exactly the Ivy, is it?'

John had to defer to his son's opinion, never having set foot inside the place. The small cafe they were sat in had an atmosphere as insipid as their teas. The surly Greek man behind the counter seemed to have begrudged them even that. He belonged to that select group within the service industry that has realised that all would be fine if only the customers could just be removed from the equation. In his hands he wound a tea towel like a Thugee scarf. The tea towel had once been printed with the Welsh flag, now the dragon was hidden beneath brown stains and every now and then the man used it to whip at his Formica counter. Perhaps, thought John, the fixtures got unruly unless he kept them on a tight leash.

'It has a charm,' he said.

'No,' Michael replied, 'it really doesn't.' He took a sip of his tea and the expression he wore on his face indicated that he regretted it. He checked his watch.

'What time is it?' his father asked.

'Ten past, still another twenty minutes.'

'Sorry, shouldn't have got here so early, you have better things to do . . .'

This was true but Michael was sensitive enough to deny it. 'Who was to know? We could have spent hours looking for the place.'

'We'd have been better getting a taxi, it's just habit . . .'

'We'll get a cab back, doesn't matter.'

This pitter-patter of politeness and muted affection was mirrored by the rain outside and their conversation faltered as both watched a woman with pram and shopping bags struggle through the pool of light shed from the cafe window. The bemused face of a toddler was pressed against the plastic rain cover of the pram, like vacuum-packed meat from a supermarket fridge. Somewhere there was the hiss of a bus's hydraulic doors

2

and a giggling group of teenage girls moved past, having been discharged out into the inhospitable night. One of them turned towards the window and pulled a face.

'What you looking at?' she shouted, stumbling as if unable to walk in a straight line while being watched by strangers.

There was a brittle flutter of laughter before they were swallowed by the dark. The pool of light in front of the two men was once again empty.

Michael took another sip of tea, having not quite learned his lesson.

There was the slosh of a car carving its way through the dirty water in the road.

'What time is it now?' asked John.

Michael sighed and checked. 'Quarter past.'

'Christ, time moves slower in Bowes Park.'

'That's Enfield Council for you.'

John smiled, trying to pretend his state of mind was nothing other than casual amusement.

His son knew him better but let it pass. 'Where did you say Ray heard about this woman?' he asked.

Ray was the IT technician at St. Ludovic's, the university where John lectured. He in psychology. Ray haunted the outside spaces of the campus, even during the hours he was supposed to be off-shift, a stolid, doughy figure trailing cotton-thin lines of smoke from perpetual roll-up cigarettes.

'She's the shit,' he had announced to John a couple of days earlier, passing him a piece of paper, 'the veritable bollocks.'

'You don't sound like a student,' John told him, with a gentle smile, 'your vernacular is as contrived as a dad at a disco.'

'They're not called discos,' Ray replied, 'not for decades, old man.'

'I am old,' John admitted, unfolding the paper with one hand and putting on his reading glasses with the other. 'So are you, getting older with each word, in fact. What is this?'

The flyer was cheaply produced, a childish drawing of stars interspersed with squiggles that John eventually deciphered as astrological symbols. In the midst of this scattershot attempt at artistry was a chunk of text in comic sans font: 'Death is Not the End' it insisted. 'Let Aida "Granny" Golding Show You!'

'Got it from one of the students,' said Ray.

'Not an English major, I hope, not with that many capitals.'

'No, the student didn't make it,' explained Ray, 'he just passed it on. That guy that thinks he's attending Woodstock.'

'That could be the entire student body.'

'No, you know him, long hair, all beiges and browns, stinks of pot and poor taste.'

John knew immediately who Ray meant. 'Shaun Vedder.'

'Shaun Vedder. He picked it up when he was doing interviews for some coursework. One of those pitiful wastes of time you old fools like to set them. Anything to get them out from under your feet.'

'That's it exactly. We care not one jot for their

education.' John looked at the flyer again. 'And why are you giving it to me?'

'Because I know you're interested in that sort of thing and, by all accounts, she's good at what she does.'

'Talking to the dead?'

'Well, I wouldn't know about that, but according to young Vedder people make a fuss over her. She's an open secret, the real thing, not like all these showy gits on cable telly, a proper medium working out of North London. So whatever it is she's doing she's doing it right.'

'You can tell by the quality of her advertising.'

'All part of it though, ain't it? She's paranormal retro chic!'

'She's a dab hand with a pack of crayons, for sure.'

And with that he shoved the piece of paper away in his pocket where it would have stayed were it not for the fact that he couldn't stop dreaming about Jane. And not just dreaming . . .

'He got it from one of the students,' he said to Michael, aware that his mind had been wandering. 'They picked it up as part of the parapsychology coursework.'

'They do parapsychology?'

'It's best to get it out of their systems early on. Once we have thoroughly denied the existence of spooks we can move on to why people like to believe otherwise.'

'And have you moved on?'

John smiled and finished his tea.

'How's Laura?' John asked as they made their way out

into the rain. Enquiring after his son's girlfriend was the surest way he knew to get the conversation back on track.

'She's fine. In fact, we're thinking of getting a place together.'

'Oh yes?' This was good news, something happy to focus on as they made their way along the pavement. The rain had filled the irregular surface, forcing them to step over puddles like children playing hopscotch. *One, two, buckle my shoe*, rattled around John's head as he listened to his son list the benefits of cohabiting with the woman he loved.

'Of course,' said Michael, 'there's a part of Laura that would prefer to remain where she is. I mean, she knows her house. You should see her move around it, you'd never know . . .'

You'd never know she was blind, John thought, silently finishing his son's sentence. Michael didn't like to describe Laura in potentially negative terms, didn't like to put anything into words that might define her as being different from anyone else. Partly this was down to Laura herself, blind since very young she refused either sympathy or concession.

'I can't imagine Laura being afraid to learn her way around somewhere new,' John said, 'in fact I can't imagine her being afraid of anything much.'

Michael smiled. 'True enough.'

They came to a junction and ahead of them, bathed in the sickly orange of a large security light, was the Queen's Road Community Centre.

'And lo, the Albert Hall,' said Michael, wiping water

from his face as they waited for a break in the traffic so they could cross.

A lorry cut its way through the semi-flooded road, an emission-blackened teddy bear strapped to its radiator like soggy road kill. Father and son had to step back to avoid a soaking. The lorry had no more knowledge of them as it sailed away into the dark than a whale might in an ocean of little fish.

'Much more of this,' John said, 'and I'll need a medium to talk to you let alone . . .' The joke soured in his mouth, bravado turned to painful awkwardness.

'Let alone Mum,' said Michael. 'Yeah . . . Let's not discuss that, all right?'

'I miss her just as much as you do,' out loud it sounded like one-upmanship, and he hadn't meant it to. Michael knew how much he had loved Jane.

They caught their break in the traffic and ran across the wet road, kicking up great splashes as they landed on the waterlogged safety of the other pavement. Neither of them stopped running, taking outrageous leaps across the puddles in the community centre car park until they finally found the shelter of the covered porch.

'No need to run,' said an old man smoking in the doorway, 'the dead aren't going anywhere.' He sliced off the hot tip of his roll-up using a long and yellow thumbnail and put the remains in the pocket of his jacket to finish off later. Giving himself a nod of pride at a job well done he shuffled inside the hall, leaving a trail of muddy footprints, like dance instructions, in his wake.

'Two is it?' asked a young man sat behind a fold-out

table. He flexed a book of pink raffle tickets in his hands as if warming them up.

'Yes please.' John had his wallet ready, the least he could do was cover the price of Michael's ticket, then at least it need cost him only his time.

'That'll be twenty pounds please,' said the young man, rather defensively as if anticipating an argument over price. Perhaps it was the disapproving look on Michael's face, he wasn't one to hide his feelings and he sighed as his father paid. He gets that from his mother, John thought, she was never shy about showing displeasure either. Many was the rude waiter or belligerent telemarketer that had discovered that for themselves over the years.

'Sit wherever you like,' said the young man, giving his raffle tickets another vicious throttling. 'But stick to the cardboard.'

John wondered what the man was talking about but as they passed into the main hall it soon became obvious: flattened cardboard boxes had been laid out as impromptu matting to soak up the wet from people's feet. There was also a leaking roof to contend with. Dotted throughout were chains of water droplets, dripping musically into strategically placed saucepans. The effect was that of an enthusiastic, if tone deaf, orchestra of children with toy drums.

'Charming,' said Michael as they filed along a row of plastic chairs near the back. They sat down and waited for the evening's demonstration to begin.

The hall was half full, with more and more coming in as the start time approached. One by one they ambled in, shaking off the rainwater and then making their way to a seat, taking stretched steps from one patch of cardboard to the next, reminding John of children playing pirates.

'Have you seen her before, dear?' asked an elderly lady to John's right. She had that flatulent smugness that ladies of a certain age were prone to, inflating her face and nodding at every opportunity for proving herself right in conversation.

'No,' John admitted, 'though I hear she's good.'

'None better, if you ask me.' She gestured vaguely around the hall. 'Most of this lot follow her around, seeing most of the demonstrations. Never been here before. Mind you,' she glanced at a nearby saucepan of rainwater, 'I dare say I won't come again either.'

'The weather is particularly bad, there's flooding in some parts of the country according to the news.'

'That's as maybe but you've got to have some standards. We like it when she does Islington, they have a better class of hall in Islington.'

'We?'

'My dear Henry,' she waved at the air as if to dis-engage a cobweb from her cheek. 'He doesn't just turn up at any old venue, don't imagine he'll lower himself to attending this place.'

It took John a moment to realise Henry was dead. 'He was your . . .?'

'Husband,' she replied with some force perhaps to rebuke the suggestion that their relationship might have been lacking in any Christian formality. 'Passed these four years now. Not that I have had a chance to miss him. I speak to him more now than I did when he was alive. You needed a loudhailer and a sharp stick to get him to the dinner table before the cancer had him; I barely get a moment's peace these days. Rattling the door handles, setting the light fittings swinging . . . then there's Islington, of course, Henry does love the hall at Islington.'

John risked a glance towards his son but Michael was either ignoring the conversation or distracted by his own thoughts, staring at the stage and tapping at his lower lip with his forefinger.

'There's another one,' said Henry's widow, regaining John's attention.

'Another one?'

She nodded towards a young woman sitting down two rows in front of them. 'Always turns up,' she explained, 'cot death.'

John couldn't think what he would want to say to that, but the elderly woman was happy to fill the silence. 'Always gets a message too,' she continued, puffing up her cheeks as if holding in her words, but there was no such luck. 'I'm at a loss as to how. I mean, it was only a baby. She should get on with her life. Girls today are far too sensitive. Mind you, this lot laps it up.'

The fact that she considered herself somehow apart from the rest of the audience hardly surprised John, her kind never felt any other way.

'I'm sure she appreciates the comfort,' he said, watching as the young girl tugged at her cheap skirt and tried to get comfortable on the flat plastic seat. He realised he was staring when his elderly companion spoke again. 'I suppose the men like her too,' she said, giving him a look of disapproval, 'she's that type.'

John couldn't help but wonder what type that was supposed to be. Attractive? She was certainly that but his attention had been drawn by something else. She reminded him of his wife. It wasn't anything so simple as looks. True, they were both blond but otherwise there could be little to compare them. Jane had been tall, perpetually thin – though never so horrifyingly skin and bone as she appeared to him now, whenever he imagined catching sight of her, as if the tumour had continued to do its worst even into the afterlife. This girl was of an average height and slightly chubby. He couldn't call her fat – even had he been insensitive enough to do so – but she had the sort of overall thick - ness that some people are born with, as if their whole body is wrapped in an extra layer. The similarities were in her mannerisms more than her appearance, he decided, the way she shifted in her seat, constantly looking around. A slightly childish impatience. Jane had never been able to bear waiting for things, to the point where she had always been late for appointments rather than endure it. That quirk had driven him up the wall when she had been alive but seemed charming now she was gone. We forgive the dead everything. There was something else too, he decided, something so elusive as to be beyond him. Like a face in a crowd that triggers recognition. Something about this girl was all too familiar.

The lights were turned off to a gentle discomfited

murmur from the audience. John supposed this was intended to replicate the dimming of theatre lights. As it was, from the snatches of conversation around him, most people seemed convinced the rain had blown the fuse. A single spotlight proved them wrong, pointing at the centre of the small stage where the young man who had been selling tickets could just be seen escaping after having placed a chair there.

'Ladies and gentlemen,' the young man announced into a radio mic, 'please welcome the incomparable abilities of Mrs Aida Golding.'

There was warm applause and out of the corner of his eye John saw Michael shake his head.

'Like bad theatre,' the young man mumbled and John found he couldn't disagree. Events like this would always fall victim to their practitioners' innate inability to play things 'straight'. Any hint of the theatrical and the verisimilitude took a pounding. At least the medium herself was a step in the right direction. She was the very epitome of the homely grandmother, wrapped up in an old-fashioned combination of tweed skirt and woollen pullover that made her look about ten years older than she probably was.

'Good evening, my loves,' she said, her voice as twee as her costume, 'thank you for coming out on this inhospitable night. Over the next hour or so let's see if we can't banish the weather with the warmth of our hearts.'

John didn't have to check whether his son squirmed at that sentiment, he knew him well enough.

'We don't need to worry what the skies throw at us,'

she continued, 'we're strong enough to face the worst of it, aren't we?'

There was a general murmur of assent, nothing as solid or confident as words. John had the absurd sensation of being adrift in a crowd of animals. No doubt this was a variation on her usual spiel, a little team-building to get her audience onside before she proceeded to 'part the veil'.

The buttering-up continued. 'There's a wonderful energy tonight,' she said, 'you bless me with your thoughts.'

'And your twenty quid,' Michael whispered.

John could have mentioned that the money had been his to spend but he chose to listen to Aida Golding.

'I can sense many familiar souls with us this evening, both in this world and the next. There are also some new faces, for which I say: welcome, it is wonderful to be able to spread the word. Tonight you will learn the most important lesson of your lives: death is not the end. All of those we have ever known, all we have loved, are still here. They watch over us. They stand alongside us. Life goes on.'

To some that may actually have felt like a comfort but in that moment John couldn't think of anything worse. He found himself imagining that the heavy breathing of the widow in the seat next to him was that of Jane. The fact that this was a familiar terror made it no less powerful. He realised that he wasn't attending in the hope of having Aida Golding's promise proven correct: he was only too convinced his wife was still with him, he wanted someone to prove otherwise.

'The dead do not leave us,' Aida Golding continued, 'they just move on to another level of existence.'

Much consolation that was. John had a sudden urge to get up and leave, his curiosity (and, yes, desperation) had brought him to an experience he was no longer sure he could endure. He was half-risen, enough for Michael to glance over, when Aida Golding cut off all possibility of a sheepish retreat.

'They are here!' she shouted, the sudden increase in volume making many of the audience jump and John drop back in his seat.

'Should have gone before you came,' said his son. John glanced over at him and just made out the ghost of a smile in the darkness.

'Too late,' he said, 'she shouldn't have made me jump.'

This momentary childishness was enough to lessen the panic that had been building up in his chest. He wasn't comfortable but he could, at least, endure.

'They all want to speak,' said Aida Golding, 'they all want you to know they're here.' She took a sudden breath, and clicked her fingers repeatedly. 'Is there a Jonah here, or Jonas . . .?'

John would take far more convincing before he would get involved, but a namesake on the front row was not so reluctant.

'Jonathan?' said the man, half getting to his feet. 'Could it be Jonathan?'

'Or Joanie?' asked a voice from further back, 'our Arthur always called me Joanie.'

'It is Joanie,' confirmed the medium, 'the voice is

becoming clearer. Sometimes it's very hard to hear and you must bear with me, my loves, try and remember I'm not holding a conversation with someone who is right here, rather we are talking across the gap between realities.'

John had to admit this was something of a departure from her earlier assertion but wasn't inclined to dwell on the fact.

'Joanie?'

'Yes.'

'I need your voice, Joanie. Can you stand up for me, my darling? When I ask you a question always reply for me, loud and clear. You can do that, can't you, Joanie?'

'Yes, of course . . .'

Aida Golding broke out of her 'trance' for a few moments, to address the audience directly. 'As those who have joined me before will know I'm a clairaudient and it's very important for me to form a strong link between the spirit and the person they want to speak to. Imagine it's like a telephone line, but there's a lot of interference and the signal is weak. Your answers, Joanie – and this goes for everyone here tonight, of course – are what keep that link strong. If you're quiet or slow to respond, the link gets weak and may break entirely. So don't be shy, shout out! Be strong and positive! Don't block this natural gift with silence and negativity, let your loved ones be heard!'

Again, there was much in this that John recognised as standard fare. Putting the onus on the audience, making them responsible for the success or failure of the night's events, instilling in them a suggestion to always reply in the affirmative. The more he heard the less he felt involved. Perhaps tonight would be exactly the cold dose of reality he had hoped for?

'It's a man's voice, Joanie. He says . . . his name, is it Arthur?'

'Yes! That's him!'

John couldn't fail to notice how much this impressed the gathered audience as several people drew in breath. He couldn't claim to be as impressed as he remembered Joanie mentioning the name herself.

'Is this your husband, Joanie?' the medium asked.

There was a slight pause at that and even in the darkness the silhouette of her body language showed discomfort. John wasn't the only one to notice.

'Only it doesn't feel like it,' the medium continued, withdrawing another gasp from her willing crowd, 'it feels more like . . .'

'He was my brother.'

'I know, Joanie, he's just told me as much! Between the two of you gossips, eh? I've got my ears full.'

There was a ripple of amusement at this as the tension was released.

'As I was saying you can often sense the family link, you can sense the call of blood even across the veil. Shush Arthur, she knows!' At that last she turned away from the audience as if hushing a man stood behind her.

'What did he say?' Joanie asked, desperate for her dead brother's words.

Aida Golding held up her hand for a moment, asking for silence so she could hear the poor, faint voice of the dead Arthur. She laughed. 'He's just telling me about when you were kids,' she said finally, 'he says he wasn't always the best brother.'

'He was a right bugger!' confirmed Joanie to much laughter, though John wondered how many siblings would have needed such a generalised comment confirmed.

Aida Golding nods as if this is all further proof. 'Ask her,' she said, 'I will, Arthur, I will . . . Do you remember the matches?'

'The matches?'

'Yes, love, that's what he's saying: the matches, the matches . . . over and again.'

'I'm not sure . . .'

'Of course she does, he says. She can't have forgotten . . . *the matches*.'

'Oh . . . I think he stole a box once, you know boys . . .'

Yes, John thought, Aida Golding did know boys.

'That's right!' the medium said. 'He stole them, didn't he? Lighting them up and nearly burning the whole place down!'

'He was trouble that's for sure.'

'He says he's sorry for that, he says he knows he was a handful.'

'Oh . . . he doesn't have to worry,'

'He misses you though, Joanie, he says he should have made more of an effort.'

'He was a busy man, I know that . . .'

'Still, he says you realise what you missed when it's gone and he just wants you to know that he loves you and he's still with you.' She held up her hand again, craning her head to grab a few last words from Arthur.

'He says he'll be a better brother for you now than he ever was.'

There were tears at that, of course, Joanie could no longer hold them in. No doubt, thought John, she wasn't alone.

'Thank you, Arthur,' said the medium, 'until we talk again.' And with those simple four words poor Joanie would be hooked, John thought, while Aida Golding moved on to pastures new.

'Trevor?' she asked, though whether this was the name of the recipient or the messenger nobody could know, 'I'm hearing Trevor?'

'My name's Trevor,' admitted a man near the back, somewhat reluctantly.

'Go on,' said a voice to his side and he was ushered upright by the woman sat next to him.

'Let me hear your voice, Trevor,' said Aida, 'the connection is always weak to begin with. It takes effort on all sides until we get warmed up.'

'I'm here,' Trevor replied, clearly embarrassed to be talking out loud in front of everybody.

'Weren't expecting a message tonight, were you?' the medium asked, her inflection neutral enough to let the meaning swing either way.

'No,' said Trevor, allowing her the point just as much as if he had said yes. 'It's been so long since—'

'Please,' said Aida Golding, having heard enough to be going on with. 'I don't wish to be influenced.'

At this point she paused and John could imagine her weighing up her options. Sometimes, he thought, it's a disadvantage to know too much about the business of charlatanism, it makes you see crookedness every-where. In this case, however, he was fairly confident that his instincts were correct. As blind as her audience may be to the fact, Aida Golding was operating a classic fraudulent medium act. Not that she was afraid to take risks:

'It's a young voice,' she said, and John had a moment to wonder how she would get out of this should it not hit its target. Would the spirit have regressed to an earlier existence? But there was no need, the bullet struck home.

'He was thirteen when he died,' confirmed Trevor, a look of absolute shock on his face.

No doubt the shock was shared by Golding herself. 'And he hasn't aged a day, he's still the same boy you remember.'

John wasn't altogether sure this pleased Trevor, the man was visibly shaking as he stared at the medium in the spotlight. John had the impression of an animal caught in the headlights of an oncoming vehicle. Was the threat of communication with this boy so terrifying? Was it the apparent proof of life after death that dis-turbed him or the thought of talking to the boy himself?

'What does he want?' Trevor asked, a funny question that would later return to John's thoughts. Certainly it wouldn't have been his first thought had the unbeliev-able occurred and Jane had made contact.

'He wants what all spirits want,' Aida Golding replied. 'He wants you to know that he's still there, that he's still watching over you, that he's still a part of your life.'

Evidently, this wasn't as reassuring to Trevor as the medium had hoped, in fact the thought seemed to terrify him further.

'What does he say?' he shouted. 'What does he say?'

John felt his son shift uncomfortably in the seat next to him.

'You always get the nutters,' muttered Henry's widow to her right. 'There's no stopping them at the door, some of them even look normal.'

John noticed the young man who had been selling tickets moving towards Trevor.

'I asked you a question!' the man continued to shout. 'What does he say?'

There was a weighty pause as Aida Golding twitched nervously in the spotlight, the murmurs of a concerned audience combining with the steady drip of the leaking roof water. Perhaps it was this constant sound that had frayed Trevor's nerves as he made a break for the door before the young man reached him.

'I don't have to stay,' he shouted, 'I don't want to hear any more, you can't make me. I just want to get on.'

He ran up the central aisle, and John saw the accident coming a moment before it occurred.

'Careful!' he shouted, just as the man's feet pushed one of the waterlogged cardboard squares in a skid across the tiled floor. Trevor fell to the ground with a cry, close to tears as his feet kicked one of the makeshift water buckets and sent a flood of its contents beneath the audience seats.

There was an eruption of panic as people jumped up, grabbing their handbags and trying to avoid a soaking.

'I just want to get on!' Trevor repeated, as the young man took his arm. 'Let go of me!'

He got to his feet and ran from the hall, mercifully staying upright this time. The large fire doors that the young man had closed in a vain attempt to keep the weather out, crashed open and John caught a glimpse of the torrents of rain outside. Then they swung back on their hinges and, like the closing of theatre curtains, the piece of drama was finished.

The young man closed the doors firmly and turned on the lights.

'Is everyone all right?' he asked, his tone making it quite clear that he wasn't all that interested in a negative answer, he'd had quite enough irritation for one evening.

'He was so scared,' announced the woman who had encouraged Trevor to stand up in the first place. 'Said he'd never been to a demonstration before.'

'Hope he never comes again,' commented a wit in the audience. There was a mumble of amusement at that.

'Such negative energy,' said Aida Golding, 'do please forgive me, he quite . . .oh dear . . .' she pulled a chair into the spotlight and sat down. 'I just need a moment my dears, don't worry, I'm sure I will be able to re-establish contact just as soon as I get my breath back. My gift leaves me very exposed.'

John could certainly agree to that.

'Such a focused wave of negativity,' she continued, 'such fear . . . well, it's almost physical in its effect. Like being stood on the promenade during a storm and being hit by a wave. Oh dear . . .' she exhaled and lowered her microphone. 'Horrible,' she added, 'just horrible. I hope you will be kind enough to give me all the positivity and love you can muster, my darlings, that's what I need to get back on my feet.'

'Of course we will,' offered a decidedly enthusiastic woman on the front row, looking over her shoulder to rally support. 'It's the least we can do, considering the comfort and love you've given us.'

Aida Golding smiled. 'You're so kind,' she said. 'Dim the lights Alasdair, let's get on.'

The young man flipped the switch and returned to his seat by the stage, watching as the medium took several slow, measured breaths. 'That's it,' she said, 'oh yes . . . that's what I need. I can feel them now, offering their love and support just as you do. I'm so blessed to have your support.'

'You got that right,' muttered Michael but John wasn't to be distracted. He was, despite his justifiable cynicism, in awe of the way Aida Golding held the room in her hands. There was no denying the genuine energy in the atmosphere; there was nothing her audience wanted more than to see things returned to normal. They wanted their medium back.

'Ah . . .' Aida Golding sighed, tipping her head back and gazing up at the unreliable roof. 'Oh, who's this? I know you . . .'

Her voice had taken on a dreamy tone and she gazed into the thin strand of rainwater that shimmered in the inherited light of the spot lamp. It was a perfect presentation, a tableau of a woman beset by angels.

'My darling girl,' she continued, 'of course your mother's here.'

There was a rustle of anticipation that made John's stomach groan. Could it be that there were so many bereft mothers here?

'It's little Emily,' said Aida Golding, 'little Emily Thompson.'

There was a gasp of breath from the young woman that had drawn John's attention earlier, though it wasn't quite enough to drown out the impatient tutting of the widow beside him.

'She always gets her bloody message,' the old woman complained, 'not fair on the rest of us.'

John was relieved to note that not everyone was so callous, the young woman certainly wasn't the only one giving Aida Golding her complete attention.

'She remembers the warmth of her sky-blue pyjamas, Sandy my love,' the medium continued and at this the young woman burst into tears. 'She's holding out her tiny hand, reaching up for the mobile that hangs above her cot . . . she likes the elephant best, doesn't she, my love?'

Sandy Thompson could barely squeeze out her affirmative answer, so choked was she with tears.

'It's little trunk is curled up, isn't it? Like the cartoons you see of elephants shooting water into the air. We could do with her here tonight, couldn't we, my loves? She'd suck up some of the excess!'

There was laughter at that but it was gentle and tainted with sentiment. John caught the same look on a number of different faces, a sort of rapt adoration, the

23

face of a disciple. It was as if nothing had ever interrupted the show, and the audience remained transfixed even once they went beyond the infantile memories of Sandy Thompson's lost daughter to other loved ones, taking in the remorse of a jilted lover, the regrets of separated siblings and the endless love of marriages brought to a close by death.

When the demonstration came to a close, an hour or so after it had begun, the hall lights came on to illuminate faces that were unswerving in their belief and admiration for Aida Golding. Even the truculent widow to John's right had a half smile on her face as she got up to leave. 'I knew Henry wouldn't come through tonight,' she told him, 'not here, not in a place like this.'

His attention was once more drawn to Sandy Thompson as she gathered her coat and handbag. Her eyes were puffy from tears and she glanced around as if uncomfortable to find herself somewhere so public. As she pulled on her coat she briefly exposed her right forearm and what John noticed there would change both of their lives thereafter.

'Can we please get out of here?' asked Michael, interrupting his father's thoughts. 'I want to be home and in the dry.'

John wasn't quite ready to leave, watching Sandy Thompson tug her coat back into place and make her self-conscious way between the rows of seats.

'Well?' asked Michael. 'Shall I call a cab?'

'Erm . . . maybe,' said John, trying not to make his interest in Sandy too obvious while also following her towards the exit.

The young woman glanced over her shoulder towards Aida Golding and the look on her face fascinated him. It wasn't the adoration he'd seen on other faces, a look he could have thoroughly understood had it been there. It was the face of a woman who both hates and fears what she's seeing, it was a resentful, bitter expression. And in a moment it was gone, replaced by dull tiredness.

'Maybe?' Michael had his phone in his hand. 'What else do you want to do? I promised Laura that I wouldn't be too late.'

'Then you shan't be.' John squeezed his son's arm. 'Call a cab, it can drop me off on the way.'

He noticed Sandy seemed also to be waiting for someone as she walked a little way down the street and huddled beneath her umbrella. A husband, perhaps, who didn't share her belief in the skills of Aida Golding?

'Why don't we head back to the cafe and wait there?' asked Michael.

'Just have it come right here,' said his father, deter - mined to hang around as long as he could. He wanted to see what happened to Sandy, he wanted to know more about her. If there was a way he could express that to his son without causing even greater despair then he couldn't think of it. He led them across the road to the shelter of a bus stop. They could keep dry and John was also in a suitably discreet position to spy on the young woman. His son soon made it clear that he wasn't to be so easily fooled.

'That's the girl,' he said, 'the one with the dead baby.'

'Yes,' his father agreed, and hoped not to have to elaborate.

'Sad,' Michael continued, 'but why are you so interested?'

John sighed, it was a mistake to try and hide your feelings from family, they knew you too well. 'I don't know,' he admitted honestly, 'there's just something about her that won't let go. Something that doesn't add up.'

'Like what?'

'I really don't know, the way she acted, the way she looked at Aida Golding.' He stretched his legs, as if he could erase his mental discomfort physically. 'And her arms were very badly scarred, she self-mutilates.'

'Are you surprised? With what happened to her?'

'Maybe. But that's just it. I'm not sure I believe it *did* happen to her.'

'You think she'd make something like that up?'

'Not her necessarily . . . here we go.'

The rest of Aida Golding's audience had departed, washed away along the streets and pathways by the rain. John and Michael watched as the medium and her young helper came dashing out of the door of the leisure centre and over to their car, an expensive-looking saloon.

'There's money in the spirit world,' said Michael, 'that's for sure.'

'Never doubt it,' his father agreed.

The car pulled out of the small car park onto the road. It drove up to Sandy Thompson, stopped briefly so that she could climb in and then pulled away.

'Well there's a thing,' said Michael, 'she was a plant.'

'I thought as much,' his father agreed. 'As a regular it was possible that Aida Golding had picked up the elaborate detail from previous visits but that didn't explain the look Sandy gave her, the clear resentment she feels towards the woman.'

'Resentment? I can't imagine she spins her story for free.'

'Maybe,' said John. 'I don't suppose we shall ever know.'

But as their taxi pulled up he had already decided he would do everything he could to find out.

Two

'Why Are You Doing This?'

John watched Ray wend his unhurried way across the campus courtyard. The rain was still with them and the irrepressibly cheerful young woman on BBC *Breakfast* saw little chance of that changing soon. The news seemed to please her, but then John doubted anything could have impinged on that plastic smile, she was a woman of infinite emotional fakery.

The IT technician had confiscated a transparent poncho from Lost Property and stood, shapeless and pale, smoking a cigarette a couple of feet from John's half-open window. He looked like a guttering candle, a thin trail of smoke struggling skywards from the conical tip of his hood, only to be smashed apart by the droplets of rain.

'Enjoying yourself?' John asked, tilting the window so he could hang out of it and yet stay sheltered.

'Some little Hitler complained about the fags again,' the technician replied, 'so I have decided to make a point standing out here to exercise my civil liberties.' Ray was always being told off for smoking within the building. 'I half hope to catch something

28

weather-related, just to rub it in even more.'

'Like what?' John asked. 'Rising damp of the lungs?'

'You mock, old man, but I need to smoke, it keeps my sense of smell in check. You think a man could work as closely with students as I do without numbing the senses?' He took a deep drag. 'It's a health precaution and the buggers on the admin staff penalise me for it. My death will nibble at their consciences.'

'You think they have any?'

'I plan on haunting them anyway, not for me the passive route, I will make life hell for them when I've gone. A never-ending assault of loud noises and sexual advances. I will be like that ghost in *The Entity*, sexual appetite uncurbed by death, desperate to throw an ethereal fuck-all up a Barbara Hershey.'

'She on the admin staff now?'

'Sadly not, which I admit will likely dilute my appetites. Even the dead can close their eyes and imagine, though.'

'A reassuring thought.'

'On the subject of the dead, how did your conver - sation with them go?'

'Well,' John settled back against the thin windowsill, trying to get comfortable, 'I wouldn't say it was a conversation exactly but it was certainly interesting.'

'She a crook?'

John didn't really doubt the answer to that but his innate politeness made him pause before answering. 'I'd say so,' he admitted, 'she used a lot of the usual tricks, misleading replies, Barnum statements . . .'

'Barnum whats?'

'"There's something for everyone", more accurately called the Forer effect. Phrasing statements in such a manner that they seem specific and yet could actually apply to lots of people. Astrologists are particularly fond of them.'

'Well now,' Ray smiled, 'you just don't believe in anything, do you?'

'I'd like to,' John admitted, 'but nothing has presented itself just yet.' Nothing except the constant presence of your long-dead wife, said a voice in his head, let's not forget that.

'That's the problem with thinkers, they're never satisfied. So you won't be going again?'

'I don't know,' John admitted, picking at the flaking paint of the windowsill.

'If she's a fake then what's the point?'

'I'm intrigued by part of the act, a stooge she uses . . . *think* she uses.'

'Well, if you need someone to hold your hand and buy drinks for then I'm happy to help.'

John smiled and nodded. 'I'll let you know.'

Ray pressed the tip of his cigarette against the wet glass, painting it with a spiral of black ash. 'Make sure you do.'

He turned and walked back across the courtyard, the rain splashing off his waterproofed body, causing a fine spray that made him appear to be smouldering.

John sprinkled the pieces of loose paint he'd picked out of the open window, feeling absurdly like a naughty child. He closed out the rain and returned to his desk to sip at a lukewarm mug of coffee and try and get his head straight.

He had pretended to be uncertain as to whether he intended to visit Aida Golding again, which wasn't in the least true. He planned on attending another of her 'demonstrations' that evening, alone this time; he was critical enough of his own behaviour without having Michael assist. Or Ray, for that matter. As sympathetic as he was he couldn't bear the idea of the technician thinking he was just a pathetic old man mooning after a broken girl. Because it was more than that, wasn't it? What was the word he had used when talking to Ray? Ah yes . . . *intrigued*.

He finished his coffee trying to wash away his own self-deception with the last sugary mouthful.

The rain still hadn't stopped by the time he left his office. He tugged a bright yellow rain-slicker over himself, straddling his pushbike and yanking the ends of his waterproofs over the handlebars. Jane had used to laugh to see him ride up the driveway, 'like a cheese on wheels' she had announced, stepping back to let him clamber through the door.

These days there was nobody to greet him but his vaguely insolent cat, Toby Dammit, a light-coloured Maine Coon that had always put John in mind of Terence Stamp, so wild was his hair and vacant his expression. Toby was not impressed at the intrusion of rainwater into his front hall and sauntered through to the kitchen to wait for food.

John hung the waterproofs on a hook by the door and

pulled off his soggy shoes. The hallway was dark and felt horribly empty and unwelcome. He looked out at the distorted reflections of streetlights through the frosted glass and gathered the strength to make the house his own.

Houses need warming up emotionally. When left to chill they become soulless places of cool brick and isolation. John knew this only too well now he lived alone. He worked his way through the downstairs, turning on lights and drawing curtains. He inserted a CD, wanting to beat away the silence. He walked into the kitchen, paying off Toby with a couple of scoops of cat meat so that he could open a bottle of wine in peace. Just one glass, he decided, to warm him up and wash down dinner. Not that he had much time to eat. He'd need to leave the house again in three-quarters of an hour and he foolishly felt the need to wash away the rain with a warm shower before heading out in it once again. He found pasta leftovers and sipped at his wine while he watched the cling-filmed bowl revolve beyond the glass door of the microwave. Tonight's 'demon - stration' was not far away at a small venue somewhere behind Euston Station, on a pleasant day it would have been an enjoyable walk.

His letterbox rattled and he stepped into the hallway to see what had been dropped through. The floor was empty. He decided it must have been the wind. Above him the stairs creaked and he glanced up through the balusters.

'Jane?' The word was out of his mouth before he had even thought about it and he pressed his hand to his lips as if shocked by their thoughtlessness. He shared the house with nobody else, of course, but still, he was not so deluded as to think it was his wife making the boards creak. He definitely couldn't catch her shape in the dark shadow that gathered towards the roof. Couldn't imagine her feet, pale blue veins running underneath the white skin, as they descended into the light, the only part of her that would dare to do so. He could see nothing of the sort. And just to make sure of the fact he went back into the kitchen where the microwave switched itself off with an earthly 'ping'. He drained his wine, poured another and refused to imagine that his dead wife was descending the stairs and making her dry and creaky way towards his turned back.

He ate quickly, shaking off his fears and nerves with every hot forkful. He was a silly, over-imaginative old man and he should know better. Had Jane taken every rational part of him with her when she died?

He forced himself upstairs, refusing to turn the light on until he reached the landing. He wouldn't be scared in his own home.

Turning on the shower he stripped off and caught a glimpse of himself in the bathroom mirror.

How ridiculous age makes us, he thought, looking at his pale, stodgy body. And not just the flesh, he admitted before stepping into the shower.

He turned on the water to as hot as he could bear, which stung and his skin glowed pink. It made him growl as he frothed his hair into a plume of foam. If only everything could be scrubbed away by hot water and soap. He rinsed the shampoo from his head and rubbed at his eyes, opening them to see something move beyond the steamed-up, frosted plastic of the shower cubicle. He froze, staring at the indistinct shape a couple of feet away. It was still now but he was sure he had seen it sway. It was a game of statues, the thing had been advancing on him while his eyes were closed but now, while watched, it was as immobile as he was, waiting for his attention to move away so it could creep forward again. But his attention wouldn't fade. He didn't dare allow it to. The shower continued to dowse him and he was grateful for the noise it made. He didn't want to know what the shape sounded like as – heedless of the fact he was watching – it began to move closer. He backed against the wall as it pressed its face up against the cubicle, a pale, grey face, split into bars by the distortion of the plastic. He could imagine her skin, dead but damp, like the soft white flesh of a verruca, ready to be pulled from the bone. One eye watched him, the other was a dark hollow, empty, he guessed, a passage for beetles, worms or whatever else made its home in a body as decrepit as this.

'Jane?' he asked. 'Jane, why are you doing this?'

His back nudged the water control and suddenly the heat was gone, replaced with a torrent of icy cold. He gave a startled cry, yanking the water tap off. The body outside the cubicle was gone, the bathroom empty.

He sat on his bed slowly drying himself off. The stress of losing Jane was considerable, no wonder it had caused side effects. Were these apparitions the sign of a guilty conscience? Certainly he had grown to wish her dead during the last couple of months. There had been so little of the woman he loved in the brittle, bed-bound creature that had shared his home. It had breathed with all the desperate agony of a woman near-drowned, each breath of air snatched from the suffocating room as if it might be her last. Her eyes had looked on delirium. She had rarely known him, thanks to the painkillers. The doctors at the hospice had assured him that everything was designed to help ease her passing but it had taken little time for him to realise that there was no dignity left for the woman he loved. Just a descent into madness and living death.

And still she wouldn't let go.

He dressed quickly, not wanting to spend any longer in the house than necessary, and soon he was back out in the rain, hiding from ghosts in the company of those who professed to be surrounded by them.

This formed the pattern of his life for some time. He made a point of visiting every demonstration Aida Golding offered that was within easy commuter distance. This in itself was no great challenge as there was enough business in London to keep her occupied five nights a week.

He watched her in public halls, gymnasiums, fringe theatres and the back rooms of pubs. She moved easily between them, from the chilly pretension of art-house stages to the beer-soaked velvet and dark wood of ancient taverns. And in every room her powers appeared on form, she passed on messages of love, advice and even recrimination from deceased loved ones, her audiences always willing to take what she offered. He found himself often seeing the same faces, eager for the next instalment from beyond the grave. Henry's widow was a regular feature, forever dismissing the venues as beneath both her and her long-suffering husband. Despite his natural reservations, John found himself talking to her about Jane, though the older woman was, of course, far more interested in talking than listening. Alasdair was there of course, taking tickets and dealing with unruly guests (which, like the panicked Trevor on the first night John had seen Golding perform, were not unusual).

And then there was Sandy. Despite the fact that he had become increasingly convinced that there was very little true about the girl's story – including her name, he had no doubt – John was just as drawn to her after repeated meetings. The only thing about her that he believed real were the tears on her cheeks and the scars on her arms, though as to the underlying cause for these symptoms he couldn't begin to say.

Every now and then he came close to talking to her but was embarrassed to find that, like a nervous schoolboy, he clammed up as soon as he got near.

But then, what exactly did he have to say? 'Hello, I've become unhealthily obsessed with you and was just wondering if you would do me the kindness of telling me what really drove you to self-mutilate?' Hardly.

So what did he expect to gain from all this? What insight could he possibly achieve other than the rather obvious one that desperate people will do anything in order to find comfort?

He certainly couldn't afford to keep attending with such regularity, at ten pounds a ticket it was an expensive folly as well as a pointless one.

Yes, all very logical, and yet still he went. Observing from the darkness as the grieving and the greedy exchanged business. It occurred to him one night, as he watched an elderly woman weep over the death of her mother some twenty years earlier, that he was no better than Jane at letting go.

Three

Lying in the Dark

'Can we meet up?' asked Michael. 'I could do with some advice.'

John shuffled the mobile from one ear to the other. 'Let me guess, you're gay?'

'That's it precisely. How about a sandwich or something? I can tell you all about it.'

'I'm free at one, that do?'

'Fine, I'll meet you at Verano.'

Verano was a little cafe just across the road from the main university building. The sort of student-orientated place that offered soup and sandwiches at a price they could nearly afford. John didn't eat there often as he always felt he was intruding into their world, crossing some indefinable line between student and lecturer. Still, he and Michael could always grab something to take away, better that than try and talk in the middle of this rugby scrum for cheese and pickle.

'Oh, hey sir,' John found himself face to face with Shaun Vedder, the student that had given Golding's flyer to Ray.

'Hi Shaun, all good?'

'Yeah, well, they've run out of vegetable tikka wraps so, no, lunch sucks but I'll get over it.'

'I'm sure.'

'You ever go see that medium?'

John was thrown by that, it had never occurred to him that Ray might have mentioned his interest. 'Medium?' he replied, more to buy time than out of any confusion.

'Yeah, Ray told me you might look into it. Writing some kind of paper or something?'

'Oh . . .' John feigned casual remembrance, aware that he was doing it badly, 'yes, something like that.'

'Only, if you need any help I'm kind of into that sort of thing myself. Be cool to do some coursework on it.'

'Well, we'll see . . . I'm not sure if I—'

'No problem.'

John could see Shaun was upset. He was the sort of kid that always wanted to impress, determined to make friends with every member of the faculty.

'I'm just not a hundred per cent on where I'm going with it yet,' John insisted, 'but I'd definitely give you a shout if—'

'Cool.' Shaun clearly wasn't fooled and left the cafe with a false smile firmly fixed in place. In the doorway he almost collided with Michael.

'Hi, ' Michael said, once he had picked out his father's face from the crowd, 'have I picked the most popular place to eat in the city?'

'Pretty much,' John smiled. 'Let's grab something and then take it back to my office, we'll have some peace and quiet that way.'

*

John's office had long since ousted human comfort in favour of expanding quantities of paper. Books lined the walls, student reports and Internet printouts slithered between magazines and journals. The whole room rustled.

'Years since I've been in here,' said Michael while he waited for his dad to clear a place for him to sit.

'Years since anyone's been in here except me,' John admitted, dumping back issues of *The Psychologist* onto the floor so as to free up a small chair that had been hiding beneath them. 'I tend to conduct interviews in the canteen, it's cleaner and serves coffee.'

'It's fine,' said Michael, sitting down and carefully unwrapping his beef and horseradish sandwich.

'So,' said John, 'what was it you wanted to talk about?'

Michael, mouth full of sandwich rolled his eyes and chewed.

'In your own time,' said John, 'I mean, some of us have jobs to do but . . .'

Michael kicked his father's shin and swallowed. 'Git,' he said, 'lunch first, talk later.'

'All right,' his father agreed, picking at a pasta salad. He had no enthusiasm for his lunch, too impatient to eat. His life seemed to be stuck in a state of anticipation and unease, his evenings filled with confrontations he wanted and yet feared. Now Michael, the most laid-back son one could imagine, 'wanted to talk'. He imagined it would be something to do with work. John wasn't blind to the fact that Michael hadn't seemed to have had any for some time. It was a subject on which he never pried, knowing that Michael's pride would put him on the defensive as soon as the subject came up. His son had been a jobbing actor for the last twelve years, having jacked in a promising career in law in order to 'follow his dream'. John had always supported the decision – life was miserable enough at times without doing a job you loathed – but he would be a liar if he didn't admit that he wished a more stable lifestyle for his son. The work, when it came, was reasonably paid but the long periods between jobs sapped Michael's confidence and John hated seeing the morose and uncommunicative man he sometimes became as a result.

'You know I said about Laura and I getting a place together?' his son said after finally finishing his food.

John speared a particularly slippery piece of red pepper with his fork and nodded.

'Well, in truth I've been suggesting it because of money more than anything else. It seemed to make sense that we chip in for one place rather than paying for two. Thing is, she's talking about buying a place but you know what my life's like, I just can't afford to commit to a mortgage. But how do I tell her? I don't want her to think that I'm having cold feet, don't want to panic her about the lousy proposition she's taking on either . . .'

'Laura's not worried about that sort of thing.'

'She should be, everyone should be these days, nobody's got any money and things are getting worse not better.'

'As true as that might be she still isn't going to run a mile because you're not Rockefeller.'

Michael smiled. 'I don't even know who Rockefeller is.'

'Doesn't matter, just being old . . . you get my point though.'

'I guess. Still doesn't solve the problem though does it? And to make things worse, Laura *has* to move. The landlord's selling the place off, wants to go and open a restaurant in Spain or something.'

'Any chance she could get a waitressing job?'

'Be serious, Dad! I'm worried.'

'I know, sorry.' John gave up on his pasta salad, slowly sealing the plastic tub closed again and tossing it into the wastepaper bin. 'What about my place?' he asked finally.

'What about it?'

'I don't need a three-bedroom house, do I? Your mother and I always promised each other that we'd sell up and get something smaller. Once you'd left we rattled around the place. We just never seemed to get around to it. Of course, once she got ill it was the least of our concerns.' He took a sip of his tea, wanting to wash away the mental image of Jane lying in bed, wilting under the sheets like rotting vegetation. 'We could split the place up, maybe. I could take the downstairs, turn the dining room into a bedroom, you could have upstairs.'

'It's your home.' Michael was shocked by the idea, uncertain of what to say.

'Wouldn't be any less so if I shared it with you, would

it? Of course I know it's not ideal, you and Laura would want your privacy, that's why I think we should turn it into two flats, give each other our space. It wouldn't be difficult. Or that expensive.'

'I don't know . . .' Michael squirmed. 'It's very kind, don't think I'm not grateful.'

'You'd want to think about it, of course. The last thing a young couple needs is an old man cluttering up the place.'

'It's not that. It's, well, it's where Mum died, you know?'

John did understand that, of course, but lied none - theless. 'Nothing haunts that house but good memories. About time it set about making some new ones too.'

Nothing but good memories.

He had taken to sleeping in the spare bedroom again. When Jane had been ill he had moved there so as not to disturb her. Their old bed, a place of life where they had made love and brought a son into the world, had become a deathly place, a compost heap upon which his wife rotted. Surrounded by the accoutrements of her disease, the drip and the respirator, the bedside table loaded with pill bottles, tissues and moisturiser, there had been no more room for him. He had moved to the lifeless guest bed, sleeping under second-best sheets surrounded by soulless decoration. Spare bedrooms are as close as a house gets to abandoned space, where none of the personality of the owner is allowed to shine through.

Now he slept there because it felt safer.

The marriage bed all too often felt like it contained more than just himself. The darkness around him was thick with more than air, it smelled of pharmaceuticals and rot. It contained the damp, mildewy breaths of the dead.

Even in the spare room his nights wouldn't pass completely undisturbed. Often he would hear move - ments coming from the other bedroom. The soft pacing of naked feet, pressing each croaking floorboard into life, groaning and whining like a forest coming to life with nocturnal predators. Sometimes he thought he could actually hear her pressing against the adjoining wall, hear the soft slide of her cheek and palms, as cold as the plaster they rested on. Perhaps she listened for his breathing, perhaps she waited for an invitation to visit? All manner of ideas occurred to him as he lay there, anything, it seemed, to keep him from restful sleep.

It seemed that the more he tried to hold onto his rational beliefs the more they slipped away from him. Was he losing his mind or was he really experiencing everything his senses told him?

Jane had mocked his refusal to believe in anything but the physical. 'For a great thinker,' she had said, 'your thoughts are so very narrow.' Her background was resolutely Catholic, though that hadn't stopped her cursing the name of her God at the end, as all must when the pain gets too much and the vastness of death overwhelms you. He had done his best to calm her, had uttered platitudes he didn't believe as she gripped his hand tight enough to bruise. He had talked of the better place she was travelling to, of the painless eternity that

44

would stretch out before her. A time of spirit and peace. He had no idea whether she knew his comments rang hollow in his throat as he uttered them. Maybe this was his punishment? Those things in which he refused to believe preying on him until he had no choice but to accept them. she forcing her beliefs on him as she never had while alive?

That night, Aida Golding was piercing the barrier between life and death at a Scout hut in Ealing. The walls were hung with powder-paint art and charts that attempted to show the difference between common British deciduous leaves. John found himself giving as much attention to a poster titled 'Flags of the World' as he did Golding's performance. His mind just wasn't in it; he should have stayed at home and dried out. He hadn't been sleeping well, too alert to the noises the house made at night and what they might mean.

'Oh dear,' said Aida, 'I can't hear this very well, it's either a John or a Jane . . .'

John didn't hear her the first time, having entered into a dreamy state, staring at the wall and swaying gently in his seat.

'Is there a Jane here? No . . . it's a Jane I have speaking . . . Yes, dear, I know, I'm telling them . . . She wants to speak to John. Is John here?'

Still John was unaware, as divorced from what was happening in the room as if he had stayed at home. It was the rustle of activity around him that finally roused him.

'It's him!' the old widow was saying, pointing at him

with one of her perfectly painted nails. 'He's the one you want.'

'Sorry?' Her words and the fact that everyone was staring at him made John feel as if he was in the middle of a dream. He was suddenly afraid, pressing himself back in his seat, away from these desperate people who claimed to want him.

'John?' asked Aida Golding. 'Is that you?'

'Yes,' he admitted.

'The message is for you. Jane is here, she's right beside you. If she were to hold out her hand she could rest it on your shoulder. And she so wishes that were possible. That she could touch you, hold you again.'

Aida was not to know how terrifying John found this thought, though even the most casual observer should have been able to tell from the look on his face. Either the shadows or her own convictions were too deep, Aida carried on: 'She's always been with you, John, she never left you. Can I hear your voice, John? She still shares a home with you, still follows in your footsteps, shares a bed. I need your voice, John, it's my connection, let me hear your voice.'

'I . . . I don't . . .'

'You miss her, don't you, John, since the cancer took her body from you?'

'Of course . . .'

'The cancer can't kill the spirit, John, it can't kill the soul. It eats away at the flesh but leaves the truth behind. She's still here, John, can you feel her?'

'I don't . . .'

'You sense her sometimes, don't you? Around the

46

house? Or when you visit places that you used to visit together? You can tell she's with you?'

'I—'

'I need your voice, John, she's slipping away, let me hear your voice . . .'

'I don't know what to say!'

Aida Golding's shoulders slumped and she aimed a beneficent smile out into the darkness. 'It's all right, John,' she said, 'she's gone, you can relax. Just know that she loves you and she will always be beside you.'

John couldn't sit still through the hubbub that followed as Aida moved her attentions elsewhere. He excused himself along his row of seating and escaped into the corridors outside the main hall. He wandered, nervous and confused, hoping to find a bathroom where he could wash at his tired, numb face in some cold water and try and bring himself back to normality. Somebody had talked to Aida Golding, that was the only viable explanation. Accepting that Golding could not – and did not – commune with the dead, she had cheated her way to the information. And really, had there been that much of it? A wife called Jane who had died of cancer. That was not so difficult, was it? That was the sort of thing anyone could have overheard during his conversations with Henry's widow. And Golding can't have known the negative effect of her words, she had sought to console him not disturb him. She knew nothing about him, he decided, nothing at all.

The corridors were dimly lit by fire escape signs and the cork boards rustled their paper notices in a slight breeze from the open front door. He found the toilets and took a drink of water from the tap, trying not to imagine the pale reflection of his dead wife appearing over his shoulder in the large mirror above the sink.

'Are you all right?'

He spilled a cupped handful of water down himself in shock as he turned to see who was speaking.

'Sorry, I didn't mean to make you jump.' It was Sandy, leaning in the doorway and trying not to smile at the panic she had caused.

John could hardly have been more awkward, rubbing at the wet patch on the front of his shirt. 'I'm a bit jumpy after that,' he admitted. 'Sorry. You must think . . .'

'I don't think anything,' she said and then her mood changed, glancing over her shoulder into the corridor. She's nervous, John realised, nervous of being caught or nervous of me? 'I just wanted to make sure you were OK, you seemed pretty shaken.'

'It's not every day you talk to your dead wife.' John smiled, trying to make light of it. Sandy didn't follow his example, just glanced once more into the corridor and then stepped back out of the doorway.

'She does smaller meetings, you know,' she said, 'at her house, once a month. You should go.'

'Do you?'

There was a pause at that question and Sandy appeared even more uncomfortable. 'Always,' she admitted. 'The less of you there are . . .'

'The more chance you have of getting a message?'

Sandy nodded.

'When's the next meeting? Do you think Mrs Golding

would be willing to have me?' In truth, now the subject of conversation had turned, John had no doubt of it. Sandy had been sent to invite him, to lure him in. At least she had the decency to appear uncomfortable about it.

'I'm sure she would,' the girl replied, shuffling from one foot to the other. 'If you want I could ask her?'

'That would be kind.' John dried his hands, feeling more confident now that Sandy had revealed herself as little more than the friendly face of a trap to lure him in. 'Can I ask you a personal question?'

Sandy looked genuinely frightened at the prospect of that but agreed nonetheless.

'How long ago did your baby die?'

'Not so long. Two years.'

'Oh, I just noticed the cuts on your arms . . .'

'What about them?' Sandy snapped, tugging her sleeves over her hands.

'Some of them just seemed a lot older, that's all.'

There was a round of applause from the main hall and the double doors crashed open, breaking the awkward pause between them.

'I'll ask her,' said Sandy and dashed off along the corridor.

John hadn't been quite sure what to do: to follow Sandy or just hang around at the door. In the end, the thought of sharing false smiles with the rest of the audience made the decision for him. He hung back until most people had made their way into the car park and then strolled out after them.

There was a brief pause in the rain, the trees dripping

heavy with it, and the tarmac shined orange from the streetlights. You could tell from the pressure in the air that the weather hadn't fully cleared, the sky was thick black, just waiting to shed once more.

'John?'

He turned to face Aida Golding who was clutching her cardigan tightly around her and offering a soft, slightly wrinkled hand. John couldn't tell if she wanted him to shake it or kiss it, he went for the former option. A heavy, silver ring pressed itself against his fingers as she clasped his hand in both of hers and held it there, refusing to let him go.

'I'm so glad I was able to offer you a message,' she said. 'We all need some words of comfort in our lives don't we, Mister . . .?'

'Pritchard.'

'Not the painter?'

If there had been a famous artist that shared his name he certainly wasn't aware one. More than likely she was fishing for his occupation. Not in the mood to be creative, he decided to give her more or less the truth.

'No, nothing so grand. I teach.'

'Oh,' Golding took his arm. 'There's nothing more grand than spreading wisdom. I like to think it's my vocation too. What do you teach, John?'

'Psychology.'

'The study of the mind? Well, a narrow view of it at least. How interesting.'

'I think so.'

'And your students must too, I'm sure.'

'I've never had any complaints.'

'And I'm sure they would be only too quick to offer them. Teenagers are never backward in coming forward, are they?'

She was fishing again, he was sure of it. Waiting for him to confirm or deny the age of his students. He decided this time he would leave her unfulfilled. He simply smiled and waited for her to say something else, which she duly did.

'Of course, it would be lovely to have you join us one night. In fact, our next meeting is on Friday, unless you're . . .'

'Friday would be lovely. Whereabouts are you?'

Alasdair presented a business card in a manner that was just a little too polished and official. Golding's manner was far superior, John thought, never letting the unsavoury taint of business fall on things. The address, in Richmond no less, would have been far better scribbled on a scrap of paper or discarded bus ticket. A business card just looked blatant and misplaced. Certainly it prompted him to ask his next question.

'How much is it? I mean . . . sorry to have to ask but teachers don't earn a fortune.'

'Oh please,' Golding squeezed his arm, 'what must you think of me? This isn't business, I charge what I do in order to cover my expenses and keep food on the table. I think it's important that I give all of my time to the cause which means, sadly, I must earn a living from it. Albeit a meagre one.'

Meagre? Living in Richmond? John thought. Come off it.

'I make no charge at my special meetings, if people

wish to make a donation then . . . well . . . that is always appreciated. But really, the important thing for me is just spreading the important message of everlasting life and love.'

'I understand completely,' John assured her. The rain began to fall again and this stirred the group to life.

'Can I offer you a lift, John?' Golding asked. 'I often drop Sandy off at the closest tube station, happy to do the same for you. It's not a night for walking.

'I'm fine,' he said, 'but thank you. I've a taxi booked so I'd better wait for it.'

'See you Friday then.' And with that the three of them dashed towards their car and John huddled beneath the awning in front of the hall to watch them go.

He didn't have a taxi booked but had wanted to save the added awkwardness of being trapped in the car with the three of them. He waited for them to leave and then began to jog up the road, trying to stick closely to the buildings and the scant shelter they offered.

Uxbridge Road was thinned out by the weather, the traffic sailed the shallow river in both directions but the pavement was all but empty. Discarded takeaway packaging swirled in the gutters. Old newspapers clung to the paving stones as if someone had been interrupted in the art of covering the whole street in papier mâché. The world felt distorted by the weather, as if so much rain had fallen that everything had simply begun to melt. He was soaked through by the time the tube was in sight. Crossing the road he paused for a moment, bathed in the lights of the stationary traffic, a straggling fish picked-out in the beam of a submersible's searchlight. Metres away, standing on the pavement he had just vacated, was his wife, the water slicking her nightdress to her skin just as the fevered sweats had. Her hair clung to her small, grey skull as if desperate to crush it, it plastered most of her face but he could tell that her lips were moving. She was talking to him. Telling him something.

First one driver beat his horn then a handful of others joined in, pulling John's attention back to the crossing where the lights had changed. He dashed across to the opposite side, the most impatient drivers narrowly missing him as they drove on. Looking back there was no sign of Jane. By the time he reached the entrance to Ealing Broadway he had just about convinced himself that there never had been.

Four

Hearing Voices

The house was oppressively normal. Far back from the river and the more ostentatious, expensive homes it stood as part of a smoky grey brick terrace. In fact, John thought, luxurious postcode aside, it wasn't that different from his own home. It was surrounded by limp privet, beaten into submission by the rain like over-blanched spinach.

John pushed open the small wooden gate, painted a particularly sickly light blue, and noticed one slight concession to the mystical: next to the plastic number plaque there was a crescent moon. It was made from plastic and the silver veneer had begun to wear off from the rubbing of reverent thumbs to expose pearlescent white beneath.

Closing the gate behind him he jogged up to the front door. Beneath the porch he took a moment to rub the rain from his face and smooth back his hair, squeezing the water into rivers that ran down his neck.

He felt perversely comfortable at what he might find beyond that door. While he could no longer guarantee the safety of his own home, or even the streets he walked, there was one place he was fairly sure ghosts did not walk and that was alongside Aida Golding. Whatever the evening might promise, whatever cons or unpleasantness she held in store, he was sure that it would all be theatre. A dark reflection waddled towards him through the smoked glass window in the door and he found himself remembering the apparition he had seen through the door of the shower. The memory robbed him of his confidence. The lock was drawn. A security chain was rattled loose. To his left, amongst the shining-wet creepers of the ivy, he became aware of pale flesh, sliding and squirming against the leaves. Was that a pair of eyes watching him, as fat and glistening as fruit?

'Mr Pritchard, welcome.' It was Alasdair who opened the door, stepping to one side to allow John in from the rain. 'If you could leave your coat there.' The young man gestured vaguely at a hatstand and stood to one side while John shucked his wet waterproofs and hung them up.

John scrubbed his shoes on the coconut-hair doormat and then followed Alasdair deeper into the house.

He paid as close attention as time allowed, walking through the entrance hall. He wanted to take this oppor-tunity to glean as much information about Golding as he could. The place was decorated in DIY store Edwardian, wipeable, dark green wallpaper and poly-styrene cornicing. The black and white floor tiles looked original enough, he decided, though the slender rug that lay down the middle of them was catalogue at best. He looked at the pictures on the wall. They were all prints, no photos, nothing personal. A watercolour of angels in flight, a fantastical meadow of the sort that unicorns have been known to trot through, a stylised rainbow's arc surrounded by stars. It was all washed-out New Age, with not a single hint of soulfulness. The images could have been printed on cheap greeting cards or a mail-order series of decorative plates. John had no doubt they were as much window dressing as everything else.

They passed the stairs and John glanced up quickly, on the off chance of seeing something. There was the slight creak of a floorboard and he realised that someone was standing directly above him. He caught sight of a young boy's face before Alasdair took his arm and led him – somewhat forcefully – into a large dining room.

The Edwardian theme continued – a perfect theatrical set for mediumship, John thought, so much easier to believe in spirits when they hover over dark walnut and antimacassars rather than Formica and glass. In the corner a massive pot plant stroked at the black and white faux velvet wallpaper. The central table was so dark as to almost be black. The brilliant white of the doily in the centre was the only thing that stopped a wrought-iron trivet from vanishing against its back - ground. The trivet was weighed down with teapot, cups, milk jug and a large fruitcake, gutted already by a large bread-knife, the fruity gore of sultanas and raisins sticking glutinously to its blade. The walls were again covered with prints and a large mirror on the wall facing the door allowed John to see what a poor sight he was, thanks to his walk in the rain.

'Good evening, John!' said Aida Golding, getting up from the table and coming over to shake his hand. 'So glad the wet didn't keep you away.'

'We'd never do anything at the moment if we let the weather stop us.'

'Too true, let me introduce you to the others.'

'I'm distinctly uncomfortable with this,' announced a man at the table. He was rubbing at his face and it took John a few moments to recognise him. It was a face he was used to seeing in newspapers and during hastily snatched television interviews outside Parliament.

'Don't mind Lord Probert,' said Golding, 'he gets twitchy in company. Don't you, dear?'

'I'm not accustomed to having my private matters discussed in public,' he muttered. 'I thought this was to be a private reading, I'm paying enough.'

'I don't do one-to-one readings, dear,' she replied, glossing over the subject of payment John noticed, 'I need the energy of a group to achieve the best results. I can assure you everyone here is quite discreet.'

'They all say that,' the nervous peer replied, 'then before you know it you're all over the bloody tabloids.'

'I can assure you I wouldn't discuss anything that goes on here,' said an elderly man sat opposite Probert. 'As far as I'm concerned these matters have all the sanctity of the confessional and I would certainly treat them as such.'

'Our envoy from God,' said Golding to John. 'Father Goss has the best interests of our souls in mind this evening.'

'A relief I'm sure,' scoffed Probert, 'and who's he?' He pointed at John.

'I'm a step down the social ladder,' John replied with a smile, 'John Pritchard, teacher.'

'Of psychology, no less!' laughed Golding, 'so our brains are to be well-looked after too!'

'A psychologist?' said Father Goss, 'I don't know about that . . .'

'A teacher,' John repeated, 'and as we're all here in a personal capacity rather than a professional one, does it really matter?'

'The man has a point,' said Probert. 'Sit down, will you? The sooner you get your feet under the table the sooner we can get on with this.'

'We still have a couple more guests to arrive, Lord Probert,' said Golding. 'Have some more tea, why don't you? It'll help you relax.'

'Tea?' the lord scoffed. 'It takes more than that to help me wind down.'

'We don't have any alcohol in the house, I'm afraid. I don't approve.'

'Only one kind of spirit in this place!' joked Father Goss. Nobody laughed.

The doorbell rang.

'There we are,' said Golding as Alasdair sidled away to let in the newcomer. 'We'll be started in a minute.'

They sat in silence around the table as Alasdair's footsteps passed down the hall to the front door. There was the sound of the door being opened and then the familiar voice of Henry's widow rolled in from the wet outdoors.

'I shouldn't be out and about in this,' she said, 'if Henry were alive he would never have allowed it. Catch my death in this I will.'

At least then she'd find marital conversation a little easier, thought John.

Alasdair showed her in and Golding introduced her as Mrs. Davinia Harris. John realised it was the first time he'd been offered her name; she was a woman who defined herself by her relationship to the dead before anything else.

'This is lovely,' she said, taking a seat, 'very nice. I'm sure Henry will be only too happy to join us here.'

'I'm sure he will too,' John announced, his voice sounding more sincere than what he felt.

'Is that everyone?' asked Probert.

'Just one more,' said Golding. 'Our group wouldn't be complete without Sandy.'

John noticed Davinia Harris's eyes roll. 'Sandy's coming is she? Well there's a surprise . . .'

'Sandy's energy is very much in tune with my own,' said Golding. 'I find her presence extremely energising.'

And informative, no doubt, thought John.

'It's good to see you here at least,' Davinia said to John. 'Finally got a message, didn't you?'

John wasn't going to argue that, in the present company at least. 'I did.'

'I was so pleased, I told Aida as much didn't I?'

'You did, dear, you did.'

'I'd told her all about you and wouldn't it be a shame if you weren't to get a message?'

Well, that solved that mystery, John thought. With

Davinia Harris around, everybody knew your business.

'I am heartened to hear that you're already a success-
ful recipient of our host's skills,' said Father Goss
leaning towards John with a diluted smile. 'I have yet to
experience the fruits of her efforts first hand.'

'I didn't think we'd met before,' said Davinia, 'and I
attend most of Aida's demonstrations.'

'Oh, I'm not completely new to all this,' the cleric
admitted, 'in fact it's something of a specialist subject,
though no doubt my parishioners would be alarmed at
the thought! But then what is the job of a priest if it's not
to pierce the veil between life and death?'

What indeed? John thought, not the most religious of
men.

'So refreshing to find an open-minded vicar,' said
Davinia.

'Well, we papal-minded ecclesiastics tend to be more
open to the wider possibilities of the universe,' Father
Goss said, 'I'm of the old church, the original you might
say!'

Davinia was clearly confused by this. 'Oh . . . what
church is that then?'

'He's saying he's Catholic,' Probert explained,
evidently becoming more impatient by the moment.

'Oh,' Davinia replied as if someone had just said
something unmentionable. 'Them.'

The doorbell rang one last time and Aida Golding
was clearly glad of the distraction. 'And that makes a
full complement,' she said. 'We can shortly begin. Let
me just refresh the pot.'

She reached for the teapot but Probert grasped her

hand. 'To hell with tea, can we not just get on with this!'

The look she gave the peer then was John's first glimpse of the real Aida Golding beneath the cosy knitted surface. 'You forget yourself,' she said. 'You are a guest in my home, not I in yours.'

Probert matched her look for a long moment. Clearly, he was not a man used to backing down, but eventually he released her hand and smiled. 'You're quite right, of course,' he said. 'Forgive me my enthusiasm.'

'Of course, dear.'

Aida walked out of the room and Probert settled back into his seat. John noticed how viciously his manicured nails dug into the wood of the chair's arm. A dangerous man, he decided. Like all people who are accustomed to getting whatever they want from life he didn't take the word 'no' well. He tried to remember what he knew of the man, recalling heated tabloid headlines and building a picture of the man's public persona. There had been affairs, he remembered, but worse than that . . . a scandal he couldn't put his finger on. He could picture the man's snarling face, elbowing a photographer aside. Crowds on courtroom steps, placards thrust skywards as protesters roared their disapproval. All the window-dressing but none of the details.

The door opened and Sandy walked in. She was the very image of functionalism, her wet hair pulled back in a ponytail, wearing jeans and a baggy, black jumper, the sleeves of which she tugged long so that only her fingers poked out of the end.

'Hello,' she said, and sat down in one of the empty chairs.

'Good evening, my dear,' said Father Goss. 'Are you a regular at these events? We were just talking about who had had messages before and who hadn't.'

'Oh, she's always talking to her little kiddie, aren't you, dear?' said Davinia, offering the young woman a distinctly false smile.

'Not as much as if he were still alive,' Sandy snapped back.

'Well, quite,' said Father Goss, attempting to be the peacekeeper around the table.

'I'm sure I didn't mean to cause offence,' said Davinia.

'Of course not,' agreed Father Goss before gamely trying to change the subject. 'We're having more tea in a minute.'

'Wonderful,' Probert sighed sarcastically.

The door opened and Aida Golding walked in, the refreshed pot in her hand. 'All here!' she announced with enthusiasm. 'How exciting. Help yourself to milk and sugar. We'll tuck into the cake afterwards.' She began pouring out a cup of tea for each of them, though Probert predictably refused his.

John stirred his cup and waited patiently for things to begin.

Golding lit a pair of large candles and placed them in the centre of the table. Then she sat down and, on her cue, the lights went out. John realised Alasdair must be in the doorway behind him, performing his duties as always. He wondered what else the young man might get up to in the dark.

'Now,' said Golding, 'I don't want any of you to be

scared. What we do tonight is not something that should be feared. It is a wonderful, natural, thing. It is the connection of love with love. We hold our hands out in the dark and wait for them to be taken by those whom we miss, those cherished souls who are lost to us in this world but alive and happy in the next.'

'I'm not sure I would class them as "alive" exactly,' said Father Goss, 'the term is philosophically complex.'

'Never mind philosophy,' snapped Probert, 'this is a seance not a discussion group.'

'I don't approve of the term "seance",' said Golding with a smile, 'it brings to mind images from horror films.'

Unlike Edwardian parlours and table rapping? John wondered with some amusement.

'Perhaps we should all agree that the terminology doesn't matter,' he suggested. 'The important thing is the attitude with which we approach things.'

'Well said, dear,' agreed Davinia. 'It is what it is and none of us would be here if we weren't comfortable with it.'

'Quite,' agreed Probert.

'Very well,' said Golding, 'then let us link hands so as to better conduct the positive energy that flows between us.'

They all did so.

For a while they sat in silence, the occasional flicker of the candle's flame the only sound in the expectant atmosphere.

'This is different to when I work with a large crowd,' explained Golding eventually. 'The connection is more pure, the link stronger. Often we should all be able to hear the voices of those who have passed, rather than just me.'

This was certainly an impressive step, thought John.

'For all that,' Golding continued, 'it can sometimes take a little longer to establish that link. It is vitally important to me that you keep your energy positive. Negativity can force the connection to wither and break. While this is a beautiful and positive gift, it's not an easy one to use and I will need your help every step of the way.'

John felt Davinia tighten her grip on his right hand; she was certainly not willing to take any risks when it came to communing with her deceased husband. To his left, Father Goss shifted slightly in his seat and altered his grip on John's hand. The priest's hand was hot and becoming sweaty, so he self-consciously gripped John's fingers so as to let their palms breathe. Not that John cold blame the man for being nervous. As much as he had been determined to maintain a cynical detachment to the night's proceedings, it was difficult now the lights had gone out. The sound of the rain outside permeated the darkness as if the weather was slowly forcing its way into the room. It made John think of what he had glimpsed amongst the leaves of the ivy. It had seemed so pale and gelatinous that he could imagine it gaining entrance easily enough. Perhaps it would force itself through the letterbox, the little black brushes drying the rain from its dead, cold skin before it fell onto those black and white tiles with a slap. He pictured it as his wife's shattered body, too long in the grave, a weathered bag of tumbling bones made soft once more in the rain.

'Steady love,' said Davinia and he realised he had been squeezing her hand even harder than she his.

'Sorry.' He loosened his grip and gave her a smile.

Aida Golding had closed her eyes and her head lolled back until it vanished into the darkness. The shadows crept down to just above her mouth which moved as she muttered to herself – at least John assumed it was to herself, he didn't like to imagine who else she could be communicating with. She gave a long sigh, the air hissing from between her lips like a last breath. Tipping her head forward once more, the breath still coming, the candles flickered and went out. Davinia gave a small yelp of concern and her hand tugged at John's.

'Don't worry,' said Golding, 'there is nothing in the dark that can harm us. We are like them, the departed, floating in the afterlife beyond the reach of senses.'

How can they hear us then? John might have asked, but there was no time as at the moment that the medium stopped talking another voice spoke up.

'Hello, dear,' it said, 'how lovely of you to come.'

The voice was barely audible as if speaking through a mound of cushions. Despite that it was recognised soon enough.

'Is that you Henry?' asked Davinia. 'What's wrong with you? Why can't you speak up?' She tutted and rolled her eyes at John. 'Typical Henry, he always was such a mumbler.'

'Sorry,' came the voice, 'I'm trying as hard as I can.'

'Well, give it a bit more ,' said his wife, 'you're in high company and I expect you to be on your very best behaviour.'

'Yes, dear.'

'Well, I must say it's been a while since you deigned to visit, hasn't it? I mean . . . I could have upped sticks and popped my clogs myself for all the interest you've been taking in me, couldn't I?'

'I'm sure Henry would have been aware had you joined him in the afterlife,' insisted Golding. 'After all, you would have been reunited.'

'And there would be a pretty way to spend eternity!' Davinia scoffed. 'Unless that useless lump has taken himself in hand after abandoning me I'd only end up looking after him like I always did. Yes . . . that would be the thing, he's probably hanging on in there hoping for just that. You got yourself in a mess up there, Henry? You in a fix?'

'I think you're being too literal, Davinia my dear,' said Golding. 'The afterlife is not really a place where you can get yourself "in a fix".'

'If anyone can, Henry can. Did I ever tell you about the time we were questioned by security in Waitrose because he'd been seen opening a Black Forest Gateau in the freezer?'

'Davinia,' said the barely audible voice, 'I don't think . . .'

'Said he wanted to check they weren't stingy with the cherries. In Waitrose, I ask you. Never have I been so embarrassed. Now he has me traipsing all over the place just to hear a few kind words. Not much to ask is it? A lady of my age? Nobody thinks of me do they? I'm all alone . . .'

'I love you, Davinia,' said the voice, 'but I have to go now . . .'

'That's typical,' said the widow. John was pretty sure he caught the glint of tears reflecting the candlelight. 'Always dashing off.'

'He's gone,' confirmed Golding.

'Bye, love,' murmured Davinia and John gave her hand a gentle squeeze. For all her ridiculous hostility it was clear she missed Henry very much.

'How romantic,' whispered Probert but Davinia chose to ignore him.

'The voices are getting more insistent,' announced Golding. 'It's becoming hard to distinguish one from the other.'

'Well, try harder!' said Probert.

'The spirits are not at your beck and call, Lord Probert,' said Golding. 'They will either have a message for you or they will not.'

He had no reply to that, simply sighed in the darkness and the table returned to silence once more.

But not for long . . .

'John? Are you there, John?'

He had imagined his response to this inevitable moment. He had decided he would make his disdain clear, he would stand up and reveal the trickery for what it was. But now, with the indistinct voice calling to him, he found he could do no such thing. It wasn't that he believed the voice to be Jane's – even muffled it carried none of the qualities he remembered – but the idea of decrying it as a sham, surrounded by those who believed in it utterly, seemed in terribly poor taste. He simply could not stamp on the feelings of the ridiculous, irritating, fragile widow whose hand he was holding.

'I'm here,' he said, and gave a polite smile at the squeeze Davinia Harris gave his hand. He was hit by a sudden wave of guilt, reminded of those last days when he had lied to Jane in order to protect her sensibilities. He felt like he was cheating her memory by playing along. Though now, once started, he found it even harder to imagine the alternative.

'Thank you for coming, John,' said the voice, 'I know it's hard for you . . .' and she was certainly right there, 'I know this isn't something that comes easily to you, I know it's something you find hard to believe.'

Despite his determination to remain logical he found himself imagining his dead wife behind him in the darkness. Not speaking to him, no, he still didn't believe this was her voice, but listening to the sham, watching him play his part. What would she think of it all? Would she be relieved to find him suddenly open to such experiences? Or would she be disappointed at how easily he was being fooled?

'But you believe now,' continued the voice, 'don't you, John?'

What to say? He could actually feel the chill of cold air on his neck. Like the breath of someone stood right behind him. Not that Jane had any breath left in her, of course. His shoulders tensed, waiting for what seemed like the inevitable: the grip of her weak hand as it took hold of his shoulder.

'Yes,' he said finally, barely more than breathing the answer, 'I believe now.'

Davinia squeezed his hand again.

Now he had said something he found the words came easier. Perhaps they had always been there, waiting for him to have the courage to utter them. In that moment, almost sure he could sense her behind him, he spoke to her as he never had before.

'I believe, Jane,' he repeated, 'and I miss you. I've missed you for years. Missed you even when you were still with me because the woman you became wasn't the woman I had fallen in love with. She was everything about you that was bad. She was every resentment, every bitterness, every little bit of hatred and anger.' And sometimes, he thought but didn't say, I think you left her behind. 'And that's OK, because we all have those things inside us. But when you became ill it was all the disease left of you. I hope you're better now. I hope everything that was good about you is back. I wish I could have you with me again.'

'I am with you, John,' said the voice and he found himself crying, because that momentary belief had passed leaving him to wish it were true. 'I'll always be with you. And now there's no pain, no anger. I'm happy, John, I'm free . . .'

'I wish I were,' he replied and then immediately regretted it, it was not a thought he had intended to voice.

'Soon, my love, soon you will be just like me.'

And with that John's session was done. There was

silence until Aida Golding snatched a deep breath as if something had yanked at her hair.

'She has gone,' she announced.

John had never been convinced of that fact ever since Jane had died. Try as he might he still wasn't.

'You all right, dear?' asked Davinia.

He nodded. 'Fine.'

Golding writhed a little in her seat as if her muscles were cramping. John looked at her and found a sudden realisation. He had never hated a person more than he did her. To create such emotions in people, to drag them through this for money. She must be sociopathic, he decided, to care so little for others.

'Ah!' she exhaled, and slumped forward in her chair. After a few moments she lifted her head. 'I need a short break,' she said, 'the energies are particularly draining tonight.'

'More tea then, is it?' asked Probert sarcastically.

'If you wish to make it,' Golding replied, 'the kitchen's just through there.'

With that she walked out leaving Probert to stare after her in shock.

'I simply can't believe the cheek of the woman,' he said once she'd gone. 'Anyone would think she was doing us a favour rather than being paid for her time.'

'I certainly haven't paid,' John admitted, only too happy to cause awkwardness for Golding. 'Have you?' he asked Father Goss.

'No,' the priest admitted, 'though I would usually make some small donation, a few pounds towards the cause as it were.'

'Me too,' announced Davinia. 'After all, it's only fair, isn't it? She gave up her job in order to be free to spread the message far and wide. The least we can do is ensure she has enough money to get by.'

Get by? John couldn't believe Davinia Harris of all people was capable of such naivety.

'I'm sure she doesn't struggle,' he said.

'Quite right, my dear,' Davinia replied, wholly missing his point, 'good for her.'

John wasn't concerned by Davinia's blindness as to Aida Golding's business practice, he did watch Sandy's face with interest though. In his current state of mind he had no issue with making the girl uncomfortable – why should the punters be the only ones to suffer?

'Have you paid?' he asked her.

She shook her head. 'She wouldn't ask.'

And John could see that was true, Sandy – or whatever she was really called – paid Aida Golding in quite another fashion. She was the 'shill', the inside man in the con. Her testimony helped lend conviction and no doubt her ears were always open for anything that could later be put to use.

He was aware that he was transferring all of his anger on to her, the safer target. Aware that he was being unreasonable and that he didn't have the first idea what had forced her into this life. At that point he didn't altogether care.

'And yet you owe her so much?' he said, sitting back down at the table so as to be able to stare right at her.

'More than you could imagine,' she replied and in that moment, all his anger, so recently built, dissipated

71

away to nothing. There was such a clear hurt in her, something that went way beyond even those scars on her arms, that he couldn't even begin to imagine how it must feel. In that moment he wondered whether this girl was the most cruelly treated of them all.

They reconvened after about ten minutes. Aida Golding wafting incense-sticks around the dining room that couldn't quite mask the fresh smell of pipe tobacco that clung to Father Goss. The cleric had loitered on the medium's front door step for a smoke, casting a silhouette like that of Sherlock Holmes across her floor tiles.

'Right then,' she announced, once they had all taken their seats, 'let's see if the rest of the evening can offer something more pleasant.'

'Shouldn't be difficult,' said Davinia, though all gathered knew she was enjoying herself immensely.

Once again the lights were turned off and the candles lit. They linked hands and waited as Golding took several deep breaths and settled into what she called her 'receptive state'.

It was only a few moments before the room was visited by its next spiritual guest.

'Is it come to this, Father?' the voice asked, 'meeting again after so many years? Is your hunger for confession so pronounced you hunt it beyond the grave?'

'Dear Lord,' said Father Goss, his voice as fragile as the thin wisps of smoke shed by the extinguished candles. 'Is that Douglas?'

'Of course, Father,' the voice replied. 'You'd know

my voice anywhere, surely? Whispered through vented confession booths, velvet curtains, the wall between life and death. It seems we'll never stop talking, you and I.'

John's eyes were starting to become more accus-tomed to the darkness. He could pick out vague shapes in the light offered through the undrawn curtains, the distant streetlights spreading their amber light thin by the time it passed through the wet glass. Nobody was moving; Father Goss in particular was rigid, his aged, bulbous profile jutting forth.

'Douglas?' the priest asked, 'what do you want from me?'

'Nothing more than your company,' the voice replied and John struggled to place where it was coming from. Was it recorded? Surely it must be . . . or maybe performed live from elsewhere in the house. Could it be Alasdair? Presumably the young man was still in the room, without shifting around it was impossible for John to tell. With the lack of light and all of them forced to maintain their positions it was impossible to be sure what was going on around them. Still, even if Alasdair was with them who knew how many other players took part in this evening's demonstration? The house could be full of people for Golding to call on.

'It gets lonely out here,' the ethereal voice continued, 'lonely and cold. It's nice just to know you're close by again. To imagine we're back in the warm velvet box, my admitting my delicious sins to you while you weep to hear them.'

'Douglas,' the priest's voice was distinctly frail,

'where is she? If you want any kind of forgiveness then tell me. Her parents have a right to bury her.'

'Forgiveness? What makes you think I have any interest in your forgiveness?'

'Think of your soul, man!' Goss shouted, 'just tell me and you will be one step closer to absolution.'

'I think not. I think I like the way things are. Anyway, who cares about her body? I have her spirit close to hand. She still likes to play . . .'

'Dear God, no!' Goss screamed the words, his hand snatched from John's as the priest jumped to his feet.

'Please!' said Golding, her voice harsh and croaky, 'don't disrupt the flow . . . ah . . .' she gave a long sigh, 'he's gone.'

'You've got to get him back!' begged the priest, 'we can't let him keep her!'

'Please, Father,' said Golding, 'try and retain your calm. I sensed the spirit's dishonesty most strongly and have no doubt that everything he said was designed to cause you upset.'

John could only agree.

'Who was it?' he asked.

'My Lord . . .' the priest shook his head and sank back into his chair.

'Alasdair, be a darling and pour the Father a glass of water would you?'

'I'm all right,' the priest insisted, 'it was just . . . Douglas Reece was a young man in my first parish, St Luke East in Tower Hamlets.'

'Charming area,' interrupted Probert.

'It had its problems,' Goss admitted, 'but where

doesn't? The majority of my parishioners were fine, spiritual people, Douglas amongst them, I had thought. He helped regularly at the services, was a very active figure in the church. He was a charming and considerate fellow.'

'Wait a minute,' said Davinia, 'Douglas Reece . . . I know that name!'

'There aren't many over a certain age that don't,' admitted Goss, 'he killed a great many people.'

'The East End Ripper!' Davinia explained.

'Not a name I would endorse,' said the priest.

'Oh come on,' scoffed Probert. 'A nutter chops up women a stone's throw from Whitechapel, what else are the papers going to call him?'

'That's as maybe, but what Douglas did . . . it's not something to be sensationalised.'

'Maybe not,' John admitted, 'but people always will, it's a common enough defence mechanism.'

'Says our resident psychologist,' Probert laughed. John shrugged.

'Perhaps,' Goss continued, 'but you must remember I knew the victims; I can't help but take the whole matter seriously. These were not statistics to me. Grainy photographs on the front of tabloids. They were people, people who were singularly dear to me.'

'Of course, dear,' said Golding, finally speaking to the man she had so disturbed with her act. 'You mustn't feel you have to discuss it.'

At the thought of this Davinia Harris turned quite pale, she could imagine nothing worse than the conversation stopping before it had even really started.

'I'd much rather we didn't talk about it,' agreed Sandy.

'It does him good to get it off his chest,' insisted Davinia, 'no use bottling these things up.'

The priest waved their comments away with a flick of his hand. 'There's not much to say, I was the one who informed the police of Douglas's guilt.'

'How did you know?' asked Davinia, positively thrilled at this turn of events.

'He told me,' said Goss, 'in unceasing detail, during the Sacrament of Penance.'

'He told you in confession?' said Probert. 'He was mad.'

'Of course he was,' agreed the priest. 'He slaughtered eight women with a set of mechanic's tools, he was extremely ill.'

'Not as ill as they were by the time he finished,' Probert replied.

'Perhaps we should take a few minutes' break,' the medium suggested, 'while I clear the atmosphere and recharge.'

'Please don't feel it's necessary on my account,' insisted Father Goss, 'I'm quite all right, just a little shaken.'

'Then for goodness' sake let's carry on!' said Probert. 'If we keep stopping it'll be midnight before you get to me.'

'And that would never do,' Davinia muttered.

'Very well,' agreed Golding, closing her eyes and gesturing for everyone to hold hands once more. 'Let us see if we can finally find someone to talk to Lord Probert.'

'Preferably not a doormat or a psycho,' Probert replied, to the audible disapproval of the others.

'It is difficult now,' said Golding, 'the air is thick with the stains left by that unpleasant creature. I must tread carefully. The other spirits are likewise cautious, he has scared a number of them away.'

'Here we go,' muttered Probert, 'more excuses.'

'Do shut up,' snapped Davinia, 'your attitude is not at all suitable for this kind of thing. One should be genteel and respectful.'

'I've never felt the need to be so in life thus far,' the Lord replied, 'I'm certainly not going to start now.'

'Hush!' shouted Golding, gripping the hands of both of them so tightly that they flinched. 'They come!'

'Helly?' asked a voice, 'are you there, Helly?'

'Oh God . . .' every ounce of Probert's pomposity was drained away.

'Helly?' asked Davinia. 'What sort of name's Helly?'

'It was her nickname for me,' Probert replied, surprisingly forthcoming, 'instead of Llewellyn.'

'I can hear you, Helly,' the voice continued, 'but I can't see you . . . why can't I see you?'

'No . . .' the lord's face fell even further. 'Her eyes, her eyes . . .'

'It's dark, Helly, always dark . . . why did you leave me in the dark?'

'Oh God!' Probert writhed in his chair, trying to tug his hand from Aida Golding's and Sandy's, they held fast.

'I didn't want this!' he said and jumped to his feet, his knees hitting the underside of the table and causing the candelabrum to topple and the candles to go out.

Once again plunged into darkness, the room was more chaotic than before, Probert still shouting.

Then one voice shouted out even louder, not a voice of one of those gathered but rather a voice they had heard only recently. Douglas Reece's voice.

'I forgive you, Father!' it shouted and then all was drowned out by the sound of a scream. Father Goss squeezed John's hand so tightly that he gave a small cry of his own, tugging free of the man's grip and massaging the back of his hand.

'The lights, Alasdair!' Golding shouted. 'Quickly!'

John was aware of footsteps in the floor above, hidden conspirators perhaps, running to assist.

The light switch was thrown but it didn't calm them, far from it. The blood it illuminated made them panic even further.

Five

Politics

Father Goss was a ruin. His throat was a second mouth, bloody lips parted as if to yawn. His chest shined with blood.

Nobody could speak, all eyes staring at the mess of blood and peeping bone that sat at the head of the table. Suddenly the priest coughed. A small black lump, about the size of a golf ball, was ejected from the hole in his throat and exploded against the surface of the table.

'He's alive,' said John, 'call an ambulance, he's still—'

But whatever life had been left in the priest's body was swift to pass. A low hiss bubbled up from the man's lungs and then ceased.

'Oh God!' cried Sandy, hands to her face, rocking back from the priest's dead body. 'Oh God, oh God, oh God . . .'

She jumped up and ran for the door but Aida Golding grabbed her arm. 'Wait,' the woman said, all pretence of soft, maternal tones gone. 'Just wait while I think.'

'We've got to call the police,' said John, looking around trying to process the obvious. 'Someone must have—'

'The cake knife,' said Davinia, pointing at where the large kitchen knife lay on the carpet, 'they used the cake knife.'

'Or he did,' said Probert, 'much more likely, don't you think? You saw what he was like. Full of guilt, the Catholics love a bit of fucking guilt . . .' The lord was getting more and more angry, clenching his fists. 'I can't be here,' he announced, 'I simply cannot be here . . . not with this . . . think what the papers . . . what everyone . . .' He roared and kicked at one of the chairs, sending it toppling.

'That hardly helps,' said John. 'We need to get out of this room and call the police.'

'I don't want the police called!' Probert shouted, his voice taking on the high-pitched squeal of an angry child. 'I can't be involved in this!'

'But you are,' said Golding, 'you are involved. And you need to think about what you do next.'

'Think about what? What are you saying?'

'What connections do you have. Who can you call? Don't tell me there's not someone on the end of a phone line who can make this go away.'

'I don't like the sound of this,' said John, 'you can't just brush this under the carpet.'

'No,' said Probert, 'she's right, that's exactly what we do. He must have done it himself, he must have . . . why would any of us . . .?'

'That's for the police to decide, surely?' said John, though he had to admit he found the idea of any of them being responsible beyond belief. He had been holding Davinia's hand, she had been holding Golding's, then

Probert's, then Sandy's then, finally, the Priest's. So the most likely culprits at the table were himself and Sandy. He knew he hadn't done it and couldn't believe Sandy had, the girl was shaking violently, Golding still holding her.

'I can't,' the girl said, 'I can't . . .' and then proceeded to throw up on the carpet, sobbing.

This is not the response of a murderer, John thought.

So what about Alasdair? Could he have done it and then turned on the lights? He certainly had a better opportunity than anyone else at the table. But opportunity or not, what was his motive? Admittedly John knew nothing about the people around him, not really. But even if Alasdair had wished to kill the old man this was hardly the way to do it. Surely better opportunities would exist than a seeming unpredictable moment of darkness in a crowded room. What about the others in the house? He knew they were not alone, he had seen the small boy at the top of the stairs and heard others running in panic after Father Goss screamed – though where they were now was another question. Had they taken a leap over the back fence in order to avoid being caught up in what was to come? Wherever they were, and however complicit they may have been in Aida Golding's performance, the important thing was that they couldn't have been involved in the murder. Let them run, he thought.

Then again, if it had been suicide – and it certainly seemed like the only viable option – perhaps they were complicit. What had driven the man to it if not the conviction that someone he feared was still reaching out to him from beyond the grave? If Father Goss had cut his own throat, Aida Golding and her team had passed him the knife and given him due cause.

'This is down to you,' he said to the medium, 'you know that, don't you?'

Probert was dialling his mobile, pacing up and down, a man of determination once more.

'I played no part in this,' she replied, 'whatever happened it's as much of a shock to me as the rest of you.'

'You set the stage,' John insisted, 'you created the mood, you gave the excuse . . . even if it was not your hand on the knife you're as guilty as hell. What did you think was going to happen, raking all that business up?'

'I can hardly be held responsible for the spirits that chose to talk through me.'

'She's right,' interrupted Davinia, 'it's not like she encouraged the Ripper is it?'

'The Ripper . . .' John was getting more and more angry by the moment, 'the Ripper wasn't in this room.'

'We all heard him!'

'We heard whatever she wanted us to hear. She's manipulated the lot of us to line her pockets and couldn't give a shit about the consequences. Whether these spirits were real or not they can still haunt us! Take a look at that poor—' he looked at Father Goss, and then at Davinia's panicked face, and frustration mixed with true misery. All of a sudden the wind was drained from him. He could have just toppled to the floor. Buried himself in the corner of the room and howled.

He looked at Sandy, still shaking, staring at him not

in fear or suspicion for once but rather a bizarre kind of relief. It occurred to him that this was one of the few times she would have seen someone stand up to Aida Golding. It was a thought that gave him back a little of his strength.

'Whatever happens,' he said, staring straight at the medium, 'I will do my utmost to ensure you never practise this charade again.'

'Oh God, don't say that!' Davinia cried. 'You can't say that! What about Henry? What about my poor Henry? You can't take Henry away from me!'

By the time the police arrived John found himself on the outside of the group, looking in. Golding, emboldened by Davinia's response had simply refused to be drawn on his accusations. She had smiled, as if conveying the greatest act of kindness, and commented that they were all bound to be feeling on edge and that she for one wouldn't take anything to heart that was said in anger and fear. There was no mileage in arguing further, that much was clear, and John had stood on the front doorstep, sheltered by the porch, watching the rain and waiting for the police to arrive.

Inside, Alasdair had ushered everyone into the kitchen where they waited in silence. Lord Probert paced up and down the hallway talking to a succession of people on his mobile. Time and again he laid out to the various people on the receiving end how he expected them to act. He outlined the questions they were to ask and, more importantly, those they were not. He clarified who should be allowed to visit the crime scene and who should not. Finally he called his lawyer and began discussing the fine details of the double injunction he wished to place on the night's proceedings. Overhearing it all, John despaired of the power money and immorality gave you in life.

'There,' said the peer as he muscled his way out onto the front step alongside John in order to wait for the police and smoke a cigar, 'I've got the whole thing sewn up tighter than an NHS budget cut.'

John couldn't even begin to stomach a reply so decided to go back inside and wait with the others.

'I wouldn't, old chap,' said Probert, holding his arm out to block the door. 'You're not man of the hour in there, you know.'

'What?'

'Your little speech about Golding set her on the warpath, you know what she's like. Tenacious little thing, wouldn't want to be on the wrong side of her myself.'

'I haven't the least interest in what she thinks of me,' John replied, 'it can hardly be any less damning than my opinion of her.'

'Yes, I heard that clearly enough. Might I ask why you bothered coming if you're such a cynic?'

'Sceptic, there's a difference. I would be willing to be proven right, just not by her . . . Her tricks were too obvious.'

'Really? She's rather impressed me. But then it doesn't matter. That's not the important thing here, what matters is ensuring you still have a career by the time you go to bed.'

'That's not the most important thing to me.'

'Really? Then you must be a damn sight richer than your supermarket anorak and chain-store jeans make you look. You said you were a teacher, yes?'

'University lecturer, actually.'

'OK, well that's better, I suppose, nobody can bear a whiff of scandal when they work with the little kiddies. Still, you think any education authority is going to want to employ a psychology lecturer who visits mediums in his spare time and has the bad luck to front the line as a suspected murderer of a priest?'

'I thought you said it must be suicide?'

'Of course it must be suicide, if any of us want to keep our position in life, precisely my point. If it's murder then we're looking at scandal so shit-deep we'll be choking for months. If it's murder we're looking at the two people who were sat next to him: the frail girl who can't stop crying or the shouting psychologist who clearly has issues over the death of his wife.'

'Don't,' said John through gritted teeth, 'don't even think of bringing her into this.'

'I won't have to, old chap, that'll be the job of the press. They'll have her photo – and yours – all over the newspapers before you can so much as say "break-down". Especially,' Probert pointed his cigar at John, 'now you've decided to make an enemy of Aida Golding. She's no stranger to fighting her corner and if it came down to which of the two of you was most capable of stitching up the other I know where my money's placed.'

'This is ridiculous. I won't be bullied out of doing what's right.'

'What's right? What rubbish! What do you hope to gain? Drag her name through the mud? You haven't a chance, you're one ranting voice against a chorus of disciples. You won't be the first bleating cynic – sorry, *sceptic* – that she's had to deal with, I can assure you, and the louder you shout the more the rest will believe.'

John couldn't deny that. Those that went to see Golding wouldn't take kindly to his calling her a fake, you only had to look at Davinia's response. He had no proof, just the conviction of his senses. And, sometimes, lately, even those seemed to be failing him.

'The important thing,' continued Probert, 'is for you to cover your own back. Not that you'll have to do anything actually as I've done it for you. As long as we all stick to the same story then none of us have anything to worry about.'

'And that story is . . .'

'That Father Goss cut his own throat. We take the heavily suspected and make it fact.'

'And if I refuse to agree to do that?'

'Then you'll have one hell of a fight on your hands. What you won't have, though, and I can guarantee you this, is a job or a house. Because, by the time I've finished with you – with the full support of the others in the room – you'll be a broken man. Not really a choice, is it?'

'I don't like being bullied, Probert.'

'Then stop putting yourself in an unpopular position. Life can be remarkably simple for those with the good sense to choose their battles.'

'Yes, remarkably simple,' John smiled, one little streak of rebellion left in him, '"Helly".'

The effect on Probert was immediate. His charm was gone, seemingly chewed away by the snarl that suddenly appeared on his face. 'Never call me that,' he said, 'or I will ruin you, regardless of what happens tonight. Understand?'

'Oh yes,' John replied, 'we're all frightened of something or someone, I understand that well enough.'

The police arrived quietly. Though whether this was at the insistence of Lord Probert or the acknowledgement that there was little left to do but mop up John couldn't tell.

The deferential manner of the chief investigating officer was all the proof needed that Probert had matters comfortably sewn up. That wasn't to say that the night passed quickly or easily – John was still awake four hours later, sat in a plastic bucket seat at the police station awaiting yet another interview – but he had little doubt the results of the investigation would be a foregone conclusion.

By the time he eventually returned home, stumbling past the front door at gone three in the morning, he was dead on his feet.

He dumped the keys on the small table in the hall and shuffled through into the kitchen, desperate for a glass of water before he shed his clothes and fell into bed for a few hours' sleep.

Toby Dammit gave him a disapproving glare then curled back up on one of the dining chairs and pretended not to have been disturbed by the return of his owner.

Filling a glass straight from the tap, John drained half in one go and then stared at his impoverished reflection in the glass of the kitchen window. He saw nothing to be proud of tonight. Nothing at all.

He was taking another mouthful when a creaking of the floorboards upstairs unnerved him.

Not now, he thought, my night has been too long as it is. Can't she at least leave me alone for one night?

Slowly, footsteps came down the stairs and John placed the glass on the sideboard. He wanted something more aggressive in his hand, something that might make him feel a bit safer. Not that there was much chance of fighting off a spirit, he admitted, grabbing a kitchen knife not unlike the one that had opened Father Goss's throat a few hours earlier. You couldn't kill the dead after all, though he wasn't sure the same could be said in reverse.

'What do you want?' he asked as the footsteps came along the hall.

There was a knock on his front door, startled he dropped the knife and it clattered onto the laminate floor.

He stared into the darkness of the hall, assuring himself that it must be empty.

The knock came again.

He drew a deep breath and walked into the hall, marching up to the front door and opening it.

The first words that came to him were the last he had spoken.

'What do you want?'

'Somewhere to hide,' admitted Sandy Thompson, 'please . . .'

Six

The Haunted

Sandy sat at the kitchen table while John made them both a drink.

'I heard you give your address to the duty officer,' she said, 'and I honestly didn't know where else I could go.'

'Home?'

'I live with her,' she didn't have to say the name, John knew it was Aida Golding she was referring to, 'and she's who I'm running away from.'

'You live with her? Why?'

'Because I have nowhere else to go and, believe me, however bad you think she is she's much worse. Aida Golding is a woman you don't refuse.'

This was the second time that had been said, John realised.

'What hold does she have over you?'

Sandy stared at him for a moment, clearly uncertain whether to answer.

'Look, Sandy,' insisted John, 'you can't just turn up on my doorstep asking for help and then not be willing to talk. Sorry, but it's all or nothing. I'll help you if I can but you need to be straight with me first.'

'My name's not Sandy.'

'You don't surprise me.'

'It's Anna.'

'Anna what?'

'Anna Golding.'

'Oh . . .'

'She adopted me when I was four. There have been years of joy ever since.'

For John it answered a lot of questions: the control Golding had over the girl, the resentment she in turn felt for Golding. But surely she was old enough to simply leave home?

'I've run away a few times, always she's brought me back one way or another. She can be very persuasive. But after tonight, with what happened . . . I just can't stay in that house any longer.'

'You think Aida Golding had something to do with the Father's death?'

'Only in the sense that you meant when you accused her. She plays with people then drops them. You wouldn't believe the things I've seen . . . the people she's cut loose because they get too much to handle.'

'The first night I saw her,' said John, 'there was a man who panicked and stormed out of the hall. You probably don't remember . . .'

'There are so many, some of them even turn up at the house. Threatening to kill her, or more usually themselves, unless she passes on a message for them. It's horrible. So much desperation, so many broken people.'

'It's not an attractive business.'

'I used to believe in her, like so many do. Even when she had me do my bit as Sandy Thompson, the grieving mother . . . she spun it so many ways. She told me that it helped offer more hope to the people in the room; that it made them more positive, which made her connection stronger; that it allowed her a little time to recharge after a particularly difficult reading . . .'

'She would pretend that it drained her more than it obviously did.'

'Yeah. "If they only knew how hard it was, girl," she'd say, "sometimes I just need a short break, just to catch my breath . . ."'

'She was an excellent liar.'

'The very best.'

'When was it you realised that she was a fake?'

'I don't know . . . honestly, I find it hard even now to say I disbelieve it totally. It's so ingrained in me. My belief in the world of spirits, that the dead surround us. Maybe I still do believe that. Maybe I just don't think *she* can hear them. I don't know . . . I just had to get out of there. Get of my life, escape into something better . . .'

'Has she ever hurt you? Physically, I mean, because if there's been a clear sign of abuse . . .'

'Forget it,' Anna shook her head, 'I don't want to go to anyone about that. I just want to be free of her.'

'But what about the others? Who else lives there? I saw a young boy . . .'

'Oh, he's all right, that's Alasdair's boy, James. She'd never hurt him, she adores him.'

'And Alasdair . . . is he family?'

Anna laughed at that. 'No! He's her partner.'

'Really?' John tried not to appear as shocked as he so obviously was. 'I just thought, what with the age difference . . .'

'I know, but she's not quite as old as she makes out to be. Still, she's twice his age, you're right.'

'Not that it matters.' John was trying to brush the matter off, feeling absurdly uncomfortable discussing it in front of her. 'So the boy's a son from a previous relationship.'

'Yeah, though she treats him like her own. Certainly gives him more attention than she ever did me.'

Was this about jealousy? John wondered. Could it be as simple as that?

'Who else is in the house?' he asked. 'I heard people running upstairs.'

'Alasdair's brother, Glen, a vicious little shit. Half the brains of anyone else in the household but he makes up for it in attitude and not caring a toss for others' opinions. The man's plain nasty but Aida doesn't mind that, in fact, she's often had cause to find it useful.'

'I can imagine, who else?'

'Glen's girlfriend, Sacha, she's not around much. Aida doesn't like her and Aida's opinion is the only one that counts.'

'And they help sometimes?' John asked. 'With the voices?'

Sandy hesitated for a moment. 'Are you going to help me? Or are you just wanting to use me to get at her?'

'We're using each other as far as I can tell,' admitted

John. He thought about it for a moment, but couldn't find the way to say no. 'I'll put you up for a few nights. Only a few, mind . . .'

Sandy smiled. 'That's great, thank you so much . . .' She drained her tea. 'Do you think we could talk more tomorrow? I've had enough of today. I just want to . . . I want to switch off, you know?'

John thought about it for a moment, suddenly uncomfortable that he had given in so easily. Was he such a pushover? Yes, he supposed he probably was. But there had been a selfish reason for letting her stay, hadn't there? 'All right,' he said. 'I'll show you up.'

He gave her the main bedroom. It was clean and empty of everything but his fears. He no longer thought of it as his room any more.

'There are clean towels in the airing cupboard, help yourself to whatever toiletries you need. You can always pick up some more things tomorrow.'

'I'll be fine.' She looked at him and her face took on that same, soft look of relief she had shown earlier when he had turned his anger towards her stepmother. 'Thank you,' she said. 'You're really very kind.' She stepped forward and gave him a light kiss on his cheek.

He didn't quite know how to respond so just stood there as she stepped back into the room and closed the door behind her.

He stood on the landing for a moment, listening to her move around the room, then went into the spare bedroom and undressed for sleep. Lying in bed he listened to the noises beyond the wall and finally admitted to himself that it was far nicer to be haunted by someone who was alive.

'And where the hell have you been?' cried a woman's voice from the bedroom.

Llewellyn Probert sighed, flung his overcoat on a chair and crept manfully towards the whisky decanter. He had been craving a drink for hours. Now, just as he could almost taste it on his lips, he had to endure an earful from the vicious creature he had the misfortune of sharing a marriage with. When would the Almighty give him a bloody hour off?

'I've been at the police station,' he shouted, pleased at the shocked response he knew such an answer would cause.

'You've been where?' The partition doors that sealed the main bedroom off from the rest of the Probert's open-plan apartment rattled apart and his wife stood, wild-eyed between them.

He looked at her, ruffled hair, silk gown awry and – most importantly – a face on her that could make a Dobermann flinch. God, he thought, I could almost fancy the volcanic sow. He knew better than to pursue that thought. A sane man didn't try to sleep with Kathleen; she'd emasculate them with a single bite of her sex. Mistresses, that was the safe way forward.

Which made him think of Thana calling for her Helly, and his mood soured yet further.

He took a sip of his drink. A large one. Then added a dash of water. All of which prevarication served only to make his wife more furious.

'Well? What's wrong with you, you silly man? Out with it!' Normally her attempts at such English phraseology amused him, given her origins across the Atlantic. The one thing Kathleen tried to hide the most was her heritage.

'I have been helping the police with their enquiries after having had the misfortune of witnessing a man commit suicide.'

'Oh, don't be so ridiculous,' she pushed him out of the way and poured a drink for herself. 'What are you talking about?'

'Just that,' he replied, going some way towards finishing his drink, eager for a crack at another. 'I was at a dinner party – as I told you – when one of the guests, a priest no less, decided he could no longer go on and opened his throat with a carving knife.'

'Absurd!'

'Quite, he didn't even have dessert.'

'Oh! How could you? What have you really been doing?'

'All flippancy aside, my dear,' he eased his way back alongside the decanter and made a solid use of its services, 'I'm telling the truth. I know it's shocking but there you go. The man obviously had a screw loose, he was involved in that East End Ripper case years ago, do you remember it?'

'East End Ripper? Oh Llewellyn, I can't make head nor tail of what you're talking about.'

'Never mind, it was a big murder investigation back in the eighties. Lunatic went around eviscerating women. The point is, this priest, Father Goss, knew the murderer. He'd been talking about it, in a rather unhinged manner. The chap got more and more excited until he just snapped, right there at the dinner table. He topped himself. Horrendous. Of course, being of some influence, I did everything I could to help.'

'To hell with helping, wait until the press get wind of it. Oh Lord . . . like we haven't had enough of their attention lately.'

'I haven't been in the papers for well over a year, dear, you do exaggerate. Anyway, I rang Howard and got him on the case. He assures me that there won't be a peep from anyone about it. On pain of a court date and sufficient damages to rupture a small country.'

'Do stop posturing.'

Probert sighed. 'Damned if I do, damned if I don't,' he muttered.

'What? It's not all about you, you know, I've been awake all night wondering where the hell you'd got to.'

'How terrible for you.' He drained his drink. 'Well, now you've found me might I suggest you get some sleep. A bit of peace and quiet would do us both some good.'

'That's right,' she said, slamming her glass down and storming back to the bedroom, 'let's not spare a thought for my feelings. They hardly matter. I'm only the one whose money keeps you afloat!'

She dragged the doors shut behind her and Probert refilled his glass and raised it after her. 'That's it,' he muttered, 'don't forget to bring up the money, and don't

– whatever you do, my contemptible little darling – choke on your poisonous tongue in the night.'

But the image of his wife's dead body, purple and bloated, only served to remind him of Thana again.

'You miss me,' he could imagine her saying, 'don't you, Helly?'

He remembered the smell of her, closed his eyes and – just for a moment – imagined how it would feel were she to walk up behind him now, just as she had done countless times in the past, place her hands on his shoulders and kiss him on the nape of his neck. He imagined he could hear the creak of leather and the rustle of plastic. He imagined what she might say as she whispered in his ear.

'They took my eyes, Helly, why did you let them take my eyes?'

He shook in his chair, looking around to thoroughly dispel the unwelcome thought that his dead mistress was somehow in the room with him. After that he decided to drink enough scotch that imagining – or indeed any thought at all – became difficult.

Davinia Harris could barely find the energy to step through her own front door.

Tonight had been a strange mixture of elation and heartbreak. My life to a tee, she thought, hanging up her coat and making her way through into the kitchen. She wanted a hot drink and then to sink into a chair and let the night's stresses slowly peel away. She also wanted to stop thinking about John Pritchard.

'Silly man,' she said, 'he seemed so nice.'

She looked around as she so frequently did, looking for a sign of her Henry, a vague glimmer perhaps, a shadow deeper than the others. 'It just upset him,' she decided, 'that's what it was. And who can blame him? It was very upsetting. I shan't rest easy for days.'

She dropped a teabag in a mug and stood close to the kettle, stealing away some of its warmth. The central heating was on a timer and had long since turned off. In an hour or so it would reignite and begin to ease the chill from this old house of ghosts. Now it was at its coldest, icy and unwelcoming in the dead of the night.

'Did you see it, Henry?' she asked. 'Did you actually see it happen? It would be a relief to know . . . if only you could tell me. If only you would say.'

She found she was crying, which only served to make her angry with herself. 'There's no time for that sort of nonsense,' she said, 'and if you were a better husband you certainly wouldn't have stood by and let me be in the same room as something like that. See what I'm reduced to, just following you around? Just for a few words of comfort . . .'

She made her tea and took it through into the lounge.

She sat down in one of her floral easy chairs, the cushions giving as deep-throated a sigh as she did herself.

'I'm sure he must have killed himself,' she said. 'That's what you'd tell me if you could, isn't it? Because there's no other explanation, is there? It can't be that . . . it can't be that . . .'

She placed her tea on the small table beside her, rather that than let her nervous hands drop it on the floor.

'It can't be that one of them who killed him . . .'

Aida 'Granny' Golding didn't wait for Alasdair to put the car away in the garage. She went straight through the front door and headed upstairs. Downstairs was for guests, every room carefully stage-managed so as to give exactly the impression she wished. Upstairs was lighter, more modern, less obsessed with the cosy and the quaint.

She shrugged off her coat and flung her cardigan on the back of a chair. Grabbing a packet of cigarettes from the sideboard she lit up and went on the hunt for something to drink. Tonight . . . no, *this morning* was definitely a time for giving in to one's addictions.

As she laid her hands on a half bottle of vodka she heard the front door close downstairs and Alasdair's feet on the stairs. She decided the vodka would be best with the remains of a bottle of Coke she found in the fridge. When he entered she was filling her glass with roughly half of each.

'Make me one,' Alasdair said.

She grunted but poured him a distinctly smaller measure and handed it over.

'What a night,' he said, before drowning the redundant statement with a mouthful of his drink. 'You think it'll be all right?'

'It'll be fine,' she replied. 'I haven't spent this many

years grubbing around church halls and sports centres to see things fall apart now.'

'People won't like it if they hear something like this has happened at one of your sessions.'

'No, Alasdair,' she replied with venom, 'they fucking wouldn't. Don't worry your pretty little head about it, this is something the adults can fix.'

'There's no need to be like that. Besides, you'd be in a right state without me so maybe you ought to remember that before having a pop.'

'Alasdair, darling, do shut up and let me think.'

Alasdair opened his mouth to argue but decided against it, storming off with his drink.

Aida smoked her cigarette with single-minded devotion. Once finished she lit another and topped up her drink. She wanted to pollute herself, to rub out the precise, puritan pretence that was 'Granny' Golding and be herself for the few hours that remained between now and sleep. She had been so busy of late. Trapped so long in the cardigans and wool-mix, soft and inoffensive beneath the tight perm. She had been 'Granny' Golding so long that the sweet old dear had become as real as her, perhaps even more so.

She looked at her reflection in the glass of the window and tried to picture the real woman beneath. She couldn't, the possession was too strong, the real Aida was no more than a ghost.

'What's going on?' asked a young voice.

Never, thought the medium, has a more important question been asked.

She turned to see young James stood in the doorway,

eyes hooded, pyjamas tugged long in both the arms and legs. A tired little man that wanted to bury himself away in the soft cottons of sleep.

Aida stubbed out her cigarette and swooped him up in a hug.

'Nothing you need to worry about,' she told him, carrying him out of the kitchen and straight across the landing to his room. It was dark but for the swirling starlight that spilled out from his night-light. She laid him down beneath this ever-moving night-sky and lay next to him for a while, watching the shapes dance across the ceiling. Five pointed stars, Saturn and her rings, the crater-pocked moon. All child-like representations of things so much bigger than a human mind could really understand. All we ever do, she thought, as little James fell asleep next to her, is sketch the universe and try and make it small enough to hold in our hands and our heads. All we want to do is make things small.

'To hell with infinity,' she muttered. 'Give me cold, hard reality every time.'

'Mmm?' James turned in his sleep, half hearing her.

'Nothing, darling boy,' she replied, 'sleep.'

Eventually, they both did.

Outside, still very much awake, Trevor Court watched the lights turning off in Aida Golding's upstairs rooms.

'Night, night,' he said, sucking the tips of his fingers. He cut the nails too short, wanting to keep them free from dirt. It was a thankless task, as often the pink tips would bleed and then he'd have to pick away the scabs, always trying to reach the pure, unblemished skin underneath. But picking them only made them bleed again. How he wished he could leave his wounds alone. Wounds like Aida Golding. They made him so sore. And there was always so much blood.

But sometimes you just had to.

Seven

The Division

John woke to the first dry skies for weeks. It wasn't only that that made him happy.

'What a stupid old man you are,' he told the distended reflection in the chrome surface of the toaster, but felt no more conviction than his double did remorse.

He poured himself a bowl of cereal and ate it while looking out of the window at his small garden. It had the hunched and tired demeanour of a man that has been beaten up and is hoping to avoid worse. The flowers had had the petals slapped from them, the bushes bent their backs and cowered like dogs, the cypress hedge needed to comb its hair, stray branches splayed at all angles. He didn't care. It was green and fresh and would soon be back on its own feet if the rain stayed away. Not that the presenter on the radio seemed convinced that was likely. 'Enjoy the break from the rain,' he said, with all the earnestness of a man giving advice to a favourite child, 'the forecasters say it'll be back soon enough.'

'Perhaps we should build an ark!' suggested the chirpy producer who seemed determined to muddle up his job description by being as ever-present on air as the DJ who had been employed by the studio for the purpose. 'At this rate we'll all be washed away.'

Something the news then had the unfortunate timing to confirm as it ran with the lead story of an elderly couple drowned in flooding.

John turned off the radio, conscious that it might wake Anna. Then it occurred to him that perhaps he should wake her. Was he really proposing to let a stranger – who he knew had been in the employ of a woman who wished him ill – have the run of his house? Did he expect to return to find his belongings in place? Surely she would be on the phone to Alasdair or Glen the moment he was past the front gate, encouraging them to come round and steal everything that wasn't nailed down before trashing the rest. What proof did he even have that she had left Aida Golding's influence?

'None whatsoever,' he announced, putting on his bicycle clips, grabbing his bag and heading out of the door.

He found not caring incredibly uplifting.

The bike ride to the campus continued his good feeling. It seemed to him that London was picking itself back up after a war. People mopping the floors of their shops, pedestrians glancing at the sky as if unable to believe such good fortune, umbrellas furled, heads dry.

He pulled into the college campus, narrowly avoiding Shaun Vedder, who was shuffling aimlessly around the place as usual. Not that this was unusual behaviour for any of the students, often you couldn't get a complex sentence structure from them until mid-afternoon. Vedder spun around to watch John ride towards his office and managed a slow wave once he realised who it was.

'Stoned out of his tree,' John chuckled, swinging the bike around the corner of the science block and heading the last few feet towards his office.

Dismounting, he carried his bike inside the building. He'd used to chain it up outside but after a spate of robberies a few months back nobody dared leave their bikes in plain sight. He'd taken to shoving his in the nest of AV cable and stale tobacco that was Ray's office. If the technician nicked it, it would only be so he could get to the corner shop and back quickly because he had the urge for a pasty.

'Morning!' he announced cheerily as he barged through the door.

'Jesus!' Ray had thrown his roll-up down the back of the desk thinking it was some less-forgiving member of the faculty. 'What's wrong with you? Are you drunk? How dare you come in here smiling at this time of term.' He dropped to his hands and knees and went on the hunt for his cigarette before it burned the desk down.

'I'm sure all the joy will be knocked out of me by lunchtime,' John admitted. 'I'm just glad to see it's stopped raining.'

'Bullshit,' Ray muttered from somewhere behind a cat's cradle of power leads, 'nobody looks as happy as you do without sex or narcotics, which is it?'

'I can't remember the last time I enjoyed either, though our friend Shaun Vedder certainly seems to have had his fair share of the latter this morning.'

'Nah . . . poor sod's mum's dead, isn't she? I heard someone talking about it in the canteen.'

'Oh,' John sat down, his good mood dented. 'Poor lad, is he heading home?'

'Not sure. From what I gather she brought him up on her own so he's not got much to go home to. He's not in a good state though, that's for sure.'

'I'll try and talk to him maybe, offer him a bit of support.'

'You do that.' Ray reappeared, cigarette between his lips, 'I'm sure that'll make all the difference.'

'You're a jaded old git, you know that?'

'Just a realist. You mean to tell me a chat from someone you didn't know would have helped you after Jane? It's just something you have to get through, isn't it?'

John nodded, though even Ray, for all his blunderbuss sensibilities, knew that John was still a long way from having 'got through' it. 'I'll still try, I wouldn't want him to feel he has no support.'

'Such a pinnacle of kindness. Why don't you help me more often? I need a shoulder to cry on too, you know.'

'About what?'

'About how little I'm getting laid.'

'Bye, Ray.'

'Get out you heartless bastard, you're no friend of mine.'

Under normal circumstances, John would have expected to see Shaun Vedder that very morning. Though when the young man didn't show for his lecture he wasn't surprised.

Talking on autopilot, John realised his heart wasn't in it. He looked out at the audience of students, some taking notes, some just staring into their own thoughts, and realised there was nothing worse in education than going through the motions.

'Psychology,' he said, completely changing the tack of his speech, 'is the science of understanding why the mind disagrees with itself. Why it will constantly fly in the face of logic and reason.' It was proof that he had been boring them that only a couple seemed wrong-footed by his sudden gear-change. 'We are at the mercy of our automatic triggers, our hang-ups and phobias. We are constantly doing the wrong thing because our minds give us no option.' He paused and then decided to go for broke.

'I'm the perfect example,' he said. 'I have spent my whole life disbelieving anything that fell beyond the realms of scientific explanation and yet, ever since my wife died, I'm convinced she haunts me. I see her everywhere. I hear her everywhere. She's not there, of course, I know that really, but knowing that doesn't make her go away. I am tortured by my own, stupid brain.'

There was an uncomfortable shuffling at that. The students were awkward at the emotional context of what he was saying. Understandable, he thought, but missing the point.

'Don't get caught up in the detail,' he insisted, 'embarrassed at the fact your mad old lecturer has a dead wife. It's not the important point. The important point is: however much I know something, the brain won't let me be. It cannot help but be an organ of deceit, working hard to convince me of things I know not to be the case but will end up believing – in that awful, vulnerable moment – because I am unable to help myself.'

He ambled back and forth, not even sure if he had a point or just wanted to shake them up.

'At its worst degree, this diversion between fact and reality is called madness. But it's in all of us, make no mistake about that. When you feel jealous of a partner, regardless of whether they've given you due cause, when you find yourself waking up in the night convinced there's someone else in your room, when you sink into depression knowing you can't complete your coursework because it's all too much work and you're just not clever enough . . .' there was a slight laugh at that, the students relieved to be on familiar, innocuous ground. 'That's the division at work. The rational voice conflicting with the panicked, instinctual, fearful voice. The one that wants nothing more than to rattle you. It's all madness, it's just that sometimes we're just able to continue functioning.'

One of the students, Jim Farrage, always the joker, pulled a crazy face and acted the loon.

'In your case, Farrage,' John said, *'barely* function.'

They laughed, nothing won back a room like gently picking on one of their number. There was a psycho-logical lesson to be learned there, too, John thought, but not today. Today they had learned enough and he had no more interest in teaching them.

'And sometimes,' he continued, 'the best way you can understand psychology is to shut up, close your books,' he tapped his temple, 'and listen to what is says in here.'

He gathered up his own . 'We'll finish early so you can do just that,' he said, and went in search of Shaun Vedder.

The campus was typical of many institutions designed and built in the seventies. The separate buildings littered the grounds surrounded by pathways and stairways that frequently led to nowhere the discerning pedestrian could wish to be. Architectural cul-de-sacs were semi-legitimised by 'free' areas turfed or gravelled and filled with park benches or picnic tables. Sometimes you'd even find students in these areas, but only if they were lost or specifically trying to avoid other people.

John found Shaun huddled on a bench in the process of being swallowed by an azalea bush.

'You mind if I join you for a minute?' he asked.

Shaun shrugged and squeezed himself into an even tighter ball in the corner of the bench.

'I heard about your mum,' said John. 'My condolences.'

Shaun nodded but chose to say nothing.

'I just wanted to offer my help,' John continued, determined to say his piece. 'You know I lost someone recently and it's difficult to deal with. I still struggle. But I'll give you whatever support I can. At least you know that I understand what it feels like. I know how it can hurt.'

They sat in silence for a moment. John hoping Shaun

might actually say something. When he eventually decided that wasn't going to happen he got to his feet and made to leave.

'You know what's really getting me today?' said Shaun finally.

John turned back to face him. 'What?'

'How it takes my mother dying to get everyone around here to give a shit.'

John shook his head. 'That's not true, Shaun, lots of people care, you know that.'

'Do I? Really? Who are my best friends, Mr Pritchard? Who do you always see me hanging around with?'

John tried to think and found he couldn't bring anyone to mind. Whenever he saw Shaun he was on his own. 'I don't know,' he admitted, 'I'm sorry.'

'You and every other stranger,' Shaun replied and shifted on the seat so his back was turned to John. It was clear he had no more interest in talking. After a moment of desperately trying to think what might be the best thing to say, John conceded defeat and left the young man to it.

The good mood he'd started the day with was slipping away. He'd been of no use to Shaun and felt embarrassed at how he'd handled the situation. Ray had been right that he should have avoided seeking the lad out. Still, having made that initial effort he felt he couldn't just abandon him entirely so went to see Tracy Lambeth, the student counsellor.

She was in her office reading a newspaper and wait - ing for her working day to end. John often wondered how someone so apparently uninterested in other people could be found doing her job.

'Hello, John,' she said when he stuck his head around her door. 'I can't hang around I've got a very busy morning.'

'Clearly,' he replied, with a smile, nodding at the newspaper.

'Can't do this job unless you're abreast of current affairs,' she said, 'you'd be surprised how much the outside world affects them. I remember a girl five years ago who swallowed a bottle of Nembutal just because the "wrong" person won *X Factor*. God knows how she got hold of some. Bought it online, I suppose. I wish one of the sods would show me how to find that sort of thing. Music, drugs and porn . . . all you ever see on this damn thing,' she tapped her computer, 'are emails and Wikipedia. God knows what I'm doing wrong.'

'Perhaps Ray could . . .'

'That smelly pervert? I'd rather have the thing thrown out of the window. Anyway . . . what did you want to ask? Out with it so I can get on with my research.' She shoved at the newspaper with a chewed biro. 'What's one of them done now? Or is it you that wants to . . .?'

'No, no, I'm all right. It's Shaun Vedder.'

'That weirdo? What's he done now?'

'His mother's died.'

'Oh, well, I suppose that's hardly his fault.'

'Of course not,' said John, 'but he's very cut up about it.'

'Well, I'm here if he needs to talk.'

John couldn't see that happening. 'I tried to talk to him myself, actually.'

Tracy shook her head in despair. 'What is with you people thinking you can just go and be a counsellor,' she said, 'I didn't train for nothing, you know. I've a diploma in grief counselling, what qualifications have you got?'

John just stared at her, not quite sure if she was joking or not.

'Oh,' she said, 'yeah . . . your wife, sorry.'

'No problem. He wouldn't talk anyway. Seems to have a real chip on his shoulder about people not caring for him.'

'Took a shower once in a while he might find his social life picks up,' Tracy laughed. 'All right, I'm only joking.'

Said in the manner of obnoxious bullies everywhere, thought John. It doesn't matter what you say as long as you insist you were joking afterwards.

'Just thought I'd let you know,' he said, getting up. 'He's genuinely suffering, maybe you could keep an eye on him?'

'Yeah,' she picked up her paper again, 'will do.'

John coasted through the rest of the day, finding he always had one eye on the windows hoping to catch sight of Shaun Vedder. He even took his lunch at Verano on the off chance he might bump into him there. No doubt he had little in the way of an appetite, for vegetable tikka wraps even, certainly there was no sign of him.

John even returned to the bench where he'd talked to Vedder. Unsurprisingly it was empty.

Perhaps, he decided, he should concentrate on his own problems and let Shaun do likewise.

Cycling home it once again occurred to him that he might be returning to a home damaged beyond recog- nition. With the carefree attitude of the morning now well and truly gone he found himself pedalling faster and faster in the need to get home and find out one way or the other. The sky was beginning to darken again, eager to fulfil the promises of the weather forecasters. By the time he returned home it was beginning to spot with rain and he ran from the side of the house where he chained his bike to the front door in order to avoid getting wet.

Unlocking his door he took a deep breath, deter- mined to deal with whatever he might find. It was as the door swung open that he realised Alasdair and Glen might be waiting for him. It could be that their revenge would be nothing less than a beating.

'Hello?' he called, stepping cautiously into the hall - way. There was definitely something different about the place, he decided, a smell . . .

Anna appeared in the doorway of the kitchen, wooden spoon in one hand, tea towel in the other. She was dancing to the music from her iPod, headphone cable swaying in time to her hips. When she saw him she screamed and threw the wooden spoon in panic. It painted an arrow of tomato sauce on the glass of the front door.

'You made me jump!' she shouted, before yanking out her headphones. 'Sorry,' she said, much quieter, 'I wasn't expecting you back for a bit yet. What time do school teachers finish work these days?'

'University lecturers finish whenever they're free,' he replied, picking up the spoon. 'Sorry I startled you.'

'I'm cooking,' she explained as he handed it back.

'I hoped that was the answer,' he replied, smiling. 'If you'd been killing my cat with a spoon I'd have been furious.'

'Oh he's fine,' she said, strolling back into the kitchen with John following, 'I fed him some tuna at lunchtime and now we've come to an understanding.'

John saw that it was true, Toby Dammit sat on the kitchen table watching Anna calmly. He glanced at John, confirming that all was under control but that supervision would continue.

'I haven't had someone cook for me . . .' John suddenly realised where that sentence was going and head it off at the pass, 'well, it's been a long time.'

'It's nothing special,' said Anna, 'because I'm a lousy cook, but I thought it was the least I could do, considering. It's pasta, anyone can cook pasta.' She stirred the saucepan of sauce. 'How was your day?'

'Fine. Actually, no, horrible. A student of mine's lost his mother.'

'That can be a blessing.'

'Not in this case, he's very cut up about it.'

Anna nodded. 'I can't even remember mine. You'd think at four I'd have some memories wouldn't you? At least he'll have that . . .'

'Or maybe that just gives him more to miss?'

'Maybe.' She dumped the spoon in the saucepan and moved over to the kettle. 'Do you want a drink? I can make you a drink.'

'You don't have to run around after me,' he said. 'It's fine.'

'I know, I just want to be . . . I don't know, a good thing in the house rather than a problem.'

'Don't worry, you're not a problem.' The phone rang, saving him from any further awkwardness.

'Hey,' it was Michael, 'how's things?'

'Fine,' said John, not wanting to discuss Anna with him over the phone, aware that his son would disapprove. 'You?'

'Not brilliant, just heard I didn't get that Stoppard thing. Didn't fancy touring anyway but, well, you know.'

'The money wasn't bad.'

'Surprisingly. I wondered if we could come round?'

'What, here?'

'Obviously there, Dad, unless you're going out or something?'

'No,' John wasn't quick enough to think of a suitable lie, 'no, it's fine. You just don't often visit so I was surprised.'

'Well, Laura and I've been talking about your suggestion.'

'My suggestion?' John's head was all over the place, imagining what Michael was going to say about Anna.

'You know, about the house.'

'You two moving in, of course, sorry . . .'

'If you've changed your mind . . .'

'Not at all, just had a lot on today, my head's not with it.'

'No change there. What sort of time would be good?'

'Whenever you like,' John decided the only way forward was to be brazen about it. 'Tell you what, come at seven and we'll feed you both.'

'"We"?'

'You'll see, tell you about it later.'

Eight

A Nice Man

'I should just go out,' said Anna, fretting over the pasta, 'give you some space for a couple of hours. There's no need for me to stay. After all, it'll only be awkward.'

'Don't be silly,' John said, grating cheese, 'it's only my son. It's not a problem. It's my house.'

'But he'll ask about last night, I really don't want to talk about that . . .'

'Then we don't have to. I'll explain everything.' He put down the grater, exasperated with his own nerves more than hers. 'For God's sake! I'm only putting you up for a couple of nights, what's the big deal?'

'Nothing,' she agreed, her voice calmer. 'Nothing, you're right.'

They carried on in silence for a minute. John glanced at the clock. It was still half an hour before Michael and Laura would arrive.

'I wish I'd packed more clothes,' said Anna looking down at the baggy jumper and jeans she was still wearing. 'I didn't think.'

'There's stuff upstairs you can borrow if you want,'

said John, dumping the cheese in the sauce. 'In the wardrobes in your room. Most of it should fit.'

'Your wife's clothes?' Anna looked uncomfortable and, now he thought about it, with good cause. What had he been thinking?

'Actually, yes . . . probably you don't want to . . . I just never seem to find the time to clear them out.' He grabbed some cutlery and began laying the table. 'Sorry, *I* didn't think . . .'

'No,' she insisted, 'it's fine, honestly. It's very kind. I mean they're only clothes I'm sure there'd be something in there better than . . .' she looked down at herself.

Relieved, he nodded. 'She wouldn't have minded. She'd certainly have lent you something had she been here.' Had she not been dead. Oh shut up, John Pritchard, he thought, just shut up.

There was a moment of slight awkwardness, with both of them looking at each other. Anna broke first.

'If you're sure it's OK, I'll grab a quick shower and get changed. I'd feel more comfortable I think . . .'

'Go ahead, please, there's nothing left to do here anyway.'

She ran upstairs and he sank back against the table, trying to convince himself that it was fine. It was only stuff, clutter he should have cleared out months ago. It really didn't matter did it?

And before he could even steel himself against it he could picture Jane, the grey, lifeless remnant of her that always lingered close by, watching as Anna ran her hands through the old clothes. He could imagine her dead eyes, almost as white as those of a boiled fish, staring on in jealousy, reaching out to stop this act of desecration.

He dropped the cutlery and the clatter brought his mind back to the present.

'You all right?' Anna shouted from upstairs.

'Fine, just clumsy.' He heard her opening the wardrobe doors and clenched his fists in anger at himself.

He picked up the knives and forks and finished laying the table.

'He's allowed to meet someone, you know,' Laura laughed, hugging Michael's arm as they walked together up the street.

Michael shifted the umbrella slightly, wanting to make sure that she was fully covered.

'Of course he is,' he agreed, 'if that's what it is. Probably it's just an old friend visiting or something . . .'

'If it was an old friend he'd have told you, wouldn't he?'

'Maybe the IT guy from the Uni, I think they're friends . . .'

'Then he would have said "The IT guy's here too."'

'Ray, his name's Ray.'

'Whatever. You know what I'm saying. You know I'm right as well. Whoever it is it was too complicated to explain on the phone.'

'Doesn't mean it's a woman.'

'Oh Michael,' Laura laughed and he was given cause once again to bask in her sheer ebullience. She went through life seeming to constantly erupt with joy. He frequently wished it was contagious.

'Well? It doesn't. But if it is then that's OK too, I'm just surprised. He really doesn't seem to be over Mum, that's all.'

'He probably never will be "over" her. Neither will you. Doesn't mean you can't get on with your life.'

'I know, it was just the way he was talking. About sharing the house and the medium thing . . .'

'Maybe he met someone there?'

'What? Amongst the gloomy pensioners and weird new-agers? I doubt it. Though there was a widow who kept talking to him, maybe she's kidnapped him.'

'Maybe. She keeps him chained up except when he has guests, if he looks panicked we'll try and break him out, all right?'

'OK.'

They stopped at the kerb, Michael waiting for a slow bus to head past rather than dragging Laura across at speed. He had learned to become a patient set of eyes for her and was proud at the trust she placed in him. He had never felt like someone who was reliable, she made him feel exactly that. With the road clear, they crossed and walked past the last couple of houses to his father's house.

'It's a nice area,' said Laura, 'peaceful.'

'Yeah,' Michael agreed, 'takes ages to get into town though.'

'Good,' Laura teased, 'it'll encourage you to stay home more often with me.'

'Like I need encouraging. Mind the step.' He guided her under the porch, turned and furled his umbrella, shaking as much of the excess water off as possible.

Laura stroked the bricks by the door, finding then ringing the bell.

'They're here!' shouted a woman's voice, audible beyond the door.

'Told you,' said Laura, ' and she sounds young too.'

'Oh God,' mumbled Michael, chuckling slightly.

The door opened and John appeared. 'Hello!' he gave Laura a big hug and a kiss on both cheeks. 'He never brings you to see me,' he moaned.

'Kiss her like that again and I never will,' his son joked.

'Come in, come in.' John stepped back to let them pass. 'Go straight through to the kitchen.'

'Such class,' said Michael.

'Only use the dining room for people you don't know,' John joked as they filed through.

'I brought this,' said Michael, handing over a bottle of wine, 'so there was something drinkable in the house.'

'I'll get you a straw.'

Michael sat Laura down at the table, noticing the four place settings. 'I didn't mishear then,' he said, 'four for dinner.'

'Ah,' said John, 'yes, I want to explain about that.'

'Hello,' said Anna from the doorway, 'shall I go away and come back in a minute?'

John couldn't help but stare. She was wearing a dark brown dress of Jane's, an absolute favourite, embroidered with small flower patterns. His wife hadn't been able to wear it for a long time as once the weight loss got so bad it hung off her. It was like looking at a happy memory.

'Oh,' said Michael, clearly shocked and incapable of hiding it. 'It's you.'

'That's not how you greet a lady, Michael,' said Laura, getting to her feet, 'God knows how you ended up with such a beautiful girlfriend.' She laughed and Anna joined in, walking over and taking Laura's hand so she didn't have to walk over and meet her.

'I'm Anna,' she said, shaking the hand gently.

'Laura, and that lump of bad manners is Michael.'

'Sorry,' Michael recovered himself, 'I didn't mean to be rude.'

'Don't be silly,' said Anna, taking his hand. 'It's fine.'

'Lovely to meet you,' he nearly said 'again' but managed to stop himself. 'I saw you at the medium thing a couple of weeks ago.'

'Yes,' said John, 'there's a bit of a story behind that.'

'I've run away from home and your father is very kindly putting me up for a couple of days while I get myself straight.' Anna explained simply.

'Yes,' said John, vaguely, 'that's the quick version.'

'"Run away from home"?' said Laura. 'How wonderfully dramatic! Tell us all.'

And, while they ate, Anna did, avoiding any mention of Father Goss but only too happy to be candid about the rest. If John had been concerned he was at his ease by the end of the meal. For all her nerves, Anna was the very epitome of social con - fidence, warm, honest and funny. It was clear that both his son and Laura were taken with her. As was he, though that was something he was certainly not willing to address for now.

'I thought I recognised the dress!' said Michael, laughing. 'You're lucky I didn't faint thinking a ghost had walked into the room.'

'I'm sure she looked better in it,' said Anna, tugging at the fabric self-consciously. 'I'm just glad you didn't mind, it was so kind of John and so stupid of me. I've never been much of a planner, I just took to my heels and ran here, not a thought about practical things.'

'Why did you come here?' asked Laura. 'If you don't mind my asking'

'Of course not,' said Anna, 'John just seemed safe, you know? I suppose I could have got myself in a lot of trouble just turning up on a stranger's doorstep but sometimes you can just tell. I knew he was a good man.'

'He's an ogre,' joked Michael, 'he beat me every day until I was twenty.'

Laura slapped him on the arm. 'Be nice!'

'I was only joking.'

'I know,' said John, 'besides, it's true. I used to lock him in the cellar and feed him on vegetable scraps.'

'He's the softest man I know,' said Laura, leaning over towards Anna as if imparting a secret, 'and the nicest.'

'Oi!' said Michael with a laugh, 'I'm sat right here, you know.'

'There's no point in arguing, son,' laughed John. 'She's right and you know it.'

'I'm sure she is,' agreed Anna getting up, 'if you'll excuse me a moment?'

She left the room, heading upstairs towards the bathroom.

'See,' said Michael, 'you've scared her off. Probably thinks you're trying to matchmake.'

'No,' said John, 'it's not like that. I just couldn't not help.'

'Of course you couldn't,' agreed Laura.

'Seems a bit weird to me,' said Michael. 'Are you sure she's not after the family silver?'

'Yes. Because we haven't got any. Besides, there's a bit more to it.' He lowered his voice. 'Last night, at a small group session at Golding's house, one of the clients killed himself.' He waved at them to keep the noise down. 'We were both there and it really shook Anna up.'

'I'm not bloody surprised,' said Michael. 'Are you OK?'

'Oh I'm fine. The point is, that was what drove Anna away so suddenly, she just couldn't stand it any more.'

'Of course she couldn't,' said Laura. 'You can tell she's a good person. None of it sat well with her.'

'So she says,' Michael said.

'Trust me,' insisted Laura. 'Blind people are excellent judges of character. I pick up stuff in her voice that you wouldn't. She's sincere, take my word for it.'

There was the sound of the toilet flushing and they all leaned back in their chairs, desperate to convey the fact that they hadn't been talking about Anna when she came in.

'She doesn't want to talk about it,' said John in a quick whisper, 'so don't mention it, all right?'

Anna came down the stairs and back into the kitchen.

'I hope you've all been talking about me?' she said with a smile.

'Of course,' laughed Laura, 'we never stopped, but we've finished now and famished for dessert.'

'They're lovely,' said Anna after Michael and Laura had gone. 'You must be proud.'

'I am,' John admitted returning to his half glass of wine, relieved that the evening had gone better than he might have hoped.

'And I think they'll move in,' she continued, 'you can tell Michael feels embarrassed by it, like it's a step backward for him, but Laura loves the idea and that's what will matter. They're very lucky.'

'To have each other?'

'No, to have you. A father that actually looks out for his child.'

'It's nothing.'

'Rubbish, it's everything. Laura's right, you're a nice man.'

John felt a bit embarrassed at that so he just shrugged and filled the sink to do the washing up.

'She seems really nice,' said Laura as she and Michael made their way towards the tube.

'I suppose so,' Michael agreed.

'"Suppose"?'

'No, she does. It's just weird, having seen her play her part at that thing. Watching her cry. Now I know it's not true . . . well, she's a hell of an actor.'

'So are you, remember?'

'True! You know what I mean, though. I just hope she is genuine. I'd hate to think of her taking dad for a ride.'

'I don't think you need worry about that,' the rain got heavier, beating against the umbrella so hard Laura had to raise her voice to be heard. 'She wouldn't hurt your dad, she's got too much of a crush on him.'

'No!'

'Of course she has, don't tell me you didn't notice?'

'I think you're reading too much into her voice.'

'And you're not reading enough. Right now he's her absolute hero, and something tells me she hasn't had many of them in her life.'

Nine

One Knock for Yes

'Is there even anyone here?' Golding asked as Alasdair pulled the car into a parking space behind the small hall.

Peering through the wet windows he had to admit it didn't look like it. With a sigh he turned up the collar on his coat and got out of the car. 'I'll take a look,' he said, dashing over to the cover of the doorway.

'The Barret-Holden Memorial Hall' announced a sign on the door 'was opened in 1984 by the Rt. Hon. Ashley Furcott.'

'Well, I wish the fucker was here now,' muttered Alasdair, rattling the handle fruitlessly before giving the wood an angry kick.

'No need for that is there?' said an elderly voice behind him. He turned to see a small, round man shuffling towards him beneath the cover of an umbrella. 'It'll stay closed as hard as you kick it, though I won't thank you for messing up the paintwork.' The man rattled a set of keys and came under the covered porch with Alasdair. 'Little thugs that live round here would break in here before you could so much as say "borstal".

We have to keep it secure or it'll be a mess of needles and whatnot.' He looked at Alasdair with a distinctly unfriendly glare. 'And our regulars are respectable, they wouldn't like that sort of thing.'

'Absolutely not,' Alasdair agreed, surprised that one angry kick had marked him down as a common lout in this miserable bastard's eyes. 'Sorry.'

'Never mind,' the old man opened the door.

'I didn't think anybody was here.'

'Clearly, dare say you wouldn't act like that to an audience.'

'I meant to open up. I thought we were stuck outside.'

'Saw you pull in, didn't I?' The old man shuffled in and begin flicking on the lights, row by row of old fluorescents illuminating the cream tiles and magnolia paintwork of the hall. 'Not waiting outside on a night like this. Put myself in bed for sure. My chest's not what it once was.'

As if to prove this he tested it out with a short coughing fit. A productive one, judging by the speed with which he produced a handkerchief from the pocket of his woollen trousers. Alasdair had no wish to monitor the man's expectorant so set to work unstacking a row of chairs from piles racked against the far wall.

'I'd help you do that,' said the old man, once he had pocketed the cotton-wrapped contents of his throat, 'but you only paid for the basic package and that doesn't include staff.'

'He can manage,' said Golding entering from the rain, 'he's a strong young man.'

'Weren't we all once,' was the somewhat inaccurate reply. 'You'll be the woman then?'

'Certainly that,' she laughed, 'Mrs Aida Golding, lovely of you to have us.'

'Oh, we'll take anybody. Even the druggies.'

'Sorry?'

'Support group they call it, Narcotics Anonymous. You've never seen the like.'

'I'm sure they do good work.'

'More than I am. I wouldn't have them near the place if it were down to me. Still, their money's as good as anyone's I suppose. Talking of which . . .'

'I'll pay the balance in cash, if I may?' She held up a small cash tin.

The old man sucked in breath and rubbed at his face. 'I suppose so, don't really like having that much cash around. The people that live round here . . . I'm not getting stabbed in my bed over a bit of caretaking.'

She counted out the money and he folded it into his trouser pocket. 'Suppose you'll want a receipt?'

'Yes please.'

He nodded and shuffled over to a stack of tables in the corner, took out a battered receipt book and begin to slowly scribble in it with a stubby pen. He held the nibbled end up for her to look at. 'Free from Argos, isn't it?' he said. 'Perfect size.'

'I'm not sure you're supposed to take them,' Golding replied before immediately regretting it. She couldn't care less where he nicked his pens from.

Alasdair gave her an exasperated look as he continued to set out the chairs. 'We haven't got long.'

She managed to resist suggesting he'd better get on with it then. Taking the receipt from the old man she slipped it under the coin tray of her cash tin and went to check on the sound system. It stood to one side of a rudimentary stage, a selection of wooden blocks surrounded by black drapes.

'Such luxury.'

She disliked performing in new venues, having to get used to a whole new set of uncertainties. The facilities in these places were never reliable, cables short circuited, PA systems cut in and out, sometimes even the lights didn't bloody work. Still, they were her bread and butter and they paid her well. Most mediums looked to breaking out in the media, shows on cable, big theatres. She'd never been convinced. Very few could last the distance, the bigger you got the more someone set out to knock you down. Better to stay small, keep it regular and intimate and you had a career for life. Even if that meant putting up with the disadvantages of public halls.

'How many chairs do you think?' shouted Alasdair.

As many as you can bloody fit, obviously, she thought. 'What's the pre-sale?'

'Ninety-four.'

'Then allow for another forty or so walk-up, new venues always bank in on the door.'

He gave a quiet sigh and dragged over another stack of chairs.

People began appearing by ten to seven, a full forty minutes before the evening was advertised to begin. In Golding's experience this was often the case. People were eager – desperate, in fact – to get in and sit down, maybe even make contact with her, hopeful that this would encourage later success. Not that she let herself be available. If anyone asked she was meditating, preparing herself spiritually for the evening ahead. In reality this meant a crafty fag out the back or, if she was feeling more virtuous, putting her feet up and reading a newspaper or magazine until it was time to begin.

Tonight she felt sinful. She stashed a pack of twenty Benson & Hedges and some breath mints in her cardigan pocket and hid just outside the rear fire exit.

'I wish you wouldn't do that,' said Alasdair as he watched her smoke.

'Worried for my health? I'll be talking to the dead soon enough.'

He refused to be drawn. Still sulking from last night, she decided. 'I think we've had all we're going to get,' he said, 'I'll give it five more minutes then knock off the lights.'

She nodded. 'Just get back by the doors, we don't want someone sneaking in while you're back here.'

He gritted his teeth and she felt a moment's worry, one day she would push him too far. Then where would she be?

'Sorry,' she said quickly, holding out a hand and managed to dredge up a smile, 'I'm just tired.'

'You and me both,' he replied but gave her hand a squeeze before heading back inside.

She finished her cigarette and loaded up on mints. Shoving the cigarettes in her handbag she took a spray bottle of lavender perfume and gave herself a good dosing. Peppermint and lavender: the scent of all good grandmothers.

She came back inside, closing the fire doors as quietly as she could and inching along behind the black drapes that afforded a narrow channel of backstage area. She was lucky to have this much privacy, some of their venues offered no stage space at all, just an empty concrete box that they had to dress to the best of their abilities. Not that it took much; she intentionally tried to keep everything to a minimum, a pretence of theatrical absence. Still she needed somewhere to avoid the attentions of the audience when she wasn't onstage, and nothing drew the focus better than a swathe of black material and a single focused spotlight.

Alasdair turned down the lights and that spot rose into being, a celestial point of brightness into which Aida Golding would emerge, God's earthly angel. The audience was still faintly lit, so that Golding could see them, her usual mixture of middle-aged and up. A couple of large groups of ladies, the 'girls', on their fun night out.

'Ladies and gentlemen,' said Alasdair into the microphone, 'please welcome the incomparable abilities of Mrs Aida Golding.'

She walked out into the hall, her best, gentlest smile in place. She kept her hands clasped in front of her, nodding and making considerable business about how shy the applause was making her feel. She held out her hands for them to be quiet.

'Thank you, thank you,' she said, giving another, intentionally humble bow of her head. 'It is always so lovely to visit somewhere new. My main aim in life is to spread this one simple message: there is no death, we all live on and I can prove it to you.'

There was the predictable murmur of pleasure at that and so she continued.

'There is nothing to be afraid of tonight. What I do is a beautiful, natural gift. It is given to me my God and I use it in the manner I believe he would wish.' To pay off the mortgage and spend three months a year on holiday, she thought with some amusement. She closed her eyes and sighed, thinking of an already booked fortnight in Cancún. A dreamy pleasure spread across her face.

'There's a wonderful energy here tonight,' she said, as always, 'you bless me with the warmth of your hearts.' She smiled and nodded as if someone had just said something amusing to her. Pretending you were one half of a conversation nobody else could hear went a long way, she had discovered, Perhaps it was because, subconsciously, nobody could conceive of anybody happily claiming to hear voices unless it were true. Perhaps it was simply that everyone wanted to believe and all you had to do was give them an excuse to do so.

'I can tell tonight is going to be a good night,' she said, 'we'll banish this horrible weather with the sunshine of our love.'

Wasn't that an old song? She thought. She really ought to concentrate, she must be on autopilot if she was falling back on song lyrics in her patter. What next? 'Walking on Sunshine'? 'I Will Always Love You'? 'Since You've Been Gone'? She smiled at the thought, not caring to hide the reaction, just another witty piece of wisdom from my spirit guide.

'I should explain that I am clairaudient: I hear the spirits, not see them. Often the sound is very faint, very muffled – not surprising, given how far they've come!'

A polite ripple of laughter.

'But in order to establish the connection and keep it strong I need your voices, all right? I need to hear your positive energies. If you understand the message I'm passing on I need to hear you say "yes". Otherwise I'll lose the connection and will have to move on. I'd hate to not be able to connect you with your loved ones just because you missed it, or misunderstood.'

That was the audience pre-conditioned then. She took a slow breath as if encouraging a trance state, in reality she was just deciding what name to go for first. Let's keep it simple, she decided, with no Anna to help bolster the responses she was going to have to play this safe until she had them in the palm of her hand.

'I hear "John" or "Joan" . . . so hard to be clear, speak up love. "John" or "Joan" . . .'

'My name's Joan,' announced someone about halfway back. Late sixties to judge from the voice, a frailty there which spoke of nerves as well as age. Though she had been quick enough to respond so, nervous she may be, but she was far from reluctant.

'Give me your voice, Joan.'

'I'm here.' Aida took a glance, she'd been spot on with the age and she was sat with another couple who matched. A couple . . . and her on her own . . . that was suggestive. Two women may accompany each other and leave the husbands at home. But if one husband was in attendance then either Joan was unmarried or divorced (massively unlikely statistically given her age), her partner was sufficiently against the idea or – and this would be the perfect solution – he was dead. Was it too early to take the risk? Perhaps one further clue.

'You're not a stranger to mediumship, are you, Joan?' she said in a slightly flat tone, so as to make the meaning ambiguous.

This could now go one of two ways . . . either:

'Yes.'

'I thought so, I could sense your nervousness. Joan, try to relax for me.'

Or, as actually happened:

'No, I've been to lots of demonstrations.'

'I thought so, you have a very open energy. It helps a great deal.'

Here on her own and a frequent visitor to mediums. The odds were now weighted enough for Golding to take the chance.

'This is your husband,' she announced, stating it flatly, brooking no argument.

'My Terry?'

Bonus. Albeit a predictable one, they always coughed up the name eventually. People just didn't think about it, using the name of a loved one in conversation was utterly natural, to withhold it would be fighting against a long-term habit. And who was fighting?

'Yes dear, he's right here.' She gave a sharp look to her left as if being pestered by something. 'I know,

Terry, there's no point in you shouting your name, love, we've gathered that.'

There was laughter. People liked this to play out in a gentle, affectionate manner.

'That sounds like him,' announced Joan, 'always two steps behind was my Terry!'

'He's laughing,' said Golding, 'he knows it's true.'

'He couldn't deny it, bless him.'

'Mind you, he says you're not always much better!' More laughter at that, of course, Terry was fighting back! 'He says he watched you when you were getting ready this evening. Says you were stood fussing for ages trying to decide what to wear!'

Lots of laughter.

'I suppose I did,' admitted Joan.

You and every other slightly nervous person in the building, thought Golding. '"Something blue!" he's shouting, oh dear he's so hard to hear, so faint . . .' Golding screwed up her face in concentration. 'Does that mean something, dear? "Something blue"?'

'I have a blue dress,' said Joan, 'lovely little thing with white flowers. He used to like it.'

Thankful that Joan was happy to make her scant details fit a bigger picture, Golding smiled and held up her hands in a positively messianic pose. 'He did,' she agreed, 'he's smiling now, trying to tell me some-thing . . .' she gave a small laugh. 'I think he's saying "beautiful".'

Joan gave a small gasp of happiness and began to cry. Got you, thought Golding, I could say anything now and you'd just nod happily. Still, this performance wasn't just for Joan, it was for everyone in the room. She was setting out her stall. Joan had sounded relieved yet slightly surprised to be hearing from her husband, which suggested another easy 'hit'.

'You've always wanted to hear from Terry, haven't you?' she asked.

'I have,' Joan admitted.

'You'd almost given up hope, hadn't you?' Joan nodded but Golding wasn't letting her get away with that. 'I need your voice, Joan, remember, let me hear you.'

'I had almost given up, yes,' Joan agreed, 'I was beginning to feel stupid for even coming.'

'There are so many charlatans out there, Joan,' Golding said, not without an appreciation of her own gall, 'they pretend to be able to communicate with our loved ones but all they want is our money.'

Joan nodded. 'I've given them plenty of that over the years,' she admitted.

'And you shouldn't feel bad about it,' insisted Golding. 'You just wanted to hear from Terry and these crooks are very clever, they can seem very believable. It's they who should feel guilty. Never regret your actions, my darling, they were done through love.'

'They were.'

'And he's here now, aren't you, Terry, my love,' she gave a small nod as if hearing his response, 'that's right, you never left her did you?'

The look of relief on Joan's face was typical. It always amused Golding how much people who claimed to want the best for their dear departed took relief in their being tethered to an afterlife of floating around after them. We all just want to be adored, she thought. Looking in Joan's eyes she saw all the adoration she would ever need,

There was a banging noise from the rear of the auditorium that broke the spell and Golding had to guard her face from snarling in anger. The doors had crashed open. No doubt Alasdair hadn't closed them properly, now the mood was broken.

'Could you see to that, Alasdair, my dear?' she asked, as gently as she could manage. There was no need, he was already en route, dashing behind the last row of the audience. In a moment of inspired thinking, Golding laughed.

'There's no need to go letting the rain in, Terry my love,' she said, 'we know you're with us.'

There was a small gasp from the more credulous in the room.

Alasdair was so tired it was an effort to stay awake in the comforting darkness. He was sat at the back, watching as Aida warmed up. Even after the four years they had been together he never lost his admiration for how she could work a room, massage emotions, manipulate information. He wasn't blind to the fact that she manipulated him just as blatantly as she did the audience, but he was a man inclined to go with the flow in life. Every snide comment he had to endure was bought and paid for. His bank account was very healthy (including a slowly growing savings account Aida knew nothing about just in case he ever needed to leave in a hurry). To Alasdair, money beat pride every single time. Thinking of Aida's hated perm and cardigan he supposed it was an opinion they shared.

When he had first met her he had been in awe of her. Then in love with her. Now . . . well, now they were more like business partners. Partners? Who was he kidding?

The entrance door suddenly came crashing open, jolting him in his chair so hard he nearly fell out of it. Who the bloody hell was that? He'd secured the doors tightly enough – or so he'd thought – perhaps it was this miserable old bastard that looked after the place, trying to sneak in for a free peek.

'Could you see to that, Alasdair, my dear?' asked Aida from the stage, as if he wasn't already halfway there.

The wind was strong enough as he pushed one of the doors closed, that he began to wonder if it hadn't blown them open. The rain was back in force, lashing at the trees that lined the avenue and bouncing off the tarmac of the hall forecourt. Then, in the darkness he saw something move, a body lying on the ground, rolling in the puddles. What the hell had happened? Were they in trouble? He was damned if he could think of another reason for lying in the wet. Annoyed at the soaking he was about to receive he stepped outside, pulling the door closed behind him so that he would at least avoid another earful from Aida.

'Hello?' he called, not speaking too loudly in case his voice carried inside the hall. 'Are you OK?'

The body seemed to spasm, arms and legs splaying out.

Shit.

He ran out into the rain. Probably it was that old bastard and now he was having a heart attack on the doorstep. As if they hadn't had enough to deal with in the last twenty-four hours.

'It's OK,' he shouted, 'help's coming.'

He reached down and turned the body face up, looking down into the snarling, rain-slicked face, an animal of plastered hair, dirt and brown leaves, stretched across its cheeks like henna tattoos.

'Not for you, it isn't,' the killer said.

It took Alasdair far too long to realise he knew his attacker. He was aware of it only a fraction of a second before the rock hit him in the temple and he toppled over into the wet, head spinning. His face smacked against the wet tarmac and he felt a tooth pop loose. What was happening? Why were they doing this?

The rock smacked down one, final time.

What on earth was the bloody man playing at? Golding wondered as she lifted her head towards the light and pulled her best 'At One With the Spirits' face. The doors banged closed and she could hear the faint sound of Alasdair shouting on the other side. If he didn't pipe down in a minute she'd have to take a break while they sorted out the problem. Barely five minutes in, it was not something she relished the idea of doing.

'Terry's leaving us now,' she announced. 'God bless you, Terry, thank you for the gift of your spirit.'

Alasdair was quiet now. She decided to take the risk and push on.

'I have a lady's spirit now,' she announced, 'a strong feminine energy, a mother.'

She sensed a portion of the audience shift forward in their seats, giving all their attention.

Doing this always made her think of the old board game, Guess Who? With every announcement you knocked out a percentage of your audience, whittling away at them until you had one left. This person is a woman, she has long hair, wore glasses, name sounds like . . . You have a winner.

'She's a big woman, too,' she added, 'she liked her home comforts!'

A polite ripple of laughter, cut short by further banging, and two loud knocks on the entrance doors.

'Terry wants to come in!' someone chuckled and Golding made a play of being amused by the interruption. She wasn't, however, it was important that she controlled the mood of the room. How could she get anywhere if their attention weren't firmly fixed on her?

'He'll have to wait his turn again,' she said. 'I have someone else here now. I'm trying to hear her name . . . Is it . . .?'

Again, a loud double tap from the doors.

'Sorry,' she said, 'I don't know what's going on.'

'I think it might be my grandmother,' said a young woman on the front row.

'Hush now, Patricia,' whispered the woman sat next to her, 'it's no such thing.'

'I'm sorry?' Golding was confused, what would this girl's grandmother be doing banging on the door.

'The message,' Patricia clarified, leaning forward

with a hopeful look on her face, 'it sounds like her.'

Steady on, thought Golding, I haven't given you much to go on yet! Still, perhaps this was what she needed to win back the attention of the audience. Anyone this eager was sure to be inclined towards positive answers.

'Oh, I hope so,' she replied, 'she so wants to make contact but with these interruptions the connection is weak. She's shouting to me, desperate to say a name . . . It's . . .'

Another bang, softer this time, little more than a tap.

'Maureen,' the young woman insisted, desperate not to lose this opportunity.

Golding couldn't be seen to give in this easily, not and retain any credulity. 'No, that's not what she's shouting. Wait . . .'

'It must be . . .' begged Patricia, 'It must be her . . .'

'Patricia!' shouted Golding just as another tapping came from the door. 'She's shouting the name Patricia!'

'That's me!' the young woman jumped to her feet. 'I knew it was Granny!'

There was an audible murmur of appreciation at that, even from those sat close enough to the young woman that they should have heard what her name was at the same time Aida Golding had.

The medium smiled, sure that she could claw this back if she could just hold their attention.

It was not to be. The tapping at the door returned but this time it didn't stop, as if someone were beating against the wood as if it were a drum, a fast, urgent rhythm.

'I'm sorry,' said Golding, 'we simply must sort this out.'

'But what about Gran?' asked Patricia.

'She'll wait, my love,' insisted Golding, stepping down from the stage and walking through the central aisle towards the door.

'Want a hand?' asked a man as she passed, getting to his feet. 'It's probably kids, up to no good.'

She looked at him, seventy if he was a day, held together by a cheap supermarket suit and the smell of damp. Much use you'd be if it was, she thought. Still, she could hardly refuse him.

'Thank you, my love,' she said. 'You're very kind.'

They walked up to the double doors and, as she reached out to open them, he placed his hand gently on hers. 'Let me,' he insisted, 'just in case.'

The tapping stopped just as he tugged at the door handle. 'It won't budge,' he said. 'Is there a lock?'

Of course there was but Alasdair had had the key, surely he wouldn't have used it though? What would have been the point in locking them all in?

'Are you sure it's not just stuck?' she asked. 'Maybe with the weather?'

'Let's have a look at this,' announced another male voice from behind her. She turned to see a younger man, broad and thick-armed. Either he worked out, she decided, or his work needed strength, a builder, perhaps, or joiner.

Whoever he was, the door shook as he yanked at it.

'It's not locked,' he said, 'look, it's opening a bit, it's as if there's something holding them together.'

144

He yanked again and the gap widened, two inches or so of air between the doors.

'Can you see what it is?' he asked.

'It's too dark,' said the older man, 'are there no lights?'

Golding looked around and, finding some switches, flicked them on to bathe the porch in light just as a tearing noise heralded the doors becoming free.

'Shit it,' said the muscular man, falling backwards as the left-hand door suddenly swung free. It was pushed by the weight of Alasdair who was still nailed to that side even though considerable effort had freed his hand from the nail pinning him to the other.

'Oh my God,' cried Aida, all pretence of gentility forgotten at the ruinous state of the young man. As the door swung back into the lit entrance his torso shed its contents in a sparkling trail across the floor. Whoever had nailed him up hadn't stopped there, they had slit him down the middle so that his innards could pour free. It was an empty carcass that hung lopsidedly on the door facing them, glistening tubes of intestine wriggling outside, like worms wanting to writhe in the rain.

Ten

The Tragedy of the Elizabeth

When the phone rang, Probert was relieved – though he wouldn't be for long. He had been unsure quite how much shoddy musical theatre he could stand before smashing his wine glass and digging out his eardrums with the stem.

One of the very worst things about his marriage with Kathleen was her insistence on spending the majority of their time in the city. He would much prefer to be lounging around the estate. Getting lost in the woods, perhaps. Maybe shooting the odd animal and pre-tending it was his wife. But no; Kathleen loved culture. As much as he tried to convince her that the majority of it was as rancid and bacterial as the name suggested, she would not be swayed. They went to theatres, opera houses, concert halls, anywhere the review columns in the bloody *Telegraph* convinced her artistry might be found. Probert hated it all. Currently he was being bombarded by five faux transsexuals exploring the difficulties of post-op psychology through the medium of the rock ballad. The lead, an imported Yank apparently famous for being in some medical drama or another, was currently straddling a large chipboard scalpel that thrust into the audience. The imagery was so unsubtle Probert's eyes were bruised almost as badly as his ears.

'What about tomorrow?' the Yank sang, 'who shall I be then?'

'An out-of-work actor if there's any justice,' mumbled the peer just as his mobile phone began to beep loudly.

'You're supposed to turn it off!' reminded his wife, with a spray of spittle that might as well be venom. It'll probably burn a hole in the upholstery, he thought and actually smiled. 'I don't know what you think's so funny,' she added, 'turn it off! You're disturbing the rest of the audience.'

'I think the cast are doing that perfectly adequately,' he replied, answering the phone and stepping out of their box into the corridor outside.

'Whoever you are,' he said, 'I'm so glad you called.' He strolled along the passageway of deep-red velvet and yellowing cornicing, like a pretentious airport tunnel leading passengers back to their real lives.

'You won't be by the time I've finished,' said Aida Golding. 'There's been another death.'

'Nothing to do with me, my dear,' he replied. 'Might I suggest you call a lawyer instead?'

'I'm making it to do with you,' she snarled, 'unless you want people digging back over what happened last night.'

'The old priest topped himself with a bread knife,' Probert said, lowering his voice when he saw the look of horror on the face of an elderly steward waiting by the entrance to the stalls. 'He can hardly have done so again so I fail to see the connection.'

'Tonight was definitely not suicide. Someone took my poor Alasdair and nailed him to the door of the venue . . .'

Her voice broke off and Probert realised that you could unnerve Aida Golding, you just had to work very hard to do so.

'That's perfectly horrid,' he said, 'and you have my sympathies naturally, but I still don't see what the connection is.'

'Douglas Reece.'

'Who? Look . . . this really isn't anything to do with me.'

'You will do as you're told!' Aida Golding shouted down the phone at him, 'or I will make your recent troubles in the press seem like fan mail.'

'You're as bad as Kathleen,' he muttered. 'It's hardly recent, I haven't been in the papers for nearly—'

'I will tell them all about how you wanted to cover things up last night,' Golding continued, 'and I'll tell them all about Thana too, because they don't know the half, do they?'

Probert shook at the mention of the name, nearly dropping the phone. Get a grip, man, he thought, you can't let the old bitch talk to you this way.

'They took her eyes, didn't they, Probert?' she continued. 'The Barrowman brothers . . . in order to teach you a lesson.'

That time he did drop the phone. The elderly steward shuffled over to try and help.

'Piss off!' Probert shouted, slapping his hands away from the dropped mobile, picking it up and running outside with it. He suddenly felt sick, his stomach clenching painfully as he emerged into the cold air. The rain was blowing in under the cover of the entrance steps but he didn't care, sitting down on the wet stone and dropping his head between his knees. How did she know? How did she know?

'Are you still there?' came the woman's voice from the mobile. 'You'd better not have hung up on me or I swear . . .'

'Still here,' he said, scared to say more in case he threw up.

'I make it my business to know all about my important clients, Lord Probert,' she said, 'so you just get over here before I have a chance to share what I know. I suggest you get your fancy lawyer on the phone too.'

She gave him the address but he could manage no more than a grunt in reply, he was sure that if he spoke he would throw up. God damn him for being so weak, if he'd been a stronger man he'd not be in this position.

The moment things went out of control for Lord Llewellyn Probert was a summer's evening two years ago.

'Well,' Probert asked, 'can you do it or not?

Jimmy Barrowman looked at the photograph and smiled a smile with a street value of around four grand, due to the gold teeth he had dotted throughout his yellowing set. Jimmy loved the sweet things in life; one day his mouth would be nothing but precious metal. 'You know me,' he said, with an East End accent so thick it could only be fake, 'I can do anything.'

That was certainly the reputation of the Barrowman brothers. Jimmy and Luke had built a thriving business on one simple principle: they could find you anything you wanted. They made no promises that it would be cheap, certainly none that it would be legal. Not that either of those factors tended to concern their usual clients, the Barrowmans aimed high with their clientele and had done business with aristocracy and the business elite from all over the world.

They operated out of The Elizabeth a grand old Edwardian hotel in north London, allegedly named after their mother rather than the monarch. It was a place that was fully booked to the casual enquirer yet always available to its special clients. You booked a room and the price was negotiable, depending entirely on what you expected to find when you got in there. Nine times out of ten the requests were predictable enough: a place where the wealthy could go and slake their thirst for pleasures they could not let their con- stituents, shareholders or wives know about. The traffic in boys of all ages was brisk, partners with unusual medical conditions, pretty amputees, feral creatures that bristled with piercings and tattoos. It was a rare night that the pristine corridors didn't catch the echo of some exotic beast or another.

'Give me a couple of weeks,' Jimmy said, 'this will take some tracking down.'

As it happened, Probert received a phone call only six

days later telling him that his order had been fulfilled. He had cancelled his appointments, offered Kathleen a lazy excuse and made the trip to The Elizabeth with a sense of excitement so strong he couldn't remember the like of it since he'd been a child.

'Good evening, sir,' said Pierre, the receptionist, 'what room is it?'

'Two hundred and twenty one,' Probert answered, checking his reflection in the blind man's large black glasses. It was an absurd affectation on the Barrowmans' part but many were relieved that Pierre, the only other point of contact for the illustrious clients of the hotel, would be able to describe none of the visitors should he be pressed.

'Certainly sir,' Pierre ran his fingers along the board of keys behind the desk, checking off each row until he came to the right key. He handed it to Probert who took it and walked towards the lift.

He was so lost in his own excited anticipation, he failed to realise the lift was descending with a passenger until the bell rang out across the lobby and the doors opened. In the past, he had made a habit of darting for the stairs in this situation, one could never be too careful and the fewer people who knew you were a client here the better, even if they could hardly know what pleasure you were seeking. There wasn't time that night and so he just kept his head down as the door opened and a middle-aged woman stepped out.

'Oh,' she said, 'do excuse me.'

Which was the first time he met Aida Golding, though he certainly didn't realise it, as lost in his own thoughts as he was. She noticed him though and made a mental note to discover more. She always made it her business to find out about the other regulars here at The Elizabeth, such knowledge was always useful and Luke Barrowman would always owe her favours, the dirty boy.

Getting out of the lift on the second floor, Probert slowed his pace as he approached his room. He pressed the teeth of the old fashioned, long-nosed key into the flesh of his thumb and tried to slow his breathing – he was actually nervous!

He opened the door and stepped inside.

The room wasn't large but as it had been cleared of all furniture except for the harness and pulley in the centre, space would hardly be a problem. His feet crunched on the black plastic that covered the carpet as he stepped inside, looking around for the companion he had asked for.

She was behind him, a fact that became clear when she curled the leather strap around his neck and yanked it tight.

'Strip,' she ordered, and though the voice wasn't quite right he did as he was told, tugging at his clothes and flinging them as far into the corner as he could.

'I want to see,' he said, forced to whisper against the tight strap, 'let me see.'

She yanked him around so he was on his back, nervous, sweating skin sticking to the plastic sheeting.

'Oh God,' he whispered, 'yes . . .'

Because she certainly did look like Kathleen, the same slim body, dark hair. He noticed that she even wore the same dark red, almost black, nail varnish. He couldn't judge further fine details, not in this dim lighting – no doubt that was the intention – but it was all too easy to believe it was his wife that currently loomed over him.

She raised a stilettoed foot and planted the heel down on his chest, twisting the point as if his nipple were a cigarette she was trying to extinguish.

'Tell me your name!' he shouted. 'Tell me your name!'

'Mistress Kathleeen,' she announced and, again the accent was a little off, there was a hint of Eastern European there. He looked down at himself, pathetic yet clearly elated, and found he simply didn't care.

'Fill me with your filth, Mistress Kathleen,' he begged.

And she certainly did.

The relationship – if that was what you could call it in those early days – grew deeper as Probert visited more often. He simply couldn't get enough of his Mistress Kathleen, she even made him appreciate the genuine article a little more, though there was little chance that his wife would ever let him indulge in the games he most desired.

His hours in Room 221 became the most important in his life, a glorious window in an otherwise banal and depressing schedule. The only thing he disliked about them was their strict limitations.

The Barrowmans' had one rule about their business: it all had to be conducted within the walls of The Elizabeth and therefore was constantly under their protection. It was forbidden for clients to make their own arrangements with their lovers, certainly they were not allowed to actively pursue a relationship with them. The Elizabeth was a place where functional needs were fulfilled; it was not a dating agency. Breaking that rule was to risk the considerable anger of the Barrowman brothers and it was said that nothing this side of the afterlife could match their ferocity.

Nonetheless, Probert wanted more.

As he showered after his sessions with Mistress Kathleen he wondered if he saw a small chink in her armour too. A moment of self-awareness, exposing a little piece of herself beyond the character he paid her to play.

'What's your name?' he asked her.

'You know.'

'No, I mean your real name. The game's over now; I want to know what you're really called.'

She stayed silent but, as the weeks went by, he kept asking. Eventually he got an answer, and a smile.

'Thana,' she said, 'now stop asking. They would not like it.'

Mentioning her employers risked ruining the moment so he chose to ignore her.

'Thana? That's an unusual name.'

'It's Hungarian.'

'Of course it is,' he smiled. 'I want to take you for dinner, Thana.'

The look on her face was pure fear, as if he had just suggested she hurl herself from one of the masked-off windows.

'I can't!' she said. 'You know the rules.'

'My darling,' he replied, 'I am a lord of the bloody realm. Do you really think I can't do precisely what I want?'

And he honestly believed that, as eventually, Thana did too.

It took precisely four weeks for the Barrowman brothers to prove them both wrong, but during that short month of grace, Probert had never known love like it. It was the marriage he had always hoped for, filled with good-humour and sweet conversation, with the aggressive sex life he needed. The perfect combination of love and abuse. He was a very happy man.

Something Kathleen certainly noticed. 'I don't know what's wrong with you,' she announced one night as she prepared for bed, putting on the silken nightwear that Probert couldn't help but think of as her battledress, the garments she wore for the constant war of attrition she fought in the bedroom. 'But I don't like it.'

'I'm just happy, darling,' he explained.

'Well stop it, it's unnerving.'.

Despite their extra-curricular meetings, Probert and Thana had of course maintained their meetings at The Elizabeth. One thing that was certain to cause suspicion, they felt, would be a lessening of their scheduled appointments. Besides, Probert enjoyed them as much as ever, and they agreed that behind the door of Room 221 there was no Helly and Thana, there was just Mistress Kathleen and her willing servant. On their last meeting unfortunately that was not the case. They were joined by two others.

'You've made me angry, you know,' announced Jimmy Barrowman as Probert stepped inside the room. 'And that is never a good idea.'

Probert's first instinct was to run but Luke Barrowman was just inside the door and grabbed the peer's wrist before he could move, yanking him into the room.

'Now look!' Probert managed, trying to regain his composure. 'I won't stand for this!'

'Then sit down,' suggested Jimmy as his brother kicked Probert hard in the thigh.

As he fell down on the ever-present plastic sheeting he consoled himself with the fact that at least Thana wasn't here. Hopefully, the Barrowman brothers would be happy to exercise their anger on him alone. The fact of the matter was that it had been all his idea.

But when he noticed the small shape in the corner, he realised his mistake. Thana was here after all.

'You see,' said Jimmy as his brother went to fetch the bound and gagged woman, 'we only ask our clients to obey one rule. That seems eminently reasonable to me.'

Probert gasped with relief when he realised Thana was still alive. She had been lying so still he had feared the worst.

Luke carried her over to the winch and pulley in the middle of the room. Probert had frequently hung from its glistening chain, whipped and spun by his enthusiastic mistress.

'I mean,' Jimmy continued, 'if you can't manage to

obey one rule what sort of person are you? It's not fucking difficult, is it?'

'Look,' said Probert, watching as Luke tightened Thana in place, hanging upside down, her eyes wide with fright, begging him to stop whatever it was that was about to happen. 'This is all my fault. Let the girl go; she was only doing what she was told.'

'But she wasn't,' said Jimmy, 'because I told her the same rule as you and she got greedy and decided it didn't apply.'

'Please,' said Probert, 'I'm a very important man, you know that, I can make it worth your while, both of you. Let's just stop this before things go too far.'

'You are an important man,' agreed Jimmy, 'most of my clients are. Which is why I have to tailor the punishment accordingly.'

Luke dragged a small chair up to Probert, picked him up and sat him on it. He then proceeded to attach his ankles and wrists to it using strong plastic ties.

'Don't,' Probert struggled but Luke punched him in the stomach and knocked the fight right out of him.

'I can't do what I want to you,' continued Jimmy, 'there would be too many questions. So I have to take out my anger somewhere else.' He walked over to Thana who was swinging violently now, fighting to free herself from the harness, 'And I am very, very angry.'

Probert had never endured the like of it. And of course, his suffering was nothing compared to hers, he only had to watch as every inch of his mistress was worked over. The brothers were not aggressive in their attentions.

Every moment of pain inflicted was done with deliberate care. They circled her wriggling body with their tools like artists, moving in and daubing a stroke before stepping back to admire their art.

'You think he's learned his lesson yet?' Jimmy asked her, lighting a cigarette. She was in no fit state to answer. Jimmy smoked for a moment, taking his well-earned break. The smell of the tobacco mixed with the slaughterhouse bouquet of blood and loose bowels.

'See how she looks at you?' Jimmy asked after a couple of minutes. He held her head so that Probert could see her eyes. Never had he seen anyone convey so much. He could see fear, anger, disappointment and, worst of all, hope. 'She's wishing she never set eyes on you, mate,' said Jimmy in the sort of convivial tone reserved for two blokes discussing sport in a bar. His mood had improved considerably over the last half an hour; say what you like about the Barrowman boys, they certainly enjoyed their work. 'Let's make you the last thing she ever does see, shall we?'

And, with the tip of his cigarette, he did just that, laughing while Probert and his lover screamed.

They called it quits after that, taking a few photo - graphs – for posterity or simply the intimidation of others, Probert neither knew nor cared. Then both he and Thana were dumped in the back of the large SUV Jimmy and Luke Barrowman favoured. With Thana pinning him down, Probert felt his lover's final breath, wet and rattling, kiss him on the forehead. Five minutes later the SUV stopped, Luke opened the boot, lifted her out and walked off. After a couple of minutes, there was a soft splash. Luke returned, closed the boot and they drove Probert home.

'Do call us again, Lord Probert,' said Jimmy, 'should you ever have an itch you fancy scratching. Next time, though, play by the rules or I'll forget my sense of national pride and it'll be you we dump in a river on the way home.' He gave a mocking bow. 'Ta ta, milord,' he said with a chuckle, 'kiss the wife good-night for me.'

They drove off laughing, leaving Probert sat on the kerb outside his apartment. He could see the lights burning in the penthouse and wondered how he would ever face Kathleen tonight. She'd want to know what had happened to him for sure, and she wouldn't be satisfied with a casual answer; it would be the full cross-examination. He just didn't know if he had it in him. At that moment he was very close – certainly as close as someone so inherently self-obsessed could be – to suicide. It seemed to him a very real and potentially relaxing solution to the night's events. To simply walk out into the traffic or jump off a bridge. The simple pleasure of being 'no more' seemed the very best he could hope for. Then his guardian angel stepped in.

'I say,' said a voice. Move along, we don't like your sort loitering around here.'

Probert looked up to see a purple-faced, chubby young man in a rugby shirt and sports jacket looking down on him as if he were something that had fallen out of the rear of a neighbourhood dog. Perhaps the attitude was unsurprising given what he looked like, but if there was one thing guaranteed to restore Probert's fighting spirit it was his inherent snobbery.

'I beg your pardon?' he asked, getting to his feet. 'Do you know who I am?'

'My local *Big Issue* seller by the looks of you,' said the plummy young thing, offering the sort of scoffing snort he had always favoured when dealing with undergraduates during his Oxford days. 'Now piss off before I call the police on you.'

As things worked out, the young man would call the police – and Probert would find himself under the considerable scrutiny of the tabloid press, not for the first time in his life – but it wasn't for loitering on pavements. It was for sticking the young man's head through the passenger side-window of a conveniently located BMW. He would claim in court that the young man had attacked him first, something his not inconsiderable influence managed to make stick legally, if not necessarily in the court of public opinion.

Probert arrived at the recent crime scene to find Aida Golding sat in the back of a police car while a handful of other officers worked their laborious way through collecting the names and addresses of all those in attendance. She waved him over and opened the door to let him in.

'Don't tell me they've bloody arrested you,' he said.

'Of course not,' she replied, 'I just couldn't bear sitting around with that lot. She pointed at the crowd of audience members that were milling around inside the hall. 'I wanted some privacy.'

He looked over towards the doors, noting with disgust where the position of Alasdair's body had been marked up prior to his being zipped up into a body bag and removed. In the light that spilled from the hall he could clearly see the dark shadow of a bloodstain that seeped across the tarmac.

'Dear God,' he whispered.

Golding lit a cigarette and for a moment he was reminded of Jimmy Barrowman.

'You're probably not allowed to smoke in here,' he said.

'Like that's the worst of my problems. Have you called your lawyer?'

'Yes, though he says – quite rightly – that you've nothing to worry about. You've got the best alibi in the world, you were being watched by a hundred-odd people while the murder was being committed. What can they possibly accuse you of?'

'I'm not worried about that,' she snapped. 'Of course I didn't kill Alasdair, why would I? I loved him.'

That surprised Probert who, like most people, had assumed their relationship to be of an altogether different nature. He was quick to recover. 'Well, what's the problem then?'

'Aside from my reputation?'

'This lot will forgive you anything, you know that. It'll take more than a few morbid press reports to keep them away.'

'You're probably right. But my main worry is far more pressing. First Goss and now Alasdair . . .'

'Goss was a suicide, surely.'

'Don't be stupid, you still think that after tonight? I'm telling you, someone's out to get me and I think I know who.'

   'Who?'

   'Let me tell you about Anna . . .'

Eleven

Picking Scabs

After the nerves of earlier, Anna begged the need for an early night. Glancing at the clock John had to admit it was very early indeed but if she wanted her bed then she was welcome to it.

He took his time clearing up, listening quietly to the radio and relishing the first time this old house of his had known warmth for some months. It would be no bad thing at all, he decided for there to be more people between these walls. He had let himself rattle around in here with his ghost for too long. The sooner Michael and Laura could move in the better. For that matter, there was no rush for Anna to move out, they'd all got along incredibly well. People, he decided, that's what I need, lots and lots of people. The more the merrier.

For a moment he thought he imagined Jane had something to say on the matter, a glimpse out of the corner of his eye and the sound of the front door latch clicking into place.

'Hello?' he called. But there was nobody there. He slipped the deadlock on the front door and went back into the friendly heat of the kitchen.

Glen Logan flicked through the channels on the TV and settled for a comedy panel game. After a few sips of his lager, staring at the telly as the same old comics plundered recent news for laughs, he realised he'd watched it only a couple of nights ago. With a sigh he went on the hunt again.

'Just leave it alone, would you?' Sacha asked, 'find something and stick with it. Or can't you manage that?'

'Been going out with you long enough, haven't I?' he replied. A thought that drove him to finish off his beer and, crushing the can, head into the kitchen in search of another one. The fridge was bare.

'Bollocks.'

'What's wrong now?'

'Out of beer.'

'Well, if you didn't drink so much . . .'

Glen didn't listen to what followed on after that, he was only too accustomed to tuning out the white noise of Sacha's complaints.

'Want anything?' he asked, grabbing the house keys from a fruit bowl in the centre of the kitchen worktop.

'Are you even listening to me?'

'If you're telling me what you want from the corner shop, yes, otherwise no.'

'Fucking pig.'

'I'll see if they've got any.'

Grinning at his joke, he jogged down the stairs, grabbed his jacket off the hook by the front door and headed out into the rain.

It was only a few minutes to the shop but he was already regretting it by the time he'd walked a couple of doors down. Was it really worth this soaking just to get a few beers down his neck? He'd need something stronger just to get the warmth back into his bones.

As he crossed the road, a car was heading up the street. Was this Alasdair, maybe? Back early? The car pulled up towards him and then drew to a halt in the middle of the road. The driver stared at him through the windscreen.

'Got a problem, mate?' he asked, returning the man's stare. Pissing down or not, you had to make your stand, didn't you?

'Oi!' suddenly there was someone beside him. A flash of movement and they punched him in the stomach.

'Motherfucker,' Glen said, never one to talk an assailant down. His attacker was dressed in a bizarre mixture of clothes. Long raincoat over a tracksuit, wool hat pulled tight over the skull. They were running right past him, not interested in continuing the fight having got in one sound blow. 'Come here!' he shouted reaching out to grab their coat. The figure turned, and again its arm lashed out, moving so quickly Glen barely registered it. His hand felt like it was on fire.

'What the fuck?' he looked at his hand and tried to understand what had happened to it. The index finger was missing entirely above the first knuckle, middle and ring fingers splayed at an unconscionable angle. His hand was streaming with blood, the rain constantly washing it away from the wounds so he could see the clean pink meat and bone beneath.

He looked down at where he had been punched and saw even more blood.

'Fucking knife,' he realised. 'Fucking stabbed me with a fucking knife.'

He tried to step forward but found his legs were shaking too much. A great stream of his blood was puddling between his legs before trickling away down the street. 'Bleed to fucking death,' he correctly surmised. 'Going to fucking bleed to death.'

'Who's Anna?' asked Probert, wafting away some of the cigarette smoke and glancing towards the hall to check on the progress of the police.

'That's the question,' Golding replied, with a smile. 'But I know. I know her better than she does herself.' She threw the cigarette out of the window and settled back into the seat.

'Anna has been helping me for years now, but that's only fair, after all I rescued her. Or maybe I never did.'

'Aida,' said Probert, his patience already fatally short after her threats over the phone, 'you're not making sense. Who is this Anna?'

'Sandy, you met her last night. Her real name's Anna, she's my foster daughter.'

'What?'

Golding ignored him. 'I adopted her when she was four, she was the daughter of Douglas Reece.'

'You mentioned him earlier, who . . .? Oh . . . the East End Ripper!'

'Yes, precisely why I invited Father Goss. Having done my research into Anna's background it seemed a waste not to put it to good use. Besides, an appearance from Reece suited Anna's special skill only too well.'

'Special skill?'

'Let me tell you about when I first met her . . .'

Aida Golding had been finally falling asleep when the shouting had started.

'What the hell is it now?' she wondered and, unable to contain the anger to her curtained cubicle, spun her legs from the hospital bed and shuffled in the dark for her slippers.

Her lower abdomen cramped with the effort of being upright and she had to grit her teeth to stop from screaming herself. The pain didn't send her back to bed, it just made her more angry. She brushed her fingers against the appendectomy scar, that awful lump of a wound. To think she had been opened and gutted. An intrusion.

She pushed her way out of the ward and along the corridor towards the sound of shouting. It was a young man, she guessed from the tone, clearly as angry as her, shouting and screaming obscenities as he was bundled away by medical staff. What the hell were they doing to him that he was kicking up such a fuss?

Turning a corner she saw a pair of double doors swing closed, several white-uniformed backs struggling through the chequered fire-glass beyond.

Abruptly the noise ceased.

'Dosed him,' she announced to the empty corridor, 'should have done that in the first place.'

She peered through the glass in the doors and was confused by what she saw. Rather than a young man, the attendants were gathering around the sleeping body of a girl, maybe four or five years old. Aida glanced around the silent corridors, surely she had made a mistake? She must have been hearing someone else. Or had an attendant been making the noise? But no. The staff here were terrible but not so bad that they would wake the patients with their swearing.

One of the nurses noticed her watching and came to the door.

'Is there a problem?' she asked, blocking Golding's view.

'I was woken up.'

The nurse's face softened. 'Yes, I imagine a number of people were, sorry. The patient was extremely delusional.'

'But surely . . .' Golding nodded towards the doors, 'I heard a man.'

'Amazing, isn't it?' the nurse replied, 'apparently she's been shouting like that since the police picked her up. Never seen anything like it. A girl possessed, you might say . . .'

'Hardly.' A rationalist through and through, Aida Golding did not believe in such things. 'Why did the police have her?'

'Can't say,' the nurse replied. 'We'd have journalists packing the place out if I did. The poor little bugger's been through a lot though, I'll tell you that.'

'Haven't we all?' Golding replied, but found herself drawn to the young girl's face again. So sweet, so delicate. And yet, so full of rage. Golding was intrigued.

Aida Golding was not a maternal woman but she was certainly a curious one. There was something about the girl that drew her attention. It wasn't just morbid curiosity, rather an innate sense that the girl represented an opportunity, albeit one she hadn't quite put her finger on yet.

'A girl possessed,' she frequently muttered to herself, rolling the idea around in her head.

She made it her business to keep an eye on the girl during the following couple of days. There was no return to the angry shouting of that first night – at least not then, though it would hardly be the last time Aida Golding heard the voice – but the girl certainly seemed a positive hive of personalities.

'She's a right little mimic, isn't she?' said one of the orderlies when he noticed Golding watching one afternoon. 'Has us all in stitches so she does. She only has to hear a voice for a little while and she copies it.' He waved at the little girl who was sat silently in a chair much too big for her, staring up into the fluorescent lights. 'Our little cuckoo, ain't you?'

'Our little cuckoo.' Once Aida Golding had been checked out, she spared no time in returning, this time as a visitor.

'So sad,' she said to the nurse on little Anna's ward. 'The poor little thing just stares at the walls, doesn't she?'

'You want to hear the things she comes out with,' the nurse leaned forward and tapped her temple. 'It's not a doctor she needs if you ask me.'

'Who's looking after her?'

'Well, we are, best we can.'

'No, I mean, where are her parents?'

The nurse looked uncomfortable. She was a terrible gossip and it was clear that she was very much divided between wanting to share a juicy piece of information and follow orders that she should keep her mouth shut. Finally, all she managed to admit was that the girl's parents were dead.

She was an orphan. Aida began to think about that.

She watched the little girl, blond hair a mess from where she pulled at it all the time.

'Piss off,' she suddenly announced in a masculine tone. 'I want to watch the snooker.'

Some argument she had heard over the channel on the television, Aida assumed.

The voice wasn't perfect. Now Aida knew who was speaking she could hear deficiencies – the girl was, after all, working with equipment that wasn't fully developed – but the change in character was astonishing.

'Never comes,' a woman's voice this time, aged and as light and brittle as an autumn leaf, 'got not time for his old ma.'

'Amazing,' Golding whispered.

'My name is Legion,' mumbled one of the patients, an elderly man who wheeled a bottle of oxygen around with him, 'for I am many.'

'Don't start with all that again, Father,' said the nurse, 'save the sermons for church, eh?'

'She's no child of God,' he proclaimed, with such vigour that he had to snatch at his oxygen mask and take a few puffs.

'That's a horrible thing to say,' the nurse replied. 'Whatever her father was like, we're all children of God.'

'My name is Legion,' the girl repeated, capturing the breathy tone of the old priest. 'My name is Legion . . .'

For I am many . . . Aida thought.

The man that had been staring at Glen had got out of his car and was running towards him.

'Need help,' explained Glen, 'need hospital.'

The man said nothing but helped him over to his parked car, leaned him against the vehicle and opened the back door.

'Got to get me to hospital,' repeated Glen. 'Fucking bleeding to death.'

There was the rustle of plastic. Jesus, thought Glen, here he was, dying on his feet and this prick wanted to make sure his upholstery stayed clean.

'Look,' he said, turning onto his side and trying to keep his intact left hand pressed hard against the wound in his stomach, 'no time. Need hospital.'

'Got to be careful,' the man replied, 'got to be clean.'

Trust me to get stuck with some special needs prick, thought Glen.

'No,' he said, trying to sound more in control than he felt, 'need to go now. Fuck the upholstery. If you're that worried, I'll pay.'

'Yes,' agreed the man, 'pay.'

He reached out towards Glen and pulled him towards the back seat. 'In.'

'Steady,' Glen argued but was too weak to kick up any fuss and toppled onto the back seat, the plastic rumpling beneath him. He listened as the driver got in and continued to drive up the street. 'Need to turn round,' said Glen, 'closest hospital is . . .'

'No hospital,' said the driver, pulling the car into an empty space further up the street. He turned the car engine off and got out.

'What the fuck?'

He heard the boot open as the driver retrieved something. Then the back door opened and the man climbed in, pulling himself on top of Glen and dumping the bag he'd fetched from the boot into the footwell.

'What the fuck?' Glen asked again, trying to push the man off. He was too weak, he could barely move as the man pushed him back against the seat. He knelt on his arms, grinding what remained of his right hand under his knee.

Glen screamed but the sound was cut off by the driver pressing his hand against Glen's mouth.

The hand stank of disinfectant, the skin was shiny and pink.

'Lucky,' said the driver, 'lucky, lucky, lucky.'

Trevor Court had never considered himself a lucky man. Certainly not as far as his dealings with Aida Golding were concerned. He should never have gone to the show, of course. He realised that now, but at the time it had seemed such a funny opportunity. He had glimpsed the poster in the church and wondered to himself about the lovely little friends he could hear from. How delicious, he had thought, imagining the world of the dead brought close enough to touch. It was a world he thought about a great deal. A world he had conducted plenty of business with. Starting of course with young Leonard. Golden Boy Leonard. Leonard whose shadow had always fallen so long and so dark. Well, he had soon stepped out from that shadow hadn't he?

And somehow she had known. She had picked him out. He'd been sat in the dark, imagining the spirits floating around him when all of a sudden he'd heard his name. Even then he might have been able to ignore it but the silly woman next to him – who had asked him his name when he first sat down, nosy, nosy creature – had forced him to speak. She had pushed him in front of Aida Golding's attention and then he couldn't get free.

And it had been Leonard, of course. He had known that as soon as he saw the look on the witch's face. Golden Boy Leonard trying to make his brother scared again. Golden Boy Leonard telling tales.

Well, Trevor would not be standing for that. He couldn't kill Leonard twice, of course, however much he might wish to. But he'd make sure the dead boy's tittle-tattle fell on deaf ears.

He reached for the sack and pulled out a long-bladed screwdriver.

'So lucky,' he repeated and went about his business.

'You wanted to adopt her?' asked Probert, 'I would have thought that was the last thing you'd do.' He thought for a moment. 'Although I suppose her condition could have advantages in your line of work.'

'It was what first gave me the idea. Up until then I'd been scratching a living in an office. Town and Country Planning.'

Despite their situation, Probert couldn't help but laugh. 'So normal, how you must have hated it.'

'It served its purpose. It offered just the sort of stability the authorities like to see when considering a foster home.'

'I dare say they lapped it up.'

'Honestly? I think they'd have given her to any-one. Considering her mental state and background, she was hardly going to be an easy prospect to live with.'

'I'm sure she was quite a handful . . .'

Anna felt as if the dark could smother her. The air was so thin and the absence of light so complete that it was like being trapped inside your own head and that was one place Anna did not want to be. If she was good and practised her voices for Mummy then Mummy would let her out later. Maybe she would even be allowed to stay out all evening.

'Bad girls get nothing,' she said in an excellent imitation of her foster mother's voice.

The older she got, the more precise her voices were becoming. And not just the voices, but the characters that went with them. Some days, down here in the dark, she would spend hours escaping the only way she knew how: into the mind of someone else.

She would become Bad Father, yelling and cursing, pounding her fists into the walls.

Or Soft Mother, singing sweet lullabies and crying and begging for things to stop.

Or Father Legion, seeing the devil in every shadow.

Or Nurse Sleepnow, pushing pills into the mouths of her imagined patients.

There were many of them, all different in tone and posture. Often, she played at them so hard she lost herself and the day went away all on its own. She would wake in the morning, let the voices come and before you knew it night had returned and with it food and the chance to stretch her legs for a while. If only she could learn to control them. That's what made Mummy really cross. When the voices came they often said whatever they wanted and Mummy didn't like that at all.

'That's no use,' came an approximation of Aida Golding once more, 'that gets me nowhere.'

Mummy didn't understand. It wasn't that Anna just copied voices, she copied people and people don't always do as they're told.

*

'I managed,' said Golding. 'Though I must admit I wasn't a natural mother.'

There was a tap on the window. 'Mrs Golding?'

Aida wound down the window to talk to the police inspector on the other side. 'Yes?' she asked.

Unbelievable, thought Probert, She owns wherever she find herself in. Has anyone sat in the back of a police car ever seemed more in control of themselves?

'You can head home now, Mrs Golding,' the Inspector said, 'we'll take a further statement in the morning.'

Golding turned to Probert. 'We'll go home and I'll finish telling you what you need to know.'

She led him through the rain to her car, both stepping automatically to the passenger's side.

'For God's sake,' Golding lowered her head, the rain plastering her perm almost straight on her head.

Probert, hardly inclined to feel pity for her given everything she had done to him, nonetheless did so. 'Give me the keys, he said, 'I'll drive.'

She handed them over and they climbed in, cranking up the heater until the cabin had the atmosphere of a sauna.

'Where to?' he asked.

She thought for a while. 'I just want to go home.'

'I can find that,' he replied and slowly reversed out onto the main road.

The audience had been released and allowed to go home and people were milling around the car. He fought to avoid eye contact, only too aware that most of them were staring inside the car, trying to see Aida

Golding. They were lost, he realised, confused and unsure how to feel about the woman next to him. Was she really the spiritual queen she presented herself as or something altogether less wholesome? Whether she was the one to kill Alasdair or not, her proximity to the terrible event made them suspicious. She must have done something to bring such horror to her door. And he was slowly beginning to realise just how much. Had he felt sympathy for her earlier? Yes, he had, but no more. She was a crook and a manipulator of people. What kind of person would evoke the memory of Thana just to line her pockets? Or Douglas Reece, for that matter. The more he thought about it, the more he began to realise that Golding deserved the very worst fate might have in store.

'You think you'll be next?' he asked, intentionally wanting to make her feel uncomfortable.

'Who knows,' she replied giving him a distinctly cold glance, 'it could even be you.'

'Me? What have I got to do with anything?'

'You were there on the night he came back. Douglas Reece.'

'You think you've brought his spirit back to life? With the seance?'

'In a way. Anna is a very complicated girl, I never really understood how deeply those personalities of hers ran.'

'Good evening, my loves, sit yourselves down.'

On hearing Mummy's voice, Anna settled her back against the wall and tried hard to control her breathing. There wasn't much space beneath the small table but she knew that the foliage of the large pot plant above her covered the rear of the table from view, so she could lean back and not worry about being seen. The main thing was to find a position she could maintain for as long as it took. Once Mummy's friends were gathered it was very important they didn't know she was there. She mustn't make a noise. Well, no noise except those she was supposed to make . . .

'What we do tonight is different to my large demonstrations,' Mummy was saying. 'The connection will be stronger, more pure. We should be able to hear the voice of the spirits themselves.'

'I say,' announced a jolly-sounding old lady, 'how thrilling!'

Anna smiled, the woman sounded nice. The sort of sweet old lady that was big and round and smelled of flowers.

'Sounds positively terrifying,' came a man's voice, pinched and nasal. Anna imagined him as the opposite to the old lady, thin and rigid, a skeleton of twigs, brittle and dusty. 'I do hope they don't appear. I'm not sure my heart could stand an actual apparition.'

'You'll be quite safe,' Mummy promised; 'I'm only clairaudient: we will hear the spirits but not see them.'

'I'm sure we have nothing to fear,' said another voice, a man again but one so vague it was hard for Anna to picture its owner. He talked in the same way she expected a cloud to, a voice that would be knocked away by the slightest breeze. A ghost's voice, perhaps. But no, she realised, he's not the ghost . . . I am!

'If we could all link hands,' Mummy said, 'that would help build a focus of positive energy. In order to achieve this I need as much energy as you can provide. I want you all to think the most positive thoughts, happy thoughts of love for the spirits that have passed, for those that are still dear to us even though they are now lost to us physically.'

'Ah, my dear Justine,' the cuddly woman announced 'I know you're still with us.'

'Erm . . .' the thin man seemed uncomfortable with this idea. Aware that the cuddly woman had set a precedent he couldn't ignore he struggled on: 'Joe, be good to talk to you again.'

The cuddly woman tutted, clearly unhappy with the thin man's effort.

'Beryl,' announced the dreamy man, before the woman could complain any further, 'come and see us, my dear. I miss you terribly.'

'Lovely,' said the cuddly woman, glad that at least someone was able to summon up enthusiasm for what lay ahead.

'Now,' said Mummy, ' let us picture them in our minds. Let us imagine them as they once were, happy and full of life. Let us see Justine, Joe and Beryl. Let us fix an image of them in our minds.'

Anna had already done so based on what Mummy had told her earlier that evening. She brought Joe to mind first, imagining the small black and white photo she'd been shown.

'He worked on the council,' Mummy had said, 'a grey man, a man of numbers and dust. He liked to smoke a pipe, his voice is low, quiet, used to the peace of libraries and empty offices.'

Anna lifted her hands to her mouth, cupping them just as Mummy had shown her, distorting her voice.

'Ah . . .' Mummy sighed and the darkness was complete, the candle blown out. 'They come!'

'Philip,' said Anna, her voice low and masculine, the image of dead old Joe fixed firmly in mind, 'is that you, Philip?'

'My God!' the thin man, said, 'is that . . .?'

'It's hard to hear,' said Mummy, 'you're so faint, Joe . . . it is you, isn't it?'

'Yes,' said Anna, a little louder now, 'it's me . . . is that Philip? Can you hear me, Philip?'

'I can!' the thin man replied, 'Oh, Joe . . . I can barely hear you but it's so good to know you're there.'

'I'm always with you,' said Anna. 'What are brothers for if they don't look after each other?'

'You always did, Joe,' the thin man agreed, 'you always did look after me. I miss you.'

'I miss you too,' said Anna before launching into the next bit of pre-prepared material, 'and Valerie. How is Valerie?'

'She's fine, just fine, she'd have come tonight only . . . well . . .'

'She doesn't believe.'

'No,' the thin man admitted, 'but wait till I tell her! I'll make her believe, don't you worry about that.'

'It doesn't matter, Philip, as long as you're here. Family.'

The thin man laughed. 'Yes, well . . . you never did quite see eye to eye, did you? She still misses you though.'

Anna continued the conversation for a few more minutes, working her way through subjects Mummy had already prepared. She talked about the recent breakdown of Philip's car, of the new house he and his wife had bought, of the holiday to Greece they were planning. All information that had been easily retrieved by a quick raid through Philip's credit card details. A couple of times she had to bite her lip to stop herself from giggling, it was going so well! The thin man really did think she was his brother and it certainly seemed to be making him happy to speak to her. Which was good. Anna liked to make people happy and if the thin man was happy then so was Mummy.

The cuddly woman came next and Anna pretended to be her long-lost friend Justine. This was an easy enough game as the cuddly woman hadn't seen Justine since she was a child and therefore knew very little about her. Having chanced upon her obituary in a newspaper, the cuddly woman had been filled with nostalgia for sunny childhood summers and set out to renew their acquaintance beyond the grave. It was testament both to the woman's gullibility and Anna's performance that the two chatted happily for about five minutes. In fact, the only reason the conversation drew to a halt was because Mummy insisted upon it, claiming that the connection was becoming frail and that they would have to let Justine go for now.

'Oh well,' the cuddly woman had said, 'we'll catch up again soon, my lovely, now I know I can get in touch.'

Anna thought the cuddly woman was very funny; she acted as if she was calling up a friend on the telephone.

The dreamy man was next, wishing to speak to Beryl, his wife. For all his wishy-washy tones it was clear that the conversation affected him deeply. Anna felt very sorry for the dreamy man and wished she really was his beloved Beryl.

Then it was over and Anna could relax.

The lights came on and Mummy slowly led her guests from the room. Anna stayed where she was just in case they should return; it was no good having played the game so well only to lose at it now.

A couple of minutes later, she heard the front door slam and Mummy came back into the room.

The tablecloth lifted and Anna looked up at Mummy's smiling face.

'Mummy's very pleased with you!'

Anna smiled, she couldn't remember ever feeling so happy. Now she knew how to make Mummy happy she'd do it all the time!

'Mummy might even let you have some ice cream as a special treat, would you like that?'

Anna nodded and crawled out from beneath the table so that she could stretch her legs.

As she stood up she felt a little dizzy and had to grab the back of one of the chairs to keep herself from falling over. She must have got up too quickly, she decided, that happened sometimes, it was nothing to worry about,

'Nothing to worry about?' asked the voice of Bad Father. 'I'll give you something to worry about.'

She looked around in panic. She hadn't heard Bad Father for a long time. She'd hoped he was gone for good.

'Don't start that, my girl,' said Mummy. 'We've had enough voices for now.'

'I'll decide when I speak,' said Bad Father, 'or do I have to teach both of you bitches who's boss?'

'Right!' Mummy shouted, 'that's that! No ice cream for you.'

Anna looked around, terrified and surrounded. Where was Bad Father? Sometimes you could see him when he talked, see his pink face, shining with sweat as he roared his law. Sometimes he was invisible, hiding on the inside.

'Fuck you,' said Bad Father and Anna could have cried to hear such language being directed at Mummy, she knew it would make her very cross indeed. Maybe even as cross as Bad Father. It looked like she might be, her face turning red as she dragged Anna out of the dining room and towards the cupboard under the stairs.

'You can spend the night in there,' she announced, 'and like it!'

'Fuck you! Fuck you! Fuck you!' screamed Bad Father and Anna wondered if he might suddenly appear and make Mummy be quiet. Bad Father liked making people quiet. He had told her often how it was done, whispering to her when she had been bad. Telling her stories in the dark.

Anna fell forwards into the darkness of the cupboard and the door was slammed shut behind her. Her knees were cut, she could feel them burning. They weren't the only thing that simmered in the darkness.

'Now look what you've done,' said Bad Father, 'always such an argumentative little bitch. Such a waste of skin and air. I should just beat you until you learn to behave. Beat you until you're dead. Then you'd be good, wouldn't you? Dead girls don't talk back! Dead girls haven't got smart mouths! Dead girls just sit quietly.'

Anna was terrified and she tried to beat at the cupboard door but the thick soundproofing absorbed her blows.

She cried herself hoarse in the soft, padded prison, Bad Father whispering to her, until eventually, tired from his rages, he fell asleep.

'Personalities?' asked Probert, staring intently through the windscreen and trying to keep a clear view of the road ahead through the rain.

'The shrinks called it multiple personality disorder.'

'Schizophrenia?'

'A schizophrenic hears voices; Anna actually becomes different people. She has a whole selection of personalities in her head, most of them based on people she met as a child. The worst of course, the most dangerous, is that of her father.

'As a child he used to come a lot. She would suddenly stiffen and then that voice, the first voice I ever heard her make, would come out. It would be full of threats – for her as much as anyone else. Details about the things he'd done or the things he'd like to do. For some time I thought we'd never get rid of him.'

'Then you asked her to dredge him back up to scare Father Goss.' Probert was at a loss to describe the despair he felt at Aida Golding. A woman so narrow-minded, so abominably selfish, he was by no means sure she fully appreciated the things she'd done to her foster child, or indeed any of them. 'And you think that Anna, when under the control of this personality, is doing the killing?'

'Who else could it be?'

'Knowing you?' Probert dug his nails into the steering wheel, 'it could be almost anybody.'

When the doorbell rang, Sacha was in no hurry to answer it.

'Let him get wet,' she muttered to herself. 'If he's too stupid to take his keys with him then a soaking's what he deserves.'

That wasn't to mention Glen's other crimes, of course, which were many. Sometimes she had to wonder why she continued to put up with him. Not only did he treat her like she was disposable but the rest of his weird family had no time for her either. It was enough to give a girl a complex. What made them so special?

All right, so Aida could talk to the dead, she supposed that was *quite* special. Bloody weird, though, and did it mean she was allowed to look down her nose at Sacha? No, it did not. You'd think a woman who could talk to dead people would be glad to talk to someone with breath in their lungs once in a while. You'd think she'd show a bit of politeness! The dead were better company, were they? Aida Golding certainly seemed to think so.

She made her slow and deliberate way down the stairs as the doorbell rang again.

'I'm coming,' she shouted, 'just wait!'

She watched the shadow bob impatiently beyond the glass in the door. She could just imagine the things he was saying about her. The thought didn't make her move any quicker. Maybe it really was time to ditch him.

She got to the front door and almost decided not to open it, so determined was she that she could do much better for herself without Glen in her life. Still, as she was in his house it was not like she had much choice.

'What happened?' she asked, unlatching the door. 'Forgot your keys?'

It wasn't Glen.

'So what are we going to do?' Probert asked, 'and why do you need me?'

'I need you to make sure that the police don't make trouble,' Golding replied, 'I don't see why you should be the only one to expect to walk away from this without consequence.'

'Without consequence?' he shouted. 'Why the hell shouldn't I walk away without consequences? None of this is anything to do with me. All I did was be gullible enough to fall for your scam. I'm another one of your damned victims. I'm beginning to realise there are a great many of us.'

'You needn't plead a blameless life, Probert, you've done your share of selfish – and criminal – acts. If you hadn't I'd have no power over you.'

She smiled at him and he found himself remembering what the Barrowman brothers had done to Thana. He never would have said that he could have wished that torture on another human being, but right now he was close. The hatred he felt for Golding was so immense it choked off his ability to speak.

'We need to track Anna down,' Golding continued, 'and make sure the mad little brat is put away where she can do no more harm.'

'What are you doing here?' Sacha asked. 'Glen told me you were long gone.'

'Not gone,' the visitor said, its voice rough and cracked, 'never gone.'

They pulled down their woolly hat, stretching the material across their face. Nice. Breath heating up inside the wool. Hot. World turned vague, shapes lit up through the haze of stretched wool.

'Run,' they said, showing the bloody knife, 'before I stab you in your slutty mouth.'

They opened their own mouth and huffed hot air, a black 'O' spreading condensation and spittle on the inside of the wool.

'You what?' Sacha screwed up her face. 'You having

a laugh? I never know what's next with you lot. You're all bloody mental!'

'Shush,' they said, and stabbed the knife exactly where they had threatened, blade chipping against teeth, gouging tongue and splitting lips.

Sacha, realising too late that this was no joke, raised her hands to her bleeding mouth and backed away.

'Don't!' she begged, the word turned indistinct by a mouth full of blood and a tongue that threatened to flap itself loose.

'Will,' they replied stabbing again and again and again.

The blade broke before their fury did.

Probert pulled the car into Aida Golding's street, his anger still burning hot in his belly. He'd hurl the hateful creature out of the door if he could. He imagined her, flailing out into thin air as he sped past. What a lovely, lovely thought.

'Slow down,' she snapped, 'or you'll go right past it.'

Trevor Court was tired. His arm and jaw ached terribly, almost so much that he couldn't bear to move them. Still, he could hardly sit here all night. If he didn't move soon he'd probably never be able to peel himself from the back seat.

'Lucky, lucky, lucky,' he said again, dropping the screwdriver back into the bag.

He felt blissfully light-headed. His work tonight had been just what he needed. He'd stayed away for too long. The world of the dead had received no gifts now for years. He wouldn't leave it so long next time; a man shouldn't fight against his strengths.

He was blissfully unaware of the real world as he eased himself up from the sticky plastic and stepped out of the car. His head was filled with songs of pain, his eyes filled with blood. He was a man outside of his own body, lost in the dirty cave of his own fucked-up skull.

Right up until Probert ran him over.

The brakes had done nothing on the wet road, the wheels locking and skidding straight forward.

The man who had just blindly stepped out of the back seat of the parked car was crushed against the door for a fraction of a second before the hinges went and both door and man went spinning backwards.

'Oh Jesus!' Probert couldn't believe it. His life was getting worse and worse by the moment. How unlucky could one man be?

When the car came to a halt he jumped out and ran back down the street to where the man's body was lying crumpled on the tarmac.

Golding stepped out after him, briefly wondering about running back to her home before anyone spotted she'd been in the car with him. But curtains were already twitching and faces were pressing themselves up against the glass.

'Oh,' she sighed, 'what have you done?'

Probert bent over Trevor Court's broken body. The man was panting, fighting to draw breath into crushed lungs.

'Call an ambulance,' Probert shouted, 'quickly!'

The man was saying something but Probert had to bend down closer to be able to hear it.

'Lucky, lucky, lucky,' the man repeated over and over again.

'Hardly,' Probert replied, glancing over to the parked car and the open back door. He could see a naked foot peering out.

'There's someone else,' he told Aida, 'in the back seat.'

He stood up and took a look, turning away in disgust as he drew closer. The streetlights didn't allow much detail, thankfully, but the little they did show had him running to the gutter to throw up.

Anna woke up in John's front garden. She was upright, her arms hanging straight down by her sides.

'What happened?' she asked, but there was nothing out here to tell her.

She looked down at the strange clothes she was wearing, the long raincoat, the tracksuit. She tugged the woolly hat off her head and dropped it on the floor. It landed on the ground with a slapping noise. She must have taken them from the wardrobe in her room. John's wife's old clothes. Clothes of the dead. If only she could remember doing it.

'You didn't do it,' said a voice, and now it became clearer. If Bad Father had something to say then things were not good. 'I did.'

She had thought she was rid of Bad Father. For years she had not heard his voice. Then the other night, in the darkness with the priest, he'd come again.

She'd asked him to, that was the ridiculous thing, she'd actually asked.

'We need something to shake them up,' Golding had told her, 'and it's about time we had Douglas at our table!'

Golding called him Douglas Reece. As had the priest. Others called him the East End Ripper. Anna had never known him as anything but Bad Father.

'Which just goes to show what a bad girl you are,' he said. Now she could see him in the furthest corner of the garden, partially obscured by plants. 'What a horrid, evil little girl.'

'I'm not.' She knew better than to try to stand up for herself, Bad Father did not like arguments. He proved as much now by the snarl on his face. She could only see his mouth, the rest of his head obscured by jutting foliage on a fuchsia bush. The buds hung like blood drops bouncing in the rain, beneath them his teeth were bared and grinding together. She could almost hear the sound of them grating against themselves. They were the teeth of an animal not a man.

'A horrid, horrid girl,' he repeated and somehow his teeth stayed pressed together, a locked gate that should not have allowed his words through. 'No matter how many times I try and teach you a lesson you will not learn, will you? When will you ever behave?'

In the distance, a group of young men laughed and shouted amongst themselves. There was the blare of a car horn that forced another roar of approval from them.

Then slowly the night was quiet again, just the sound of the rain drumming against the leaves.

'Night Music,' said Bad Father, 'I always did love the Night Music.'

Water was cascading off his chin, a thick silver rope glistening like drool as it tumbled past his chest.

'You shouldn't be here any more,' said Anna. 'You were gone and it was much better. I could get on with my life, be my own person. Why did you have to come back?'

'You needed me,' he replied, 'that's what I think. Spending your life playing your silly games in the dark. Lining the pocket of that old crook. You hadn't the gumption to leave. You hadn't the strength. You just sat there and did as you were told. I think you wanted me to come back. I think you want me to take you away from all this.'

'I don't need you. I have John. John will make things better.'

'The old man who wants you to dress up like his dead wife? Yes. I'm sure he will.'

'You don't know him! He's a nice man, a kind man!'

'That's what you think after spending five minutes in his company. So pathetic . . . always trying to find a daddy.'

'Maybe if I'd had a better one in the first place.'

'Don't you say that! Don't you badmouth me. I was the father you needed. The husband your mother needed. It's not my fault they took me away.'

'They didn't take you away! It was your choice!'

'Don't argue.' Don't.' But his voice was a little weaker now and she saw that second smile appear beneath his clenched teeth. That last smile he had given her when the police had kicked down their door. The small knife that he had drawn across his own throat, the hot blood that had poured down into the cot, thickening in her hair as it cooled. The police sergeant desperately trying to wipe it off with his handkerchief. The shouting of the other officers as they held Bad Father down while he kicked and thrashed his way to death.

'You left me,' she said, 'and I wish you'd just stay away.'

'I'm here,' he said, his voice now little more than a whisper. 'I'm always here.'

The blood continued to flow from his throat and she thought of the priest. Coughing as his life bled out. The slow hiss of air from the severed oesophagus like a puncture in a bicycle tire. Was she always to be shown that final smile? Did she somehow crave it?

Thinking of how the carving knife had felt in her hand as she had sat there in the dark, the voice of Bad Father lingering like the scent of a snuffed-out candle, she thought perhaps she did.

'What are you doing?'

She turned around to see John stood in the doorway of his house. 'I heard your voice,' he explained. 'You were shouting.'

'Sorry.' She looked towards the corner of the garden where Bad Father had stood. He had gone.

'There was someone else out here.'

'No.' She ran towards the door, desperate to get in, wanting to rub away the rainwater and the memory of her conversation.

'I heard them,' John insisted, 'a man's voice.'

'There's nobody here but me,' she said and on some level, deep down, knew it to be true.

Twelve

The Fruit

'What were you doing out there?' John couldn't fail to ask. 'I thought you'd gone to bed.'

Anna shivered in the hallway, her clothes so drenched she could only be drier without them. 'I don't know,' she admitted, 'I sometimes get . . . blanks. I'm so cold.'

John sighed. 'Get in the shower. I'll fetch you a drink of something.'

'Sorry,' she said, her head drooping down like that of a child who knows she's been bad.

'You don't have to be sorry,' he said, pausing in the doorway to the kitchen. 'But you do have to discuss it. Get yourself warm first.'

She nodded and ran upstairs.

Going through to the kitchen John dug around in one of the cupboards for a bottle of brandy he knew he had gathering dust.

Even with the surprise of finding Anna outside, he clung to the positive mood of a few hours ago. It could hardly be a surprise that Anna had issues. If those issues resorted in her being in his front garden when she had thought herself in bed then, yes, they needed addressing. He could – and would – help her do that. Maybe even recommend someone for her to discuss it with. If she was as serious about wanting to make a fresh start as she seemed to be, then he was only too happy to give her the support she needed to do it.

He took the bottle of brandy, poured a little into a glass and tested it. Rough around the edges but it would knock some of the chill off. He poured a decent measure into another glass and leaned back against the worktop, listening to the sound of the shower upstairs.

He should tell Anna that she could stay as long as she needed. It would offer her a bit of security. Of all the things that must be preying on her, he could at least remove that concern.

He took another mouthful of the brandy. Was he being too soft again? The girl had been here twenty-four hours, he barely knew her and yet he was willing to keep her for as long as she needed. He thought about what Laura had said earlier, about him being a nice man. Maybe it was true, or maybe he was just naive. Or maybe he hoped for more from Anna, was that it? Was he lusting after a woman half his age? He'd hardly be the first man to do so. And she certainly did remind him of Jane when she had been young. Yes, Anna was attractive. Still, he thought his feelings were more complex than lust. He wanted to save her, that was the truth of it. The look in her eyes when he had stood up to her foster mother, to her he was a hero. That had been a feeling he hadn't experienced for years. He was so used to being a quiet man, a background character in his own life, he'd forgotten what it felt like to be powerful, to have someone look up to you.

'Oh, you silly old fart,' he said out loud, 'you'll fall flat on your face one of these days.'

Except, he didn't actually believe it. He thought he might finally be stepping out from the shadow of Jane's death and the relief was so profound, the potential so exciting, he could hardly believe he had lived such an empty life for so long.

Upstairs the shower switched off.

He topped up his own glass and made his way upstairs.

'I've got you a brandy,' he shouted. 'Is there anything else you want?'

There was a long moment of silence and John wondered if she'd heard him. Then the bathroom door opened and Anna stepped out.

'Yes,' she replied, forcing him up against the wall and kissing him on the mouth.

After running upstairs, Anna had gone straight into the bathroom, tugging at her wet clothes as if they were attacking her.

The thought of Bad Father still lingered and she half expected to see his face staring back at her when she looked in the mirror above the sink. But it was just her, hair limp, skin cold and pale. What a ruinous thing she was, not something you could ever love.

'Oh, hush now,' said Soft Mother and Anna was relieved to hear a friendly voice. At the same time she panicked that Soft Mother was speaking loud enough for John to hear. She didn't want John to know about the voices, that's why she hadn't told him about the real tricks she used to play for Aida Golding. If he knew she had been the voices in the dark, the voices of the dead . . . Well, she was sure he would never forgive her.

'Oh now,' said Soft Mother and Anna quickly turned on the shower to help cover the noise, 'he would understand, I'm sure. Besides, he likes it when you pretend to be Jane doesn't he? Didn't he ask you to dress up in her clothes?'

'It wasn't like that,' Anna insisted. 'He just wanted me to have something to wear.'

'Shush, my love,' Soft Mother replied. 'A girl knows. What about the look on his face when you came downstairs in that brown dress, eh? He fell in love with you on the spot!'

Anna laughed, embarrassed, and climbed into the shower cubicle.

'He doesn't love me, silly,' she said. 'He barely even knows me. He's been very kind that's all. He's a kind man.'

'Bless you, but you don't know men like I do, my girl. None of them are just kind, they want that fruit between your legs!'

Anna was embarrassed at this, partially at the childish, prudish way it was expressed, partly by the thought of John overhearing. She hushed Soft Mother, busying herself with sponge and soap.

Soft Mother wouldn't be quietened.

'There's nothing wrong with it, you know,' she said while Anna dunked her hair beneath the shower head.

'Sometimes that fruit is the best thing a girl has to keep her safe.'

'It didn't work for you, did it?' Anna replied and then bit her lip. She didn't want to upset Soft Mother, she was just being defensive.

'Well, dear, your father didn't really like that sort of thing. His attitude towards women left a lot to be desired.'

It occurred to Anna that thinking they were little more than sex objects, as Soft Mother seemed to do, left a lot to be desired too. She didn't say as much though as she didn't want to argue with Soft Mother. Soft Mother couldn't help being a bit backward in her beliefs.

'I don't think John wants that,' she repeated, 'I think he just wants company, and someone to look after. John's a very sad man.'

'Indeed he is,' agreed Soft Mother, 'but I think it's you that doesn't want more than company.'

Anna didn't reply to that, just cupped her hand and filled it with shampoo.

'Is it such a terrifying notion?' asked Soft Mother. 'Is it more than you can bear to do in order to keep hold of him? Won't you regret it when he tells you to leave because you didn't give him what he wanted?'

'He wouldn't do that.'

'Are you so sure? He certainly wouldn't throw you out for offering though, would he? What man is offended by the idea of a woman wanting to crawl on top of him, eh? What man could fail to be flattered?'

'I don't know . . .'

'Yes you do! Listen to your mother for once, if you

want a man to love you then you need to loosen up a little.'

Anna leaned back and forced frothy shampoo from her hair. Could Soft Mother be right? She had nothing against the idea of sex, whatever Soft Mother might think, though she certainly had very little experience in it. Living in the prison of Aida Golding's house her opportunities had been virtually non-existent. She'd still be a virgin were it not for the fact that Glen Logan couldn't keep his hands to himself once he'd had a few drinks.

She thought about it. Imagined what it might feel like with someone softer and more considerate than Glen. Someone who might actually care about how it felt for her.

'You know I'm right,' said Soft Mother as Anna leaned back against the tiles and gave in to a her imagination, letting her fingers wander.

Perhaps she was.

Anna turned off the shower and reached for a towel. She looked at herself in the mirror. Was it such a bad face? Such a bad body? Maybe not. Maybe it was some - thing she could offer John in return for all his kindnesses.

She heard him coming up the stairs.

'I've got you a brandy,' he shouted to her. 'Is there anything else you want?'

She dropped the towel, walked over to the door and opened it.

'Yes,' she replied, standing naked in front of him – and didn't that feel exciting and liberating? She took power from the way he stared, his eyes unable to hold onto her face, wandering irresistibly down her body. Of course he wanted her! Soft Mother was right, as always.

She walked across the landing and kissed him.

John had no idea what to do. Yes, he had thought about Anna while waiting downstairs. Had admitted to himself that he found her attractive. But could he really allow himself to give in to such an idea? He was more than twice her age and she was clearly not in control of her actions.

His mind went blank for a moment, unable to process anything but the taste of her mouth and the way her body felt pressed against his. She was hot, straight from the shower and steam was actually rising off her skin as she pushed him back against the wall. He felt his clothes dampening. Felt himself stiffening, the thought of her becoming aware of his erection both thrilling and shocking him out of the sensation.

'No,' he said, pulling away. 'I can't.'

Her face fell instantly and he wished for nothing more than to take back what he had said, she seemed so crushed.

'I thought you wanted . . .' she looked like she was about to cry.

'I'm sorry,' he insisted, 'it's not that I don't find you attractive. Of course I do. I just—'

'Forget it,' she said, pushing past him and into her room, closing the door quickly behind her.

John stood there, both drinks still in his hands.

*

Anna climbed straight into bed, wanting to hide under the sheets where nobody could look at her.

'I told you he didn't want that,' she told Soft Mother, pressing her face into the pillow to deaden the noise. 'I told you.'

'Yes dear,' Soft Mother replied. 'Stopped him asking any more awkward questions though, didn't it?'

John sat down on the edge of the spare bed.

'*Fuck*,' he said, absolutely at a loss as to how the night had gone so wrong so quickly. He drank his own drink. Then, still angry with himself, he drank hers.

He put the empty glasses on the bedside table, stripped and climbed into bed. His chest burned with cheap brandy and embarrassment.

'Fuck,' he repeated. He closed his eyes and reached under the duvet to imagine how things might have gone if he had only said yes to Anna.

Thirteen

'They'll Kill Someone One of These Days'

The following morning, John left for work before Anna got up. On his return both of them moved politely around each other, steadfastly refusing to mention what had happened the night before. After a while both of them relaxed, he telling her about his day, her asking questions about all his students. She seemed to find every detail of his working life thrilling, which it wasn't, but he couldn't help but enjoy the attention.

That night they went to their separate beds he smiling, she laughing about a particularly innocuous joke he'd made.

It had clearly been decided, by mutual consent, that the night before would simply not be mentioned.

This set the standard for the days that followed. John went to work; Anna became the old-fashioned housewife. After so long looking after himself – and since Jane had worked more hours than he did before her illness forced her to retire he had always taken the lion's share of the housework – John found it awkward to begin with. Everything was always immaculate, a drink pressed into his hand as he came through the door, food laid out on the table shortly after. He felt like he'd taken residency in a seventies' sitcom. He realised she was trying to be useful, no, more than that . . . *essential*, so that he didn't decide to revoke his invitation for her to stay. He tried to explain that it was unnecessary, that she could stay as long as she liked and that she certainly didn't have to repay him by becoming the house slave. She would just laugh and tell him not to be so silly, she liked helping out, liked keeping busy, what was the matter? Did he not like her cooking? At which point, backed into a corner, he would simply confess that he liked it just fine and stopped complaining.

Of course, there was a great deal of truth in what she said. Anna was desperately avoiding finding herself at a loose end. She wanted to be busy, focused on simple tasks, dashing from one place to another. As long as she had that she could ignore the voices – for the most part at least – and convince herself that life really was no more complex or threatening than a series of rooms to tidy and meals to cook.

Michael and Laura visited again and John was pleased to see that the first night hadn't been a fluke, the company was easy and everyone got on well. In fact, Laura and Anna made plans to see each other during the following week, for 'girls' adventures' they said, laughing together as naturally and confidently as if they had known each other for years.

Anna didn't suffer from another of her 'blanks' – at least, John admitted, if she did he was unaware of the fact – and he found he was in no great hurry to discuss it any more. Life was too comfortable. After feeling uneasy in his own house for so long he couldn't bring himself to rock the boat. Let things continue as they were. He was happy.

Plans for Michael and Laura to move in continued, helped, John was sure, by the clear friendship developing between the two women. They began to discuss how the house might be split, how they could best afford to double up on the amenities. While sketching out a plan of the rooms, John realised he had included space for Anna without even thinking about it, she had become part of the household in his head and therefore needed to be accounted for. How easy it is, he decided, to change your life completely within the space of only a few weeks.

Laura and Anna made regular trips into the city, both of them insisting on 'doing the tourist thing'. Anna was only too happy to visit the well-worn old haunts, despite having lived in London all her life she had seen very little of it. Not that she would have minded even if she had, to be able to live a normal life, with a friend on her arm, was more than she had ever hoped for.

Michael got a job touring an Agatha Christie play around provincial seaside towns. The money wasn't great but it was better than nothing and he joked about the pleasure of killing members of his cast on a daily basis (twice during matinees).

'They're all failed soap stars,' he said, 'or creaking comic turns from the eighties. You've never known a more poisonous group of people, they deserve every - thing I give them, with knife, axe and garrotte!'

While he was on the road, Laura moved in with John and Anna. She was perfectly capable of looking after herself, she insisted, but it seemed pointless not to make the most of their company when they were all getting on so well.

It was a shame that it was all to be lost so quickly. But lost it would be, and it started with a visit from Lord Llewellyn Probert.

Probert found John alone at the university. He and Anna had travelled in together (as had become something of a habit of late) and to his relief Probert arrived just after she had left his office to do some shopping. John hated to think how she would have reacted had she been present for the conversation between the two men, no doubt it would have done much to ruin her current contented feelings.

'You free for a chat?' asked Probert, catching John between his office and the main lecture hall.

'Actually, I'm lecturing in a few minutes.' John felt absurdly embarrassed at the sight of the Lord here at his place of work. It was as if something private had been brought out into the open. He glanced around in discomfort, wondering who might be watching.

'It's important, I'm afraid. Is there somewhere we can talk privately?'

'I can't just go wandering off,' John replied. 'Can it not wait?'

'Not really. Leave them a note to say you'll be late.' Probert seemed almost as uncomfortable as John when he admitted: 'It's about Anna.'

That was enough to beat down John's complaints and he passed on a message to one of his students that he'd be there as soon as possible.

He led Probert to his office, finally regaining some of his confidence once they were out of the public eye.

'How did you find me?' John asked, then brushed the question away. 'You know, forget it, I'm sure it's not difficult for someone like you.'

'No,' Probert agreed with a smile, 'it isn't. I just asked the police.'

'Why then? I mean, is everything all right about that night? About . . .?'

'Father Goss? Yes, at least in the way you mean. There's quite a lot you don't know, I imagine, unless you read about Alasdair?'

'What about him?'

Probert tried to get comfortable on the small chair he'd been given, stacks of books and magazines in his way. 'Is there nowhere with a little more space?'

'Alasdair,' John repeated, 'what should I have read about Alasdair?'

'He was murdered,' Probert replied, giving up and resting his left foot on a stack of old test papers. 'During one of Golding's demonstrations. His skull was caved in and then he was nailed to the door of the meeting hall. The murderer took a knife and . . .' Probert mimed a cut from groin to throat. 'When they opened the door he spilled out everywhere.'

John couldn't think what to say to that so he kept silent.

Eventually, Probert continued. 'Golding dragged me

in because she was convinced that whoever had murdered Alasdair intended to kill her next. In fact, she thought it was Anna.'

'She thought what?' John was genuinely confused; he couldn't place the two ideas together in his head. 'She thought Anna was next?'

'No.' Probert sighed, clearly finding all this exceed - ingly unpleasant. 'She thought Anna was the murderer.'

'Ridiculous.'

'Perhaps. It certainly seemed so later. I drove her home and . . .' Probert shifted awkwardly again, 'we actually apprehended the likely culprit.' He saw no need to explain that he had done so with the bonnet of a car. 'Apparently, after having dealt with Alasdair, he had driven to Golding's house meaning to carry on the good work. He killed both Alasdair's brother and his girlfriend. Presumably he would have then lain in wait to kill Golding when she returned home.'

'Who was he?'

'A fellow by the name of Trevor Court. History of mental illness, there was some question of his being implicated in the murder of his brother when they were both children. Nothing could ever be proven of course but he's been in and out of institutions and care programmes. Apparently he attended one of Golding's demonstrations and became convinced, after she claimed to have a message for him, that she knew something about his past. He ran out of the place screaming his head off.'

Trevor, thought John, remembering the look of panic on the man's face at that first demonstration, the one he had attended with Michael. What had he said? He'd been terrified at the notion that Golding was talking to someone that had a message for him.

'"What does he want?"' John said.

'Sorry?'

'I was just remembering. I was there on that night. "What does he want?", that's what the man kept shouting. I thought it was strange at the time.'

'Well, the man was obviously deranged, the things he did to them all. He didn't just kill them, it was drawn out and cruel, he took real pleasure in it.' Which in turn made Probert think of the Barrowman brothers and he lost himself for a moment. 'Sorry,' he said, pulling his thoughts back together. 'I found the body, you see. Alasdair's brother Glen, that is . . . in the back of Court's car. He had spent a long time working on it with a screwdriver.'

The two men sat in silence for a moment, the words needed to settle down before either was willing to step over them.

'I don't know what to say,' John admitted finally. 'I mean . . . well, it's just horrible. I don't know how I'm going to tell Anna.'

Mention of her name shook Probert out of his funk. 'Well, yes,' he admitted, 'but there's a lot more about her you need to know first.'

Anna was getting used to freedom. Some days she couldn't quite bear the idea of wandering around out - side, big open streets, crowds everywhere, it was too much. It was an environment a person could get lost in, maybe lose their sense of solidity and float away into that endless sky. Other days, *better* days, the wide open was what she craved. Those were the days when the memory of that soundproofed cupboard beneath the stairs was fresh in her head and the only thing she could do to brush it away was to get out in the bright light and noise of the city. Now the weather had finally take a turn for the better walking was a pleasure. She would head out and take her time over planning what she could cook for John and Laura. She made it an event. Something to make a fuss of. It was a simple act, something she could control and focus on, getting better each and every day one meal at a time. Small steps. The presenter on one of those morning chat shows had talked about the importance of those: 'Walking back to mental health takes small steps,' they had said, looking into the camera in that earnest way they all had. Anna could sense the charlatanism in most of them, she'd lived with one long enough after all, but she still enjoyed having the shows on. It was another little freedom she could allow herself, even if Laura would insist on turning the volume down whenever she walked in the room. 'It's like having a football crowd in the house,' she would say.

Anna stopped at a farmers' market and lost herself in a stall selling homemade jam.

'Who knew you could make so many different types, eh?' asked a voice behind her and she turned around to see Davinia Harris.

'Oh,' said Anna, startled by the woman's presence. For a moment the world pressed in on her: the jumble of

stalls, the shuffle of the customers, voices everywhere
. . . were they all in her head or were some of them on
the outside?

'Sorry, dear,' said Davinia, 'I didn't mean to make
you jump.'

The older woman reached out and took Anna's arm
to stop her falling over.

'It's all right,' said Anna, slowly getting herself back
under control. 'I was miles away.'

'No bad place to be these days,' said Davinia. 'Let me
buy you a cup of tea to say sorry.'

'Oh don't worry, there's no need . . .'

'I insist,' said Davinia, 'there's a lovely little place on
the next street along, they do cakes to die for!'

Feeling she could not refuse, Anna followed Davinia
out of the market and around the corner to a small
teashop. It was laid out over three tiny floors of a
Victorian terrace. Bored waiting staff stared into thin
air. Perhaps, thought Anna, all of their clientele had
finally given up and died of old age.

Clearly the archaic nature of the place appealed to
Davinia. 'Like they used to be,' she said, gesturing
around vaguely. 'Would you like a scone? Or a toasted
teacake?'

'No, I'm fine thanks. Just a cup of tea.'

'Oh,' Davinia sounded disappointed. 'Well, I might
just have a little something . . . an Eccles cake or a bit of
shortbread perhaps. Tea's too wet without a little
something.'

'Eccles cakes are nice,' Anna agreed, feeling she ought
to say something.

'Quite right dear, that's the spirit,' Davinia replied and promptly ordered two Eccles cakes and a large pot of tea. 'Let's go upstairs,' she suggested, 'it's full of old things.'

Anna guessed that Davinia meant this as a recommendation and followed her up a narrow, dark wood staircase that led to a second floor. It was, indeed, filled with old things. A perfect hiding place for lace or faux Wedgwood, there was so much of it already there nobody would notice more. The walls were covered with prints of old London street maps. On one, a fire - place dressed in heavy green tile was decorated with knick-knacks and dusty teddy bears.

'Lovely,' confirmed Davinia, settling into a chair near the window.

Anna ran her finger along the mantelpiece, looking at the row of pretend antiquity. There was a selection of china rabbits, a cut-glass perfume bottle, a satin pin - cushion that held a cluster of long hat-pins. 'It's very nice,' she agreed and sat down.

'It's ever so funny I bumped into you,' said Davinia, 'as I was only thinking about you the other day. I wonder how dear Sandy is doing, I thought.'

It hadn't occurred to Anna that Davinia didn't know her real name and she was grateful for the fact that it had been pointed out.

'If anyone's seen dear Aida of late, I thought,' continued Davinia, 'it'll be her.'

'Actually I haven't,' said Anna 'I've . . .' she had been about to say 'left' before correcting herself, '. . . stopped going to see her.'

'You and me both, dear,' said Davinia, 'She's vanished off the face of the Earth. There was a bit of fuss over a night she did at the Barret-Holden Memorial Hall in Bermondsey only I didn't go.' She leaned over and spoke in a whisper. 'My Henry won't be seen anywhere south of the river my love, he's a terrible snob like that so when Aida's down that way I just don't go.' She leaned back again. 'But things seemed perfectly normal the next few nights. She was on her own, mind, no sign of that nice young man that helps out . . . And then, a few days ago . . . nothing! All the shows on the website are cancelled, she won't answer her phone. Who knows what's happened to her?'

Anna shrugged. 'I'm afraid I haven't seen her since that night.'

'Oh yes,' said Davinia gushing with enthusiasm, '*that* night. Who can forget that, eh? Though the police certainly seem to have. I haven't heard a peep from them. That clever Lord Probert, I imagine, had something to do with that. He did say he was going to sort it all out, didn't he? I must admit I didn't take to him on the night but he certainly seems to have a bit of clout. Click of his fingers and the police were rushing around like he was the Chief Constable. Or is it Chief Commissioner? I can never remember. My Henry refused to have anything to do with the police . . . ever since those riots with the blacks. Said they were as bad as the crooks half the time. I dare say he was right. Here's our tea!'

The waitress laid it out for them – paper doilies on the plate, Anna noticed, as if you couldn't risk the Eccles cake staining the china.

'Enjoy,' she insisted with a slight Hungarian accent and vanished back down the stairs.

'Oh I think we will,' agreed Davinia, taking a big mouthful out of her Eccles cake and chuckling through a shower of pastry crumbs.

'I'm sure Anna will tell me everything about herself that she thinks I need to know,' said John. 'I don't think it's fair to hear personal details from you.'

'Oh, don't be so bloody pompous,' Probert replied, 'I'm not just here to gossip, it's important, I'd hardly bother otherwise. Anna is not quite the woman you think she is.'

'I know all about that,' said John. 'Aida Golding adopted her, she told me.'

'She told you about her parents?'

'She doesn't remember them.'

'She remembers them only too well,' Probert replied. 'Her father was Douglas Reece.'

'Who's Douglas Reece?' The name was vaguely familiar but John couldn't place it.

'Douglas Reece was the East End Ripper, remember? We allegedly heard from him that night.'

John tutted. 'We heard from no such person, it was just one of Golding's confederates putting on a silly voice.'

'Yes,' Probert agreed, 'it was Anna.'

'Anna? Don't be ridiculous, she was sitting right next to you.'

'Indeed she was, in the dark, if you remember, Golding is always very careful to ensure that we can't see a thing at these affairs. Anna had been working with her for years, she's always had a skill for voices. No, more than a skill really . . . perhaps a better word would be affliction.'

John stood up. 'That's enough. I have a lecture to get to and I don't have time to sit listening to this twaddle. I presume Golding put you up to this did she? Trying to get her own back? Stir up some trouble?'

Probert didn't move from his chair. 'Oh, I'm sure she'll make a nuisance of herself soon enough,' he said, 'but I've come of my own accord.'

'A likely story.'

Probert snapped, that calm, noble air he so liked to affect was replaced by genuine anger. 'I don't make a habit of interfering in other people's business, Pritchard,' he shouted, 'but this whole mess has gone on far enough. If I can help make sure nobody else is hurt – or worse – then I shall do my damnedest to see that it is so. Whether given your permission or not. Now sit down, you stupid man, it's better for Anna that you know about all this because if Golding's right then someone needs to be keeping an eye on her.'

John hesitated for a moment then resumed his seat. 'All right,' he agreed, 'but only for Anna's sake. And that's not to say I believe any of it . . .'

But he did, of course, he believed it all.

'I can't stop thinking about what happened that night,' said Davinia, much to Anna's unease. The last thing she wanted was to discuss the death of Father Goss. 'It was just so awful, wasn't it?'

'Yes,' Anna agreed, 'it was. I'd really rather not talk about it.'

'Well, naturally,' agreed Davinia, 'who would? All that blood . . .' she rolled her eyes as if feeling faint. Of course, in reality she was more alive than ever, there was nothing that invigorated Davinia more than the grotesque. 'And the East End Ripper!' Davinia gasped with pleasure, too wrapped up in her own excitement to notice the discomfort the conversation was obviously causing Anna.

'I don't suppose you remember it?' the older woman continued. 'You'll have been far too young when it happened but the whole country was up in arms about it. "You make sure you get a bus home," my Henry used to tell me, "don't go walking around at night on your own, not with a lunatic like that on the loose." Not that I would have been walking in the sorts of areas he tended to pick on, of course, we've always been North London, the closest we get to the East End is Albert Square! Do you watch *EastEnders*, dear?' she asked. 'Henry never used to allow it on but I have to say I never miss it now he's gone. They're addictive, aren't they, the soaps? Moving wallpaper, that's what Henry called it, nothing but moving wallpaper.'

'I don't really watch much television,' Anna said, grateful of the change of subject.

'Oh, very wise,' Davinia replied, 'rots the brain, I'm sure. Or the eyes, one or the other. You must excuse me.'

She rose to her feet and wandered purposefully up the stairs in the direction of the toilet.

Anna was left quite alone in the empty tearoom,

staring at the steam that rose from the spout of the teapot.

'What a gobby old bitch,' said Bad Father, taking a seat at the table.

For a moment, Anna could say nothing, her fingers slapping her lips in shock as she looked around to make sure nobody else was here to see or hear him.

'Go away!' she begged him. 'Go away! Go away!'

She hadn't seen or heard from Bad Father since that night in John's garden, had hoped, in fact, that he was gone for good, washed away by the rain.

'It's you that keeps bringing me back,' he said, dabbing at pastry crumbs on the table with his finger, 'thinking about me, talking about me . . .'

'That was her, not me. I didn't say a word.'

'I noticed. Didn't exactly stick up for your old dad, did you?'

'Oh please . . .' Anna began to cry, turning to look over her shoulder, terrified that Davinia would return at any minute and see them. 'Please leave me alone.'

'She's a horror,' he said. '"My Henry" this "my Henry" that. I bet he would have loved to shut her up. I bet every night he dreamed about taking an axe to the bitch just to stop that flapping mouth. I don't know how he could bear it. I should kill her now, as a favour to him.'

Anna sobbed as upstairs the toilet door opened and Davinia began to descend the stairs.

'Douglas Reece was an extremely disturbed man,' said

Probert, 'textbook loon, thought he was doing God's work by getting rid of all the "fallen women".'

'There's no such thing as a "textbook loon",' said John.

Probert shrugged. 'You're the expert. What would I know?

'He wrote letters to the police,' he continued, 'just like the original Jack the Ripper. That's how they caught him in the end, a thumbprint on one of the envelopes. He had previous form after a rape accusation in the seventies. They tracked him down, religious mania, history of violence, he fit the bill. They stormed his flat one night, typical heavy-handed Met operation, clomping boots on the stairs, kicking in of doors. He was alerted and he beat his wife to death with a poker before they could enter.'

'Oh God . . .'

'He was likely planning on doing the same thing to his daughter, four-year-old Anna. They kept her in a cot in the living room, she was far too big for it, curled up in there like a panda in a cage. Makes you sick. When the police burst in, he changed his mind. Cut his own throat over the cot.'

John put his hand to his mouth, unable to say a word.

'Dowsed the poor thing in his blood before the officers pulled him away and he bled out on the carpet. One of the men grabbed Anna, did his best to wipe the blood off her and got her out of there. Chap's name was Sherwood, as in the forest, works in private security now. Passed over one too many times for promotion. I talked to him at length. He was relieved to know the girl was still alive, I don't think he held out much hope for her. By the time they handed her over to social services she was screaming her head off.'

'Hardly surprising.'

'What was surprising was the voice she was using to do it.'

'"The voice"? What are you talking about?'

'Dissociative identity disorder, isn't that what you lot call it? Anna hears voices and they trigger changes in her personality. Douglas Reece was the first of those personalities to take shape, presenting himself that very night. When they dragged her into the hospital she was shouting at the staff in a man's voice – or as good an approximation of one as a girl of four could make. Over time more and more personalities developed, most be-nign, some, like Reece, the trigger for violent behaviour. As she grew older, her control of them increased, mainly under the instruction of Aida Golding.'

'Who used her as a prop for her seances?'

'Absolutely. Hateful little beast, isn't she? Not an ounce of morality in her.'

John shook his head. He was thinking about the voice he had heard outside the house, the night he had found Anna standing in the rain. But it hadn't happened again, had it? Was she better away from Golding's influence?

'She's better now,' he said to Probert, hoping very much that that was true.

'We on our own?' asked Davinia once she was back at the table. 'I could have sworn I heard someone else up here.'

Anna didn't dare to speak. She stared at Bad Father, watching him as he licked the pastry crumbs off his finger.

'She doesn't even acknowledge the fact that I'm here,' he said. But that wasn't altogether true was it? As soon as he had spoken, Davinia's face pulled a confused expression and she looked at Anna.

'You what, love?' she asked, 'you got something stuck in your throat?'

'Stuck?' laughed Bad Father, 'you'll soon have something stuck in you, all right.'

'It's clever,' said Davinia, 'I'll give you that. Very good. Is that what I heard? Were you practising while I was upstairs?'

'I don't need practice,' said Bad Father, 'I know what I'm doing. I'm doing what poor Henry would have wanted.'

'Now love,' Davinia said, 'don't get nasty. I'd rather you didn't bring my Henry up, I'm very sensitive about him, you know.'

'Oh God,' Anna couldn't believe her eyes, her hands grasping at her face in shock.

'It's all right, dear,' said Davinia, 'you don't have to fret, I'm just saying.'

But it wasn't Davinia Harris's words that had so shocked Anna, it was the appearance of a fourth person at their table. Another man, but one who made no secret of his time spent in the grave. His flesh was powdery layer upon layer, great chunks missing to expose the darkness within. It was as if he were made of old plaster. As he leaned forward it was with a dusty crunch of decaying bone.

'Look at him,' said Bad Father, 'and he was hardly much worse when he was alive. Drained day by day. A shadow of a man. All because he lived with that.' He inclined his eyes towards Davinia.

'Sandy, my love,' said Davinia, 'you're starting to worry me now. Do you want me to call someone?'

Anna looked first to the resurrected Henry and then to her own Bad Father. The latter placed his finger to his lips and slowly shook his head. Anna realised there might yet be an opportunity for her to make everything all right.

'I'm fine,' she said to Davinia, 'sorry. I just . . . sometimes I . . .' Try as she might, she couldn't think of an excuse for what the old woman had heard.

Davinia took pity on her, 'Forget about it, dear. Finish your tea and we'll say no more about it.'

'She'll certainly be better for being away from Golding,' Probert agreed, 'though you'll forgive me if I point out that someone as damaged as she is can hardly be cured overnight.'

'No,' John agreed. 'Of course not. She'll need a lot of time. And a lot of help.'

'Help you can hopefully give now that you know what you're facing.'

John nodded. 'Thank you.'

'Forget it,' Probert got to his feet. 'I don't make a habit of giving two shits about anybody but myself but I thought I'd try it for once.' He smiled. 'Besides, I cannot begin to tell you how much I loathe Aida Golding.'

'You and me both,' agreed John.

'Well,' said Davinia with a good deal of forced cheerfulness, 'I can't sit here chatting all day. I'm sure we've both got things to be getting on with.'

Anna nodded. She was scared to speak unless absolutely necessary, convinced it might encourage Bad Father or Henry, who were both still at the table with them. Henry had dipped two crumbling fingers into Anna's teacup, a greasy swirl of oil spreading out from where the desiccated stumps were rehydrating themselves.

'I'll pay,' insisted Davinia. 'It's been lovely to have someone to talk to.'

She got up and headed for the stairs, Anna cautiously following. Bad Father and Henry stayed in their seats.

At the till, Anna thanked Davinia, still glancing around but finally daring to believe she had left their demons behind.

Out on the street the bustle of people and the heavy traffic served to knock away some of the fear she had been feeling. Watching the big double-decker buses, delivery vans, speeding taxicabs and motorbike couriers that whizzed past as she and Davinia reached the main road, Anna couldn't believe that this was a place she could be haunted. This was the noisy, electric, petrol and steel real world. This was not the muddled confines of your own head or the lonely, empty night.

'Drive like lunatics, don't they?' said Davinia, shaking her fist at a white van that nearly clipped the kerb at the crossing. They'll kill someone one day.'

'Indeed they will,' said Bad Father and Anna screamed as she saw the crumbling remains of Henry leap forward and shove his wife into the road. There was a pointless squeal of tyres from the traffic as Davinia bounced off the bonnet of a UPS van, connected face-first with the rear window of a taxicab and then flipped back to be folded and pressed flat beneath the braking wheels of the traffic that, even now, was rear-ending each other in an attempt to avoid the inevitable.

Anna screamed. After a pause while the information soaked into the crowd around, she was joined by the sound of other, horrified voices. She ran. Nobody watched her go, they were all focused on the road, a great sweeping wave of people descending on the site of the accident, to help, to look, to *know*. There's nothing that fascinated people more than looking at death, Aida Golding knew that.

She ran back through the market, twisting and turning at random as the city squatted over her. Her lungs tightened, her head whined like metal against metal. Finally, turning into a small green square, she tripped and came to land in a pile of damp leaves. She lay there, a scared animal waiting for the predator to move on. But the predator was there with her, its fingers sliding in-between the leaves to poke and prod at her. 'We got her!' Bad Father chuckled. 'And soon we'll have them all!

John walked out with Probert, agreeing that he'd keep in touch, knowing that was a lie.

'I hope it's all right,' said the peer. 'It would be nice to think she could get back on her feet after everything Golding's put her through.'

'I'll do my best,' said John, 'at least she's safe from her.'

'For now.'

'For ever, there's no way she knows where I live. I'm ex-directory and they won't give out addresses here. Unless you've told her?'

'No, and I never would. Still, as far as Golding's concerned I'd never be sure of anything. If she wants to find you – and I'm sure she probably does – then she will.'

Fourteen

The Life and Death of Shaun Vedder

Eighteen months ago

'Psychology, eh?,' the old woman said, shifting in her bed and releasing a gust of flatulence from within the yellowing sheets, 'what's the point of that?'

'It would help me understand you,' Shaun might have said but, tired and not in the mood for a long argument with his mother, he chose to say nothing.

'I mean, Christian's got sense, hasn't he?' she continued, 'he's getting a City and Guilds in electricity. He'll be straight into a job with that. Psychology? Waste of three years, if you ask me.'

'I didn't' was the next thing Shaun could – but did not – say.

'Still,' his mother relented, ferreting in an eiderdown for her Silk Cut, 'keeps you off the streets.' She found the pack, lit one and sent a mushroom cloud of smoke up towards the light brown ceiling. 'And the less money you have the less smack you can afford.'

'Pot, mother,' Shaun finally chipped in. 'I was caught smoking a little pot, not doing smack.'

'Pot, smack, they all sound fine until you end up on *Jeremy Kyle* slapping your wife about.'

'I won't end up on *Jeremy Kyle*, Mum.'

'No, I don't suppose you will. No bloody drive, that's your problem.'

Sixteen months ago

'You Shaun?'

'Yeah.'

'I'm Bobby, we're sharing.'

'Cool.'

'Yeah . . . Hope you don't fucking snore.'

Fourteen months ago

Shaun watched as Mr Pritchard began to map out a diagram on the overhead projector. For a couple of minutes he was lost in the sweep of the bright red pen reflected across the white wall of the lecture hall. He wished Mr Pritchard could just draw on it all day, filling the whole room with spirals and squares and circles and—

'Shaun?'

Shaun snapped out of his daydream, having slid forward on his seat and nearly fallen on the floor.

'Sorry,' he said, spilling his books and sending his biro flying several rows forward.

'You all right?' Mr Pritchard asked, smiling.

He was a gentle man, Shaun thought, a nice man. There was no malice in that smile. The same could not be said of the sniggering from all around him.

'Wanker,' someone whispered and there was a ripple of laughter.

'Fine,' he replied, gathering his books and reaching forward to take his pen after it had been passed back up to him. 'Just slipped. Sorry.'

'Surprised he doesn't stick to the fucking chair,' someone else whispered, he thought it was Bobby. 'Cunt never washes.'

One of the girls released a theatrical 'Ewww!' before Mr Pritchard held up his hands.

'Enough,' he shouted, 'you should be paying attention to me not Mr Vedder.'

He began to explain the diagram and Shaun grew more and more embarrassed, skin glowing hot in the dark as he knew everyone was thinking about him.

Twelve months ago

'Vedder, can you keep your shit over on your side?'

'Sorry.'

'Place is a fucking mess.'

'Sorry.'

'No way am I sharing next year, certainly not with you anyway.'

'No.'

'Place smells like fucking vegetables.'

'Sorry.'

'Like a broccoli rolled over and fucking died in here.'

'Sorry.'

'Whatever.'

Ten months ago

They thought the common room was empty when they started to talk.

'You'll never guess.'

'Tell me!'

'I can't, it's too embarrassing . . . seriously I was *wasted*. I've never been good on vodka, I think I'm allergic or something. I passed out in the garden once, knickers on my head, sat in leftover barbecue food. I had burger dimples on my bum, gave me a rash.'

'Who was it?'

'No, seriously, if anyone found out I'd have to leave Uni. My reputation would be screwed.'

'You haven't got a reputation, well, you have . . . but not a good one.'

'Piss off.'

'Just tell me.'

'I didn't even know what I was doing. It's like I was half asleep and the next thing I know I'm snogging some bloke and he's got his hand down my jeans.'

'Yeah right, I'm sure you didn't encourage him at all.'

'Well, maybe I was trying to cadge a few joints off him, I can't remember. It's the vodka. I'm allergic. Oh I could die . . .'

'Who was it?'

There was a pause.

'Shaun Vedder.'

There was a longer pause.

'Fuck!'

Both girls burst into hysterical laughter and Shaun,

sat on the sofa just around the corner, wished he could crawl between the cushions, bury himself in sponge and dust, and never, ever, come out again.

Eight months ago

Shaun sat in the gardens and smoked. He knew the place like the back of his hand now, knew all the best places to keep out of sight and wish the rest of the noisy bastards away.

If only he could stay here.

He'd tried to change. Cut his hair, wear more modern clothes, tried to talk about the things everyone else seemed to talk about. They'd despised him all the more for it. He'd despised himself too.

The only one who had seemed at all impressed was his mother. 'Finally,' she said, 'he gets himself a haircut and uses a comb. What next, I wonder? Might he get a job?'

At least he had his own room now. Somewhere he could get inside and shut the rest of the judgemental bastards out.

He was becoming lonelier by the day.

'Hi, Shaun.'

Shaun dropped his joint in panic as Mr Pritchard appeared, strolling past on his way to the IT department.

'Hi,' Shaun replied, uncertain as to whether he should pick it up or ignore it. Could Mr Pritchard smell it? Was it obvious from the look on his face?

'Pick up your joint, Shaun,' the lecturer said. 'I'm not going to tell anyone.'

Shaun did so, thanking him awkwardly.

'You all right?' Mr Pritchard asked. A question Shaun wasn't used to.

'Fine,' he lied, 'just getting some peace and quiet, you know?'

'I know. It shows. Your last paper was excellent.'

'Thank you, I liked it. The subject, I mean. It was interesting. It's all interesting.' Shaun floundered, not knowing what he should be saying.

'It's not *all* interesting,' Mr Pritchard laughed. 'Some of it's deathly dull, but we have to cover it.'

'Overall, though,' said Shaun, 'I'm glad I chose it. As a subject.'

'Good!' and with that Mr Pritchard grinned and carried on walking towards the IT block.

It was the first conversation Shaun could remember that hadn't involved, in one way or another, him being insulted.

Six months ago

'Shaun.'

'Hey.'

Shaun watched his brother flip the switch on the kettle and then stare out of the window. Christian tapped his fingers rhythmically on the worktop. Click - ing his tongue against the roof of his mouth. Shaun tried to think of something to say. He racked his brain for subjects he knew interested the younger man, things he'd heard him discussing with his friends. Surely if there was one person he should be able to talk to it was his own brother?

The kettle switched off.

'How's it going with the course?' Shaun asked in desperation.

'Fine,' his brother replied, walking out of the room.

Four months ago

'Ray.'

'Shaun.'

A long pause, the click of a pair of lighters, the soft crunch of immolating tobacco.

'Shit weather,' said Ray, King of Small Talk.

'Yeah.'

'Don't suppose you know any mediums?'

'What?'

'You know. "Is there anybody there?"'

'No.'

Another long pause. The holding of breath.

'Why?' Shaun's voice was pinched, refusing to exhale.

'Pritchard's on the hunt for one. Probably hoping to find out where his wife left the cash.'

A final long pause. Then the release of breath, the sigh of contentment.

'Oh,' said Shaun, wondering where you'd go to look up local mediums.

Two months ago

'And she's supposed to be good, is she?' he asked the librarian.

'Well, she replied, pulling her glasses down to look over the top of them as if this was somehow more discreet. 'They say she really has got the gift.'

Shaun smiled. 'Really?'

'Well, if you don't believe . . .' the librarian leaned back and, for a moment, Shaun thought she meant to snatch back the flyer.

'Oh, I'm open-minded,' he insisted, 'I mean, that's why I ask . . . there are so many crooks out there, aren't there?'

'There are at that,' she agreed, 'but Aida Golding's the real thing, I tell you. A real power!'

Six weeks ago

'Hi Shaun, all good?'

Shaun smiled at Mr Pritchard. He'd been wanting to chat to him but felt it would have been over-eager if he had just hung around after a lecture. Much better, he'd thought, if they could just casually bump into one another. He'd been loitering around the campus all day hoping for the opportunity.

'Yeah,' he said, shrugging, before thinking he really ought to make more of a go of it than that. 'Well, they've run out of vegetable tikka wraps so, no, lunch sucks, but I'll get over it.'

'I'm sure.'

Mr Pritchard seemed distracted. Shaun was aware that he was losing his attention. 'You ever go see that medium?' he asked, deciding it was best to get straight to the point.

He could see that Mr Pritchard was thrown by this. Perhaps Ray hadn't even told him who it was that had found the flyer. Probably he'd claimed that achievement himself.

'Medium?' Mr Pritchard asked, as if confused. He wasn't a good liar. Why was he making this so difficult?

'Yeah,' he replied, struggling to keep his voice even, determined to maintain the pretence that none of this of this was important, just a casual conversation. 'Ray told me you might look into it. Writing some kind of paper or something?'

'Oh . . .' Mr Pritchard pretended to have remembered. Shaun was annoyed. Why was he being like this? Did he have so little respect for Shaun's work that he wasn't even willing to discuss the subject? Had he been lying when they'd spoken months ago? 'Yes,' the lecturer added, even more dismissively, 'something like that.'

Shaun fought to contain his anger. This was not how he had imagined the conversation going. By now they should be chatting enthusiastically on the subject of parapsychology, swapping ideas and agreeing to work together. Why was Pritchard being so evasive? He decided he should be even more blatant, make one last effort.

'Only,' he said, finding it really hard to keep his voice casual now, 'if you need any help I'm kind of into that sort of thing myself, be cool to do some coursework on it.'

There, he was in the open. Surely Pritchard wouldn't refuse him?

'Well, we'll see . . .' He was! He was dismissing him just like everyone else! 'I'm not sure if I . . .'

Shaun had no interest in listening to excuses. 'No

problem,' he said, pushing his way past the lecturer, just wanting to get out of there.

'I'm just not a hundred per cent on where I'm going with it yet,' Pritchard said, trying to back track, 'but I'd definitely give you a shout if—'

'Cool.'

Shaun wasn't going to give Pritchard the satisfaction of seeing him hurt. He didn't need him. Didn't need any of them. He offered a false smile and virtually ran out the door.

Five weeks ago

'I'm sorry, Shaun,' said Dr Walker into the receiver. He rubbed at his face, Christ why did he have to do this? Was there no friend of the family that could take the job on? 'It's your mother, Shaun. I'm afraid she's . . . well, she passed away last night.'

There was silence on the other end of the line. Shocked probably, Walker thought, though he must have known this was coming, the woman smoked enough after all. 'Shaun?' Nothing. 'Shaun?'

He looked up as the receptionist entered the room. 'Do you know,' he said, putting the phone down, 'I think the little bastard hung up on me!'

Four weeks ago

'Oh dear,' said Aida Golding, 'I can't hear this very well, it's either a John or a Jane . . .'

Shaun shifted in his seat, trying not to show his disappointment. He wasn't here to listen to other people's messages. It was his own he needed.

'Is there a Jane here?' she continued. 'No . . . it's a Jane I have speaking . . . Yes, dear, I know, I'm telling them . . . She wants to speak to John. Is John here?'

If he was, Shaun thought, he should pipe up or let someone else have a go.

'It's him!' shouted a woman at the back. 'He's the one you want.'

Shaun turned to look around and was shocked to see the woman was pointing at Mr Pritchard.

'Sorry?' the lecturer said, clearly bemused as to what was going on.

'John?' Aida Golding asked, 'is that you?'

'Yes,' he replied.

About time, Shaun thought.

'The message is for you. Jane is here, she's right beside you. If she were to hold out her hand she could rest it on your shoulder. And she so wishes that were possible. That she could touch you, hold you again. She's always been with you, John, she never left you. Can I hear your voice, John? She still shares a home with you, still follows in your footsteps, shares a bed. I need your voice, John, it's my connection, let me hear your voice.'

'I . . . I don't . . .'

Pritchard had no idea, did he? Shaun felt his eyes sting with frustrated tears. What he would give to be in the lecturer's position.

'You miss her,' Golding continued, 'don't you, John, since the cancer took her body from you?'

'Of course . . .'

'The cancer can't kill the spirit, John, it can't kill the

soul. It eats away at the flesh but leaves the truth behind. She's still here, John, can you feel her?'

'I don't . . .'

Shaun was tempted to jump to his feet and bring a halt to this. What was the point? He saw the young mother a few rows in front of Pritchard, Sandy, the woman who had had the lovely message about her daughter. She was looking as uncomfortable as Shaun felt. She was probably offended, he decided, by the lack of care the idiot seemed to feel over something so important.

'You sense her sometimes don't you? Around the house?' said Golding, desperately trying to drag a response from the man. 'Or when you visit places that you used to visit together? You can tell she's with you?'

'I—'

'I need your voice ,John, she's slipping away, let me hear your voice . . .'

'I don't know what to say!'

And that was that. Aida Golding's shoulders slumped, defeated by the man's apathy. 'It's all right, John,' she said, 'she's gone, you can relax. Just know that she loves you and she will always be beside you.'

Good for him, thought Shaun. But where does that leave the rest of us?

Two weeks ago

'Hello,' Shaun hopped awkwardly from leg to leg.

Long-haired tit looks like he's wetting himself, Aida Golding thought. What was wrong with kids today?

'Hello, my love,' she replied, 'thank you so much for coming.'

'Oh, no problem, I've seen you a few times now. Wonderful.'

'Thank you, my love, that's so kind of you.' She moved towards the door, determined to escape. She had no patience any more, had no time for the lot of them, not since . . .

'It was actually my lecturer at Uni, John Pritchard, who recommended you,' said Shaun, hoping this might convey enough worth for her to stay a little longer. Why did everyone race to leave his company?

It certainly held her back. She turned to face him, a wide smile on her face. 'Did he now?' she said. 'How good of him.'

'Yes, he used to come all the time, didn't he? I saw him sometimes. But then I suppose he's so busy with Sandy.'

'Sandy?'

'The girl who lost her baby? She comes with him to Uni sometimes, I think they're living together. That's what people say anyway.' Fuck knows what she sees in him, he didn't add. He must be twice her age.

'Does she really? How lovely. It's nice that they have each other to rely on.'

'Yeah, I suppose.'

Golding pulled her most casual face, a soft mask of delicate indifference. 'Do you know I had a book I wanted to give to Sandy. A lovely little spiritual thing that I thought would help her. Only she never comes these days, does she?'

'I could give it to her next time I see her at Uni if you like?' he offered, grateful for the opportunity to be useful.

'No,' Golding shook her head, 'I really should give it to her myself. If only I had his address . . .'

'I'm sure I could get it for you.'

'Oh I wouldn't want you telling him, I'd like it to be a surprise.'

'That's all right, I don't need to ask him for it, I could get it easily.'

'Really?' she reached out and cupped his cheek with one, well-moisturised hand. 'You are a dear. I'm sure someone in the spirit world loves you very much.'

'I don't know about that,' he admitted. 'My mother never really made that much of me. Besides, she only died recently.'

'That doesn't matter, dear, there's no waiting list, you know! I'm sorry to hear of your loss, though.'

'Cancer,' he admitted. 'We knew it was coming.'

'Doesn't help, though, does it?' she said. 'There's always things unsaid, isn't there?' She smiled and took his hand. 'You come again, bring that address, I'll just bet I can make contact for you.'

Shaun left that night happier than he'd been for months.

Last night

'And you're sure this is right, dear? I'd hate to send it to the wrong place, the book's out of print now.'

'Positive, I got it from the office.'

'They just let you take it did they?'

238

'Oh, they didn't know . . .' Shaun laughed nervously, he could hardly admit it had taken him this long to get it because he had had to wait for the opportunity to sneak in and steal it. Perhaps a half-truth wouldn't hurt. 'There was nobody in so, well, I just looked it up. Not as if they wouldn't want you to have it, is it?

'Of course not, dear, they'd be only too pleased. Now you sit down . . . I'm sure we'll have a message for you tonight.'

Six hours ago
'I love you, Shaun,' his mum had said. 'I know I didn't always tell you but I do. You're such a good boy. I couldn't be more proud . . .'

Shaun lay back in the bath, wiping the tears from his eyes.

There was a knock on the door.

'Oi,' someone shouted, 'you going to be long?'

No, Shaun, thought, as he cut a deep groove straight down his wrists. He lay back in the water as it bloomed red around him.

I'm not going to be long at all.

Fifteen

Born Bad

John didn't say a word to Anna about his discussion with Probert. Whenever he thought about bringing the subject up – or any small part of it – the words felt as big and sharp as rocks and he couldn't bear to utter them.

Besides, it was clear that Anna was not in the same happy mood she had been when he'd left her earlier. She was silent and nervous, constantly twitching at every loud noise. Something has spooked her, he decided, let's just hope it wasn't the voice of her dead father.

'I'll cheer her up,' Laura announced after Anna had gone to bed. 'We're having one of our girls' adventures tomorrow.'

'Where are you going?'

'St Paul's . . . I want to say rude things in the Whispering Gallery and terrify the priests.'

He laughed. 'If anyone can shake her out of it, it's you.'

'I'm sure it's nothing,' she said, 'she's obviously had one hell of a life. She's been a different woman lately, much more self-assured. But you don't get there overnight, something set her back a bit. That's fine. To be expected. It was probably something tiny, something she overheard, the face of someone in a crowd . . . who knows? She'll be OK. Between the two of us we'll make sure of that.'

He took her hand. 'Thanks. I really appreciate that, you know.'

'I know. And so does she.'

John decided to change the subject. 'How's Michael?'

'Fine, suffering a week of matinees and evening performances in Weymouth. He's never been so cold, apparently.'

'Or tired I imagine.'

'It's not so bad, apparently the matinees are really only to offer pensioners somewhere warm to sleep. I think the cast sometimes joins them.'

'And on that note.' He got up, meaning to head for bed.

'Sleep well St John,' she said with a smile, 'for tomorrow's a new day!'

He kissed her on the cheek, thinking, not for the first time, how lucky his son was to have found such a wonderful woman.

He climbed the stairs, quietly leaning his head against Anna's door. Had he heard the muffled sound of talking? Or was she just snoring. Or, more likely, was he imagining things?

He went to bed.

Anna had bundled herself beneath the duvet and

wrapped the pillow around her face. Anything to stop hearing the voices.

They were back in force now, Bad Father, Soft Mother, Father Legion . . . all of them arguing with one another, all of them wanting her to themselves.

And the blank periods were back. One moment she was in the leafy square, the next she had been stood outside the university with no memory of how she had got there. Checking her reflection in a shop window, she had gone into Verano, bought herself a coffee and snuck into their bathroom to tidy herself up. There had been pieces of leaf in her hair and grass stains on her knees. At some point she had broken a nail, though whether that had been falling over earlier or during some unremembered accident since she couldn't say.

She drank her coffee and tried to put on a natural smile in time to cross over and pick up John.

It would be fine, she convinced herself. There had been an accident, that was all, and it had triggered an episode. She was getting better, for sure. Getting much, much better.

But she couldn't believe it, not with the glimpses of Bad Father she had suffered for the rest of the day. He had been peering through the kitchen window, standing in the airing cupboard, loitering beneath the street lamp opposite the house. He was everywhere. He would never let her go.

'You need me, girl,' he had whispered, lying next to her in the bed, curling himself around her, spooning beneath the duvet. 'You need what I can do.'

'No, no, no . . .'

She gripped the sheets and held on, terrified that if she loosened her grip for a second he would have her and she would find herself somewhere else. Maybe even in John's room with a knife in her hand . . .

'We'd teach him a lesson, my girl,' said Bad Father, 'wouldn't we?'

She bit into her tongue and fought her way through until dawn.

'Why are you still here?' Laura asked the following morning. 'You can't come, you know.'

John was sat in the lounge flicking through the free newspaper that had been abandoned on his front door mat that morning.

'I don't have to go in till later,' he explained, 'and I know I can't come, I'm not girly enough for girls' adventures.'

'Precisely. You might encourage Anna along though, she still hasn't come out of her room and we need to get there before twelve.'

'God's not going anywhere.'

'Maybe not, but he's not allowing tourists after then, they're closing off the galleries for a service.'

'How is poor God to earn a living?'

Laura squeezed his hand and walked out to the front door. 'I'm just popping to the post office,' she grinned and held up a small parcel. 'Emergency provisions for Michael in Weymouth! I'm sending him some Kendall Mint Cake, a miniature bottle of scotch and a porn mag.'

'A life-safer, I'm sure,' said John, getting to his feet. 'I can take you.'

'You sit down, John Pritchard,' she said, opening the front door, 'I'm perfectly capable.'

'I wasn't suggesting otherwise,' John insisted, putting his hand on her shoulder, 'but I'm still only too happy to go with you.'

'You just make sure that woman's ready,' she replied. 'We leave the minute I return!'

Laura grabbed her cane and stepped out of the door. John watched her walk along the path and admired her every step of the way. She had already become familiar enough with the distance between the front door and the gate that she barely needed her cane to get herself out onto the pavement and strolling down the road in the direction of the shops.

If she can overcome her difficulties, he thought, we all can.

He pulled the door closed just as someone stepped through his front gate. He watched the distorted image creep closer through the smoked-glass window in the door. For a moment he thought of Jane. Not the real Jane, the one he had loved and lost, but the terrible shadow she had left behind to haunt him.

He opened the door and came face to face with Aida Golding.

'Hello John, my dear,' she said, 'and how have you been keeping?'

Aida had been watching the house for about an hour. She had sat in the car, chain-smoking cigarettes and trying to decide whether John had left early for work or was still there. It would be easier, she had decided, were she to confront Anna on her own. After all, Anna was weak and easily controlled. She had no doubt that she could have the stupid girl doing whatever she wanted within a few minutes of coming face to face with her. Not that she didn't want the chance to get back at John too, she was not a woman who bore any aggressor, however ultimately small. But Anna first. She'd drag that snivelling creature back into line if she had to half-kill her to do so.

She had briefly considered calling on the Barrowman brothers. She'd maintained her relationship with Luke throughout her time with Alasdair. Luke's needs were unconventional and she enjoyed fulfilling them. She had known that all it would have taken was one brief phone call and both boys would have been around here last night teaching John and Anna what happened when you took sides against Aida Golding. On the whole, though, it had felt too easy. After what had happened to Alasdair (and Glen and Sacha, she reminded herself, though who really cared about those two?) she had increasingly felt the need to reassert herself. Frankly, she wanted to smack the world in its mouth.

She saw a young woman appear at the front gate and, for a moment, she wondered if she had the wrong house. The girl was obviously blind, tapping her way towards the gate with her stick. Maybe he had a blind daughter? She decided there was only one way to find out.

She got out of the car and made her way along to the front gate. The door was just swinging closed as she walked down the path and she recognised the indistinct shape beyond the glass as John.

It *is* the right house, she thought, and we'll have to start with Pritchard rather than Anna, after all.

The door opened again, John had clearly seen her too.

'Hello John, my dear,' she said, 'and how have you been keeping?'

He actually went to shut the door in her face. She saw his shoulders tense in preparation. She shoved forward, refusing to let him.

'I wouldn't, darling,' she said. 'We need to talk, you and I. It will be a lot more painless for you if you manage not to piss me off any further.'

'We have nothing to discuss,' he replied, nonetheless forced to let her past. It was either that or physically throw her out and she guessed rightly that he wouldn't be able to do that. No, however angry he might be, John was old school.

She walked through into the living room, sat down in one of the chairs, pulled out a cigarette and lit it. She was like a cat, marking her territory.

'I don't allow smoking in here,' John said, his voice getting louder before he seemed to get a lid on it. She noticed he made a tiny upward glance before shutting the lounge door. Oh yes! That was it, Anna was upstairs and he didn't want her to know . . . He thought he might be able to get her back out of the door without the little bitch even twigging she'd been here.

'Never dictate to guests, dear,' she replied, 'it's not polite.'

'You're not my guest out of choice,' he said, 'and if

you don't leave straight away I shall call the police.' He reached for the phone.

'And tell them what? That you refused a mother access to her legally adopted child? Good luck with that.'

'After they hear about the way you treated her I'm sure that won't be a problem.'

'Happy to talk about that, is she? Really? The bitch has grown some claws at last.'

'With my help we'll see you serving a sentence for abuse.'

'Always making threats aren't you?' she replied, '"I will do my utmost to ensure you never practise this charade again." That's what you said that night after the seance, remember? All riled up and manly. You wanted to ruin me, didn't you?'

'I did,' he admitted, 'and still do. I find you contemptible.'

'Clearly. Enough to steal my daughter!' she raised her voice at that, intentionally wanting it to carry upstairs, to reach Anna and make her afraid.

'I didn't steal her, she came here for help.'

'Or to hide after killing Father Goss?'

'Don't be ridiculous. I met with Probert, I know all about Trevor Court.'

'Do you now? And how exactly do you think he managed to sneak into the room, cut the priest's throat and then vanish again? He may have been to blame for Alasdair . . .' her voice cracked slightly at the mention of his name but she was damned if she was going to lose strength now, 'but Goss was killed by someone else.'

'By himself then, like we all said.'

'Or by Anna . . . consumed by the personality of her father. She's a very sick woman you know. Very sick.'

'Thanks to you.'

'Oh, I didn't start her off, dear, you know that. I think some kids are just born bad, don't you?'

'No, I don't, but I think a lifetime of sustained abuse is enough to make people sometimes do bad things.'

'Oh, so you are willing to admit she's bad then?'

'No!' John paced up and down, frustrated by her presence. 'Just get out, I'm not having any more of this conversation.'

He began dialling the phone as she stood up. Might he actually call the police? Aida wondered. If he did she'd fight but, really, she had little ammunition, just hot air and a lot of determination. Perhaps a sustained period of intimidation would be better. She doubted it would take long for Anna to come running home if she made a habit of calling round.

'I'll be back,' she said, 'don't worry about that.' She opened the lounge door and turned back to offer him a smile. 'A mother has a right to visit her daughter.'

'You're not my mother!' Anna screamed, hurling herself through the doorway.

'Anna!' John shouted, seeing the kitchen knife in her hand, 'don't!'

But Anna couldn't hear anything but the pumping of her own heart and the laughter of Bad Father. She slashed the knife across her foster mother's throat in one smooth movement, like running a bow across the strings of a cello.

'Oh God!' he said, dashing forward, 'please don't!'

'Shut up!' she shouted her voice deep and rough.

That's the voice, he thought, the voice I heard outside, the voice at the seance. That's Douglas Reece.

She got to her feet and he held his hands out towards her, trying to reassure her, trying to calm her down.

'Please,' he said, 'we can fix this, it's fine. Let me just call an ambulance.'

'Call it for yourself,' she said in that same rough tone, and stabbed him in the stomach.

He doubled over, shocked and winded, a small circle of blood growing larger on his shirt front. 'Anna?' he asked.

But Anna was long gone, now there was just Bad Father.

Sixteen

The Dead Are Not Jealous

Bad Father dropped the knife on the floor where it was absorbed by the fast stretching pool of blood from Aida Golding's throat.

'Anna,' the old man said again, reaching out towards her.

'No,' Bad Father replied, walking out of the room and closing the door firmly behind him.

The front door was still wide open and he stepped outside, taking a deep breath of fresh air and wondering what exactly to do with himself.

There was a soft tapping noise coming along the street and he walked up the path to look. Of course, the blind girl, Laura. They had an adventure to go on didn't they? They certainly did.

He went back and closed the front door to Pritchard's house before calling out to her.

'I'm ready when you are!' He took extra care over the voice, making sure it sounded like his daughter.

'I should hope so!' she called back, holding out her arm for him to take it. He did so.

'You all right?' Laura asked, 'you sound a bit funny.'

'Fine,' Bad Father replied, 'perfect in fact.'

'That's all right then, let's have an adventure!'

'Yes,' Bad Father replied, 'let's.'

John tried to control his breathing, pressing his hands against the wound in his belly. There was a lot of blood. He felt light-headed. Staring at Aida Golding's dead body he felt his vision blur and his head topple.

Then he was awake again. He'd passed out.

Probably shock as much as blood loss, he decided, need to get myself together, stop the bleeding and . . .

And stop Anna.

Yes, that was the thing, wasn't it? He had to stop Anna. And unless he kept his wits together . . .

He carefully undid his belt and pulled it free of the waist-loops of his jeans. Reaching for a cushion from the sofa, he gave an involuntary shout of pain and sat back for a moment to build up courage for the next movement. He stripped the cover from the cushion, folded it and, using the belt, strapped it as tightly over the wound as he could. He couldn't help but cry out as he yanked the belt tighter but he knew that it was useless unless he cinched it hard. The pain actually motivated him a little. Adrenalin, he realised, my body's trying to help out.

He slowly got to his feet and walked as slowly and as carefully as he could out of the lounge and into the hallway for the phone.

'Ring Laura first,' said a voice from the stairs and, glancing up he saw Jane's feet stood near the top. Not the terrible, long-dead feet he had glimpsed before. This was the real Jane, *his* Jane, here to help. 'You need to warn her,' she continued, 'as soon as you can.'

'Yes,' he agreed, 'warn Laura first.'

He dialled her mobile number.

Laura could tell something was wrong with Anna but chose not to pry. One way or another she'd shake her out of it. Wasn't that what friends were for?

'What time is John back this evening?' she asked, thinking they might all settle down with a takeaway rather than Anna cooking.

'I don't know,' Anna said, 'I didn't think to ask.'

'I can just ring him,' Laura said reaching for her phone in her pocket. 'Oh . . . I left it on the kitchen table. I thought I'd be going back to the house before heading off.'

'I was too eager!'

'You were. Never mind. It's not important.'

Laura's ringtone came dancing through the house, a jolly Katy Perry tune that had no place in this quiet house that reeked of death.

'Shit.' John hung up.

'OK,' said Jane, 'that's OK, ring the police next.'

'Yes, the police.' He dialled again.

'Emergency. Which service?' Janice Tilsley had been working an eight-hour shift by the time the call came through. The little patience she possessed had been worn down by a series of prank calls over the course of the morning. 'They should send the little bastards to prison,' she had told Simon, who manned the desk next to her. 'I think they do,' he replied before taking another call of his own.

'Police,' replied the voice on the other end, so quietly Janice had to strain to hear it.

'Was that police, caller?'

'Yes, someone's been stabbed.'

'Sounds like you need an ambulance to me, then.'

'I probably do, yes.'

'Connecting you now.' Janice routed the call through to the Emergency Medical Services. 'Connecting 020 7840 8400.'

'That's my number,' said the caller.

'I know, dear,' said Janice. 'I'm talking to the Medical Services. Says someone's been stabbed.'

'They have,' the caller insisted, 'me. And a woman. Had her throat cut.'

'Who am I talking to?' asked the Medical Services operator, taking the call.

'John Pritchard, I live at—'

'We've got your address,' chipped in Janice, trying to be helpful.

'You've been wounded?' the Medical Services operator asked.

'Stabbed, yes. But that's not the problem.'

Sounds like it to me, thought Janice, the poor bugger could barely speak up.

'I'll have an ambulance on its way as soon as possible,' the operator promised, 'do you want to hold the line?'

'I want the police. Laura's in trouble.'

'Laura?'

'My daughter-in-law . . . she's gone with her and if someone doesn't stop her then . . .' the line went quiet and Janice strained to hear. It sounded like he was talking to someone else. 'I'm telling them,' he was saying, then someone's name? Jay?

'I'll call the police,' said Janice.

'Shall I hold the line?' asked the Medical Services operator.

'I can manage,' Janice replied, irritated.

'Ambulance will be with you in approximately twenty minutes,' the operator announced, then disconnected.

'Connecting you with 020 7840 8400,' said Janice.

The police operator answered. 'Hello, what's the emergency?'

'He's been stabbed,' said Janice, 'but we've called an ambulance.'

'You need to get Laura,' the caller was insisting, the two of them talking at the same time, 'she's going to St Paul's.'

'Is he delirious?' the police operator asked.

'Who knows?' Janice replied. 'Apparently Laura's in danger.'

'Who's Laura, caller?'

'Are you talking to me?' asked the caller, his voice fainter than ever.

'Yes,' the police operator replied, 'who's Laura?'

'My daughter-in-law. She doesn't know that Anna's dangerous. They're going to St Paul's. Anna's going to kill her.'

The caller gave a cry of pain and the phone clattered out of his hand.

This is the stuff, thought Janice, this is what you signed up for, not those nasty kids with their pranks.

'Caller?' asked the police operator.

'His name's John,' Janice offered.

'John? Can you still hear me John?'

There was another cry of pain plus the rattle of something against the phone receiver.

'I think he's dropped it,' suggested Janice, 'can't be easy if you're stabbed, can it?'

'We'll send a car,' the police operator said and disconnected.

'Did you hear that, caller?' asked Janice, 'the police are on their way.'

John finally managed to pick up the phone just as it cut off.

'The police are on their way,' he told Jane.

'How long will that take?' his wife replied, 'you can't wait for them. You've got to do everything you can, haven't you?'

'Yes,' he agreed, 'everything I can. God it hurts. Hard to think.'

'I know, darling, the pain gets the better of us all in the end, I remember the names I called you, the threats I made.'

'Doesn't matter.'

'Call a taxi. Quickly.'

John had the local firm on speed dial. 'Sladen Cabs?'

'I need a taxi straight away, to St Paul's. It's urgent.'

'Done something you need to confess?'

'Sorry?'

'You must be! Only joking, pal. What's the address?'

John gave it to him. 'How long?'

'With you in a couple of minutes, we're all sat on our arses till the schools kick out.'

The operator hung up.

'Any minute now,' he said.

'Well done,' Jane replied, 'that girl's right, you know, you are a good man.'

'I'm a dead one.'

'Probably. But not yet. I'd put a coat on. Try and hide the state of you. Taxi's not going to want to take you anywhere looking like that.'

'Maybe the police will get there in time.'

'Maybe. Maybe not. Think of Michael.'

'I should call him.'

'And tell him what? Put a coat on.'

'I will.'

John struggled towards the coat rail by the front door, tugging a waterproof jacket of the hook and slowly pulling it on.

'She can't help it, you know.'

'Anna? I know. She's not a bad girl.'

'But you've got to stop her.'

'Yes.'

'Do you love her, do you think?'

'Don't ask me that, Jane.'

'I just wondered. You kept going to those meetings hoping to talk to her, moved her in when she asked.'

'Just trying to help.'

'I wouldn't mind. The dead have no right to be jealous after all.'

There was the sound of a car horn outside.

'It's here.'

'Yes.'

John opened the front door and waved to the taxi driver. He turned back for a moment.

'You might be right,' he said, 'I might love her.'

'I know. Go on. Be quick. Save her.'

John walked out to the taxi, the door hanging open behind him. As he turned to get in the car he could see his wife, sat on the top of the stairs.

'Haven't closed the door mate,' the driver said. 'You'll have the place empty by the time you get back.'

'It's never empty,' John replied, and carefully climbed in.

'Not far,' said Laura as they climbed up out of the tube station. 'I can't believe you've never been.'

'To St Paul's?' Bad Father replied. 'I've been lots of times.'

'You liar! You told me you'd never been allowed.'

Bad Father cursed himself. He had to remember who he was or she would get suspicious. But it was so hard. There were so many people in Anna's head, it was hard to hold on.

'All right then,' he replied and smiled before realising that Laura wouldn't be able to see it so it didn't matter. 'I've never been.'

'I can't wait to have a good look around,' Laura said, laughing at her own joke.

They walked along Cheapside before turning into the park and cutting along to the main entrance of the Cathedral.

'I'll pay,' said Laura, 'that's if they still let us in. What time is it?'

'Half eleven,' said Bad Father looking at the watch on his wrist. He stared at the wrist for a moment, rubbing it with his fingers. Anna's wrist, he thought, not my wrist. These aren't my hands. None of this is mine.

He felt a surge of disorientation and he squeezed Laura's arm even tighter.

'You all right?' she asked.

'Just wobbly for a minute.'

'Probably being in the sight of God!' Laura joked.

Was that it? Bad Father wondered. Was God trying to tell him something?

He found it so hard to listen these days. God spoke much more quietly than he had used to.

He would have to listen very hard.

'Why St Paul's then?' asked the cab driver. 'You meeting someone is it?'

John had started to feel cold, even though he was aware that he was sweating. Self-consciously he mopped at his forehead with his fingers.

'No,' he replied. 'It's my daughter-in-law; she's in trouble. That's why I have to be as quick as I can. Can you drive fast?'

'So the cameras tell me. What sort of trouble?'

John couldn't decide whether to tell him or not but then realised that the more the cabbie knew the harder he'd try and help.

'It's a long story,' he said, 'and the short version will sound ridiculous. But she's with a woman who suffers from severe mental problems. I'm afraid the woman might hurt her, maybe even kill her.'

'Aye,' the taxi driver agreed, 'some women will do that.'

'The police are on their way, but they don't know either of them so I'm trying to get there as quick as possible. Try and stop her.'

'Well, if the police are involved they can hardly give me a ticket can they?' the driver reasoned, putting his foot down.

Constable Tony Hinds parked up outside John Pritchard's house and strode along the path to the door.

'Hello?' he called through the open door, 'hello? Mr Pritchard?' He could hear the sound of the ambulance en route. The siren jogged him along and he stepped inside. 'John Pritchard?' he asked again, pushing open the lounge door just as the ambulance pulled up and two paramedics came running up the path.

'We need a stretcher?' asked one of them, spotting Hinds.

'Not for her,' the constable replied looking at Aida Golding's body. He reached for his radio. 'On site now, control,' he said. 'No sign of Pritchard, there's a dead woman here though.'

'Bonus,' came the voice of control, 'the caller also mentioned St Paul's I'll route a car there now.'

*

'I'm sorry but we're closing the galleries early today,' the woman in the ticket kiosk explained, 'we have an early service.'

'Oh but we've come such a long way,' Laura lied. 'Please? It's bang on half past now, if we'd been just a minute earlier you'd have let us in.'

'I'm not allowed,' the woman insisted. She looked at the blind girl and felt guilty. The woman seemed so sad. Her carer didn't look much better, pale and sickly. That I spend my days doing this, she thought, cashing in on a house of God and then turning them away when they really want to go in. She looked around, trying to see if her supervisor was nearby. Derek Porter could be a horrid little jobs-worth when the mood took him. She remembered him ranting for five minutes over the theft of some pencils from the gift shop. The fact that he would refuse these two was the deciding factor.

'All right,' she said, 'but be quick and don't tell anyone I let you past.'

'Thank you so much!' Laura said, laughing and squeezing Anna's arm. 'We won't be any trouble.'

'How much longer?' asked John, as worried about whether he would last the journey as arrive there in time.

'Who can tell with this bloody traffic?' the cabbie said, slamming on the horn. 'Ten minutes maybe?'

Ten minutes. With every jolt of brakes and swerve of the wheel, John felt weaker. He wanted to check his wound but knew that if the driver saw that he'd stop immediately. He was pretty sure it was bleeding again.

'You'll manage,' said Jane from the back seat, 'you're stronger than you give yourself credit for.'

'I'll have to be.'

'Have to be what, mate?' the driver asked.

'Nothing, just thinking aloud.'

'So what's wrong with this woman, then?'

'She hears voices, controlling her.'

'I know how that feels,' the driver said, snatching for his radio as it barked at him. 'Ten minutes,' he told it, 'I'm on a lifesaving mission.' He dropped the handset into the ashtray, ignoring the sound of laughter coming from the speakers.

'I always think though,' he said to John, 'you know, when you read these stories in the papers and that, people who say voices told them that Tom Cruise was the son of the devil and must die. What I always wonder is this: what if the mad buggers are right?'

'Have you ever climbed so many steps?' Laura asked, as they arrived at the Whispering Gallery. 'It reminds me of the time I walked up from Covent Garden station rather than use the lift. How bad can it be? I thought. By the time I got to the top I could barely walk, my legs had gone numb. I walked out onto the pavement and just toppled over!'

Bad Father didn't reply, just stepped through into the gallery and stared out into the open space. It was like being in the mouth of God, he thought. 'Wonderful!' he said and savoured the sound of his voice echoing out into the void.

'Give me your arm,' asked Laura, 'or I'll trip over something and panic the priests.'

Bad Father led her away from the entrance, staring up at the alabaster statues looking down on them.

'There's always someone higher up,' he said, staring up at their cold, imperious faces. 'But at least they're blind too.'

'What are you talking about?' said Laura, laughing and patting his arm. 'Describe it to me! Let me see it!'

'It's big,' he said, struggling to put the place into words. 'So big.'

'You don't say! Let me sit down so that you can go to the other side and then you can whisper it to me.'

'All right,' said Bad Father, putting her down on the bench.

'You have to whisper though,' she said, 'if you speak too loudly it doesn't work. Talk to the stone and it carries all the way around,'

'I know,' Bad Father replied, irritated at the way she was talking to him. Like he was stupid. Like he was a child.

He kept walking, listening to the sound his footsteps made as they echoed around the dome above them. Were they perhaps sounding out in heaven even now? If so it can hardly have been the first time his actions had been heard among the Great Host.

'I am a child of God,' he said, thankful to be using his own voice once more, feeling stronger for it, more in control. 'And I will do anything in the name of the father.'

*

'Thank you!' John got out of the car and nearly fell over. His legs were so weak now, he was by no means sure he could even work his way around to the main entrance.

'Only way to find out,' said Jane, standing just behind him.

'True,' he agreed, paying the driver and making his steady way around the building. 'Do you think the police are here?'

'Let's hope so,' she smiled, 'it's not like you're going to be up for much of a fight, are you?'

'No,' he admitted, 'I think it'll be all I can do to bleed on her forcefully.'

'They'll be in the dome, the Whispering Gallery.'

'How do you know?'

'Laura's blind, darling, think about it. It's what made her want to visit in the first place.'

'Oh, yes . . .'

'Do you remember when we went?'

'Yes, years and years and years ago.'

'When God himself was young. I know. Do you remember what you whispered to me?'

He did. 'I said I'd be with you for ever.'

'You got that right. There, the ticket office, see it?'

'It's closed. Last admission was at half past eleven.'

John looked at his watch and then had to put out his hand against the wall to stop himself falling over.

'Can I help you, sir?'

He looked up to see a small, ginger-haired man walking towards him. 'Derek Porter' was the name on his official name badge, 'Sightseeing Supervisor'.

'Could you tell me if two girls went up to the Whispering Gallery recently?'

'Not unless they were here before half past, sir,' Porter replied. 'We close early today.'

'Can we check?' A stab of pain forced him to cry out and Porter's face fell. This is not a sympathetic man, thought John. He's worried I'm going to make his life difficult, that's all.

'Can I get you some medical assistance perhaps sir?' Porter asked.

'I'm fine,' John insisted, rather idiotically as everyone could see he was far from it. There was a trickle of people heading towards the main body of the cathedral and a number of them were turning to look at him.

'Please,' he said, 'a girl's in danger, you have to help me.'

Porter remained dubious. 'What girl?'

'The police should be here already,' said John looking around.

'We have security if that would help?' suggested Porter, only too happy to pass John on to someone else.

'Aaah!' John cried out, the stabbing sensation from his gut more than he could stand. He reached for the zip of his jacket and tugged it open.

Porter, a suspicious and fearful man registered one thing only: this weirdo had been hiding something under his coat, something strapped to his front. 'Security!' he shouted, 'this man's got a bomb!'

Bad Father heard shouting coming from below. Looking over the edge of the balustrade he saw people running across the cathedral floor towards the main entrance.

'Run little mice,' he said, 'run before God stamps on you and cracks open your tiny skulls.'

He sat down opposite Laura and tilted his head towards the wall.

'Can you hear me?' he asked, using Anna's voice again.

'Yes!' came the excited reply.

'I'm not who you think I am,' he whispered and allowed his voice to change back to his own. 'There are so many of us in here! He said. We are legion!'

'Stop messing about!' Laura replied, 'it'll take more than a creepy voice to scare me.'

'How about a little history then? On the twenty-third of August 1983 I followed Dinah Stapleton home from where she worked at the Three Hounds. I forced her around the back of the shared house she lived in and killed her with a Stanley knife. I opened her up and defecated in the hole. Because that's all she was worth, Laura, that's all she was.'

'That's horrible . . . Anna!'

'Not Anna. No. Douglas. On the fourteenth of October 1983 I killed Katie Brasslow. I did it in her own room because that way I could take my time. She thought she was going to get fucked for cash, the dirty whore. You should have seen her, off her head on pills, fawning over me and telling me what I could have for my money. I tied her up using her own handcuffs and then gave her what she wanted, I filled her stinking hole for her, filled it with a broken bottle.'

'Stop it!'

Laura stood up and began to run for the door.

'Yes!' he shouted, jumping to his feet, 'run if you can!'

'Ridiculous!' John shouted, as two security officers grabbed him from behind and forced him to the floor. He screamed in agony as his stomach hit the ground. His vision blurred and he felt himself beginning to pass out. If that had been explosive, you bloody idiots, he thought, we'd all be dead by now. As it is, maybe it's only going to be me . . . his eyes closed.

'John!' his wife shouted. 'Stay with me, John! You can't stop now!' He tilted his head and looked right into Jane's face as she lay on the floor next to him.

'Everybody back!' One of the officers was shouting. 'Keep clear.'

'I don't think it was a bomb actually,' said Porter, 'maybe you'd better check?'

'She needs you John,' said Jane and he was stuck dumb by how beautiful she was. She was the wife he had shared the very best of his life with, the woman who had given him worth, who had made every experience better simply by being there with him. 'You've got to find the strength,' she said, 'somehow . . .'

The security officers turned him over and one of them let go of his arm and stepped back. 'Fucking hell,' he said, 'look at the state of him.'

'Do you mind,' said Porter, 'do try to remember you're in a church.'

'On your feet, my love,' said Jane, 'one last push . . .'

*

Bad Father reached Laura just before she could get to the exit, grabbing her by her hair and yanking her towards him.

'On the twenty-ninth of November 2011,' he said, 'I took a blind girl in the house of God and made her beg for her life.'

'Anna!'

'Not Anna. Never Anna. I took a blind girl and I squeezed the life out of her,' he grabbed her by the throat, 'squeezed the life out of her slowly . . . so she could see again, looking into the face of God.'

'Please Anna!'

'Not Anna. Not Anna.' But his voice was changing, becoming softer, more feminine.

'You leave her alone,' said Soft Mother, 'you've had your day, just leave them all alone.'

'I killed you once, woman,' Bad Father replied. 'Wait your turn and I'll gladly do it again.'

'In a church!' shouted Father Legion, 'how could you do such a thing in a church? Have you no shame?'

'Your God is not the same as my God,' insisted Bad Father, 'mine loves what I do.'

'If you squeeze like that,' warned Nurse Sleepnow, 'you'll irreparably damage her windpipe.'

'Precisely the point!' Bad Father shouted. 'Now will all of you leave me alone?'

But they wouldn't. He fell back against the wall, the whispers swooping in from both sides. Every voice he had ever shared a head with, swooping around the cool plaster like nesting swallows.

LEAVE HER ALONE! KILL HER! KILL YOURSELF!

SHUSH NOW! MAD FOOL! BAD BOY! CRAZY BITCH! DIE NOW!

'Shut up!' he screamed.

GOD'S DEAD! YOU'RE DEAD! MUMMY'S DEAD! ALL DEAD! WE ARE THE DEAD! WE ARE THE DEAD! COME AND JOIN US! WE ARE THE DEAD!

He was drowning in a sea of ghosts.

Laura began to move, climbing to her feet meaning to run past him. But he swung his foot into her shins and she fell back against the balustrade.

'Don't kill her!' Anna screamed. 'Please! I can't bear it! Don't kill her!'

But Bad Father was stronger and he reached forward, eager to topple the blind girl over the edge where she could crack open on the tiled floor beneath, spilling out like the filthy bag of offal they all were.

Then John Pritchard shouted.

He was on his feet, one of the security guards actually helping him now they could see he was no threat.

'Now, John!' Jane shouted, 'everything you've got! Now! Now! Now!'

He roared in pain as he pushed the security guard aside and ran into the main body of the cathedral.

'Anna!' he shouted, 'Anna!'

Above, Bad Father looked down and, as John looked up, their eyes found each other's.

'Not Anna,' Bad Father whispered. 'Not Anna.' He took hold of Laura's shoulders and squeezed, pushing her back against the railing. She screamed.

'Anna!' John shouted again. 'Please listen to me! It's

me, it's John, and I need you. Can you hear me?'

He fell to his knees, no more strength left in his legs. 'Oh God,' he toppled to the floor, aware of people running towards him. He looked up at the dome way above him. 'I'm dying.'

'Yes, darling, said Jane, lying down next to him and taking his hand. 'Now tell her that.'

'I'm dying, Anna,' he shouted, 'but that's OK. Sometimes there are worse things aren't there?' He convulsed in pain, unable to speak for a moment. Jane squeezed his hand until he got his breath back.

'Keep talking,' she said, 'you can do this my love.'

'I used to be scared all the time, Anna' he continued. 'I saw death in everything. And I ran from it, terrified.'

'John?' Anna's voice. Finally, Anna's voice, calling down from above. 'I get scared too.'

'I know you do,' he replied. 'I know.'

Out of the corner of his eye he became aware of the security guards pushing back the crowd and barking into their radios. They've seen her, he thought. See, Porter, I wasn't so mad after all, was I?

'I know you get scared, Anna,' he said. 'But you don't have to be. Not any more. Not now I'm here.'

Anna sobbed and the noise bounced around the dome like a trapped bird. 'I just want to be free,' she said. 'I want to be empty.'

'I know, love,' he said, holding out both of his hands to her. His vision growing darker and darker.

'Nearly there, baby,' said Jane, resting her head on his shoulder, 'we'll look after you.'

'Come here, Anna,' he said, his hands shaking as they

reached out towards her. 'Come here and let me make it all right.'

He saw her let go of Laura, climb up on the railing and hold out her hands. 'Thank you, John,' she said. 'You're a nice man.'

'You are at that,' said Jane and blew him a kiss.

Anna jumped and he prepared to take her in his arms.

ALSO AVAILABLE FROM HAMMER

Kronos
Guy Adams

**A new novelisation of the classic Hammer film,
*Captain Kronos Vampire Hunter***

*'What manner of monster can wreak such damage?
I only hope you know how it can be stopped.'*

The peace of an English village is shattered when a young girl
withers before her friend's eyes, becoming but dust and bones.
Witnessing this terrifying transformation, local physician Dr Marcus
fears the village has been cursed by the presence of evil. He
immediately summons his old army friend, the mysterious but
powerful vampire hunter, Kronos.

Together with the help of his assistant Professor Grost, Kronos has
dedicated his whole life to destroying vampires. He knows that
there is nothing so varied and deadly. With a vampire nothing is
certain, especially how one might be able to kill it.

As more and more villagers fall prey to this deadly curse, time is
against him. And when it comes dangerously close to home,
Kronos is faced with a terrible choice...

AN EXCLUSIVE MEDIA COMPANY

Twins of Evil

Shaun Hutson

**One of Hammer's classic films, novelised by one
of the UK's best known horror authors**

Karnstein Castle stands like a bird of prey on the highest point of
the hills that surround the village below. A huge monolithic
reminder to all those who see it of the power of the family who have
lived there for centuries.

By day the village of Karnstein is a peaceful place, but by night, an
unimaginable evil roams free. Villagers are found dead, their
throats ripped open and bodies drained of blood. Young girls
disappear and are never seen again. Rumour has it that they are
taken to the castle for the pleasure of Count Karnstein, the last
surviving member of the family.

Into this strange place, come beautiful identical twins Maria and
Frieda. While Maria lives a blameless life, Frieda is drawn to the
castle and Count Karnstein. A man rarely seen in daylight, a man
steeped in Satanic ritual and the blood of beautiful young girls.

Before long Frieda and Karnstein unleash a reign of bloody
terror on the villagers, and no one, it seems, is strong enough
to stop them.

HAMMER

AN EXCLUSIVE MEDIA COMPANY

About Hammer

Hammer has been synonymous with legendary British horror films for over half a century. With iconic characters ranging from Quatermass and Van Helsing to Frankenstein and Dracula, Hammer's productions have been terrifying and thrilling audiences worldwide for generations. And with the forthcoming film, *The Woman in Black*, there is more to come.

Hammer's literary legacy is now being revived through its new Partnership with Arrow Books. This series will feature original novellas which will span the literary and the mass market, the esoteric and the commercial, by some of today's most celebrated authors, as well as classic stories from more than five decades of production.

Hammer is back, and its new incarnation is the home of cool, stylish and provocative stories which aim to push audiences out of their comfort zones.

For more information on Hammer,
including details of official merchandise, visit:
www.hammerfilms.com

HAMMER

AN EXCLUSIVE MEDIA COMPANY

Wake Wood

K.A. John

Released in 2010, *Wake Wood* was the first of Hammer's new releases

Still grieving after the death of their young daughter Alice in a frenzied dog attack, Patrick and Louise Daley leave the city to try and find some peace in the Irish countryside, and the village of Wake Wood seems like the perfect place to start again.

But the residents are guarding a terrifying secret: they can resurrect the dead. However, the rules are strict, they will bring Alice back only if she has been dead for less than a year; and, after three days, she must be buried.

Desperate to see their daughter again, even for just three days, the Daleys agree to everything. But they have been lying from the start. And by the time the villagers realise, it's too late. Alice is alive and she does not want to go back . . .

HAMMER

AN EXCLUSIVE MEDIA COMPANY